I saw him walking towards my car. His face was shadowed, because the lights above the sidewalks didn't project enough light. Tall, lanky, and as he got closer I started feeling really nervous. He opened the car door, and got in.

"Hi, Cilla," he smiled at me. Oh my god, was all I could think. Every deity must have been watching over me and smiling down on me for bringing us together at this moment. He wasn't cute. He was devastatingly gorgeous. Model-hot. He was so out of my league that I felt like a short freak next to him.

"Hi Todd," I parroted back to him.

We both looked at each other and laughed a bit nervously.

"Well, we both look like our pics, so that's good, right?" I asked.

"Yes, though you're even more beautiful than in your pictures," he said, still smiling.

"Thanks, you're really hot," I said, blushing . . .

The Unflingable Fling

Jenny Baskwell

Published by Jenny Baskwell
www.jennybaskwell.com

Printed by CreateSpace, an Amazon.com Company

ISBN: 978-0-9899703-0-3 (pbk)
ISBN: 978-0-9899703-1-0 (ebook)

September 2013

Contents

"Being deeply loved by someone gives you strength, while loving someone deeply gives you courage."
- Lao Tzu

"If I could but know his heart, everything would become easy."
- Jane Austen, *Sense and Sensibility*

1

Happy Hour, or Dear God, Help Me to Forget This Work Week!

I sat there at a table in the bar area at Typesetters, people-watching. Older blue-collar workers at the bar, religiously watching the sports channel on the bar TVs, drinking whatever basic beer was on tap. Younger and older office workers seemed to be on a work-mandated happy hour meet-up, because that table of eight looked really awkward at making small-talk; I theorized their office was a too formal and micromanaged environment, so they didn't want to socialize when it concerned off-work topics. Or maybe they had an early mandatory holiday party, which nobody seemed to be into, judging from body language that seemed more suited to a doctor's office waiting room.

Couples milled around the bar here and there, some looking happy, others looking only a little awkward, so maybe they were on dates. And me, sitting alone at a small table near the huge windows and waiting patiently for Hillary, but not being approached by anyone.

My cellphone pinged with a text from Hillary: "Hey, I'll be there in 5. Snag a table for 3, Kara's joining us."

Kara was a friend of Hillary's, very nice but a bit opinionated. She usually chose the less intelligent opinion, but I always wisely kept that to myself, since I wasn't out to be mean to anyone's face.

Glanced at my phone, and read the previous text from my girlfriend Hillary, from two days ago, "Want to go to Typesetters on Fri?"

Typesetters was a local upscale modern restaurant and bar in the Princeton, New Jersey, area that we frequented on occasion for happy hours. It attracted a lot of people leaving their office jobs at the end of a busy day, unwinding with coworkers or friends, or people out for an evening, so a good amount of handsome men in business suits were there. However, we didn't go to Typesetters to go cruising for men, instead we would just catch up and girl-talk for hours. At times, we'd notice our surroundings and people-watch, but mostly we were sharing something important, interesting, or completely outrageous. Some might say that was an untapped opportunity to look for men, but I always saw it as a very important chance to strengthen a great friendship—after all, half-price wines made everything better, right?

"Yes, definitely," had been my text back to Hillary on Wednesday.

Somehow, she and I were always on the same wavelength about getting together. We went out every two months or so, and it was always as if we picked up our conversations and rolled with it; time and life didn't diminish the friendship at all.

"Can't wait to catch u up on my latest . . ." I had texted to her, before she could reply.

"Cool, tell me who they are Fri night, seeya then," she had replied.

Good thing about her was that she always knew when my news concerned guys, or lack of them.

I looked up from my cellphone and put it on the table. Almost went back to people-watching and thinking, but a waitress came by, so I ordered a white wine, then requested menus for myself and the two friends I was waiting for. After she left with my drink order, I looked around and saw a number of open tables. It was mid-December, and I was glad to be relaxing at Typesetters, rather than at the insanity a few miles south on the highway, also known as the mall. I had finished my holiday shopping a few days ago, and I was eternally grateful for the gifts that I had been able to purchase online.

After my half-price wine was delivered, some of the tables started filling up. Twice people spoke to me, only because they wanted to take the extra chairs at my table. I held onto the two extra chairs until my girlfriend Hillary finally arrived to claim one of them. Now the hour was officially happy!

"Ok, spill," she ordered after giving our appetizer order and her drink order to our waiter, who had come by a few minutes after Hillary's arrival. "Who are they, and are they good?"

"It's great to see you, too!" I responded, dryly.

"You too!" she smiled, looking as happy as I felt that it was finally Friday, with a weekend ahead of us. Her red wine arrived, and she lifted her glass.

"Here's to catching up!" Hillary said, as we clinked glasses. "You start, I'm dying to know!"

"Well, Adam broke up with me–" I started.

"–oh no, that sucks," she said. I took a sip of wine.

"By text," I clarified. She paused, then rolled her eyes.

3

"Seriously?"

I nodded in reply.

"He's a dick, and an immature one at that. He doesn't deserve you, and you'll find someone so much better than him!" she said emphatically.

"Thanks, Hilli, I appreciate that," I said, taking a big sip of my wine. "I agree that he's a jackass. He wanted me to commit, then he decides to do other things instead of wanting to be with me instead of enjoying the fact that we're committed. He didn't even want to do anything special to celebrate that we're committed, which means that he definitely sucks."

"So, any new prospects yet?" she asked, digging into the appetizers that a different waiter had just brought to our table.

"Actually, I was thinking of a different approach," I said, in between bites of crostini that I had been dipping into the organic red pepper marinara sauce. "I was thinking of possibly doing a hookup or two, because dating's really burning me out on men."

Hillary's response was to snag some of the free chipotle-cheese-topped mini-crabcake sandwiches from a passing tray of samples, then handed one of them to me. We ate them, then I knew I had to ask her opinion.

"What do you think, now that you've absorbed my new approach?" I asked, then started on the mini lobster raviolis, so Hillary would have to speak.

"Are you sure about this? Just sex is a bit different than dating. You have to worry more about your safety, and still have to think about emotions. And, you have to be assertive— don't let the guy walk all over you or push you into something that you're not mentally comfortable with. All I'm saying is, think about this from different angles," she said.

4

"These tips are really good to know," I said slowly, "Thanks! I know I'm definitely a bit more naive when it comes to guys."

Hillary asked, a bit loud since it was packed in Typesetters by now, "What are you expecting, by doing this, instead of just going on dates?"

"Well, I was thinking that I could enjoy myself, without having as many emotional expectations getting in the way. And, I could feel a bit more comfortable around guys, if I'm more physical with them on purpose. If sex is less of a big deal, maybe I'll feel a bit more confident, and then I can focus on building something real with a guy," I explained.

"It could work," she mused.

Just then, Kara showed up, to hug each of us. I signaled the waiter.

The waiter took Kara's order, then quickly returned with it and with refills for Hillary and me. After we all had full wine glasses, Hillary held her glass up.

"We already toasted," I protested. "Sorry, Kara."

"No problem," she said, smiling.

Hillary insisted, "Raise your glasses, ladies! It's Friday, the weekend is ahead of us, and I'm toasting to good times, as we always have!"

Glasses clinked, to her satisfaction, and we all drank the delicious, half-price wines.

"Ok, so catch me up in what I missed," Kara pleaded.

"I got dumped by text, and I'm sick of dating," I said succinctly. "That's it so far."

"Ok, details," Kara requested.

"Fine, ugh," I started to complain. "I'm getting tired of online dating. It was working out for a while, but at this point I'm just fucking tired of having to sort through the perverts, creeps, and people who I'm clearly not compatible with because I'm not sure they even graduated eighth grade."

"Do you know how much of a snob you sound like?" Kara teased me.

"No," I replied haughtily, "But perhaps you need to explain it to me. Are you honestly saying that I should lower my standards, that I'm too picky?"

Hillary laughed, then replied, "Nah, we're teasing ya! So, tell us more about the insanity that is online dating!"

I took a hearty sip of wine, then started, "It's spending a lot of time, sorting through, well, the crap, to get to the decent guys. In terms of hard numbers, I've probably looked at more than eighty guys' profiles, been in contact with at least forty of them, and weeded out twenty-five of those forty. Out of the fifteen left, we chatted to try to become acquainted with each other, to see if we're compatible. Sometimes the messages just fade out at this point, or they continue without the guy making a move to meet in person.

"Otherwise, if he does ask me out for a real date, we meet up and get to know each other and see how it goes. Sometimes, in person, they're not the person they said they were. Or, they're exactly who they said they were, which doesn't always mean they're compatible with me. Only sometimes does it even work out to a second date or even contact after meeting.

"And, sometimes the guy just wants sex, and blocks you on the website after the sex. That way, you can't contact them on the website. Which is actually more than a bit dumb, since usually I already have their cellphone numbers. I can think of one or two of those guys that I'd want to be vindictive to, and contact them again to tell them I have herpes or something, and that they should be tested."

Kara gasped.

Hillary looked stunned, but asked anyway, "Holy shit, how did you get that?"

I waved the seriousness away and smiled, "Girl, I'm only messing—I don't have herpes or anything. But, I'm just thinking random evil thoughts. Did I ever tell you about the one guy who I actually messed with?"

"No, tell us what you did to him!" Hillary leaned in, then so did Kara, since it was getting very crowded in Typesetters and we didn't want to have to yell out personal stories.

"Well, he was that guy eight months ago," I started on the story. "The one I told you I met at my condo closing."

Hillary tapped her index finger against her wine glass and suddenly remembered, "Oh yeah, the title company guy?"

"Mortgage company guy," I slightly corrected. "Not my loan officer, but a new employee that brought the papers. They should have just sent those to my lawyer. Would have saved me from ever meeting him. Anyway, he was the first person who arrived for the closing, and I arrived right after him. We were sitting in the waiting room, just chatting, and he turned a little flirty with me. It was nice, especially since I was so nervous.

"Afterwards, he ended up talking to me in the parking lot, and asking me out. We went out to dinner that weekend, and I had a nice time there—we went to Moonlight Café, you know, that really good café downtown?"

"Of course, it's really good," Hillary confirmed, "especially for dinner. He sounded nice, refresh my memory on how it went to crap?"

"As I said," I continued, "Dinner was nice, he insisted on paying, then after dinner he asked what I wanted to do—did I want to go somewhere else, or to his place, or to show him my place, or call it a night? He was nice about it, no pressure. I said, how about if we go to my place, so I could give him the tour of my new condo, although I hadn't moved in yet. So, we went to my place, he oohed and aahed over it, then we're standing in the middle of my empty living room and he kissed me. It was nice, then he asked me if I want to go back to his place with him. I told him I did, but that it might be easier if I drove myself, in case I got too tired."

Kara interjected, "Ok, all of that sounded fine. Except, if you hadn't moved in by then, where was your car?"

"Oh, my car was there," I confirmed. "I did have a few things moved over there already. And, I had been there all day, cleaning and getting ready for painting and other fixes I was going to start on the next day. So, that's where he had picked me up from, for our date.

"Anyway, I get his address, we go outside, I lock the door, then we get into our cars and drive to his place. I didn't have a clue that his idea of 'hanging out' over his place was sitting next to him while he got high and we watched TV. Apparently, after he was sufficiently high, he wanted me to get naked, give him a blow job, then masturbate while he watched."

"Oh, gross," Kara replied.

"He sounds like a loser," Hillary chimed in. "Was he too high to actually put the effort into having sex with you?"

"Yeah, I really think so," I said, remembering how bizarre the moment had been. "Or at least he was too high and lazy for it. He kept talking about the blow job he wanted so much, and when we were sitting on his sofa next to each other, more than once, he pushed my head down to his crotch. Really classy, right?"

"What did you do? *Please* tell me you didn't agree to his creepy bait-and-switch-laziness?" Hillary asked.

I took a few bites of my lobster ravioli, shaking my head no.

Swallowed, then continued, "Don't worry, I told him to just go with my ideas. I told him to stand up, and I took his hand and led him to his bedroom. I saw a bandanna on his dresser, and I told him to take his clothes off and lay down on the bed. I tied the bandanna around his head to blindfold him, then told him to wait a few minutes and I'd start pleasuring him. I put his stereo on, then I quietly closed the door behind him."

"That's it for your revenge?" Kara asked, surprise in her voice. "Did you put a pillow under his neck so it wouldn't cramp up? Jesus, Cilla, I would have hoped that you stabbed him or something, the way he was acting. What a colossal asshat."

"Let me finish," I chided Kara gently. "I waited a few minutes, until I could hear his snoring. Then, I went back out to the living room of his condo, which was an open-style room with the dining area and kitchen. He had a *huge* bag of weed sitting on his kitchen counter, right next to his cellphone. First, I grabbed a clean baggie from another drawer of his, and poured most of that into the baggie, which went into my purse."

"What the hell are you doing with someone's weed?" Hillary gasped. "You stole from his stash? Did he ever show up to kill you or at least accuse you of it?"

"I'm almost done!" I continued. "I went into his spices and pulled out his oregano leaf one, then poured half of that into his remaining weed stash, and mixed it up really well. Then, I put the spice jar back, grabbed a paper towel, and wiped the outside of his cellphone off very well, so it was nice and shiny. No fingerprints or anything. Then, I held it by an edge with the paper towel, and swiped it. Repeatedly."

There was dead silence from both Hillary and Kara; they just sat there, not even drinking their wines, waiting for me to elaborate.

"Where did you swipe the phone?" Kara spoke up, confusion evident on her face. "I don't get it."

"Ok," I hesitated to explain, "this is really unladylike of me, but . . . buttcrack, a few times."

"Holy fuck!" Hillary exclaimed, loudly. "You did this? You???"

"Yup! I put the phone back on the kitchen counter, then threw out the paper towel. Next, I checked the bedroom door, and the asshat was still asleep, so I left, very quietly," I finished.

"Did you ever hear from him again?" Hillary demanded. "And what happened to your bag of pot?"

"Never heard from him again. He didn't even block me from the dating website. The bag of weed went to my movers. I knew one of them from college, and knew he'd appreciate it. I paid half of what the normal rate usually was!" I replied proudly.

"Now that's a happy ending!" Kara exclaimed, then she and Hillary started laughing. "I can't believe you did that, stealing his drugs."

I shrugged. "Well, the date had been nice before he started smoking pot. That changed the entire evening. He was stupid enough to leave his stash out on his kitchen counter like that with a complete stranger, so he deserved it."

"And swiping his phone," Hillary added as she drank the rest of her wine.

"Like a credit card!" I grinned.

Hillary choked on her wine, then started laughing after. Kara was hysterical, fanning herself and trying to breathe. I couldn't help laughing too.

After a few minutes, Hillary got it together enough to comment, "I can't believe he didn't contact you or anything. He didn't mess with your mortgage or financial info?"

"Not that I know of," I replied. "Besides, when you sign mortgage papers, that's when things can happen. Everything gets locked in based on those mortgage papers. He had the signed papers back in his office the next day, and the info would have been in the system before the date happened. Plus, I've checked my mortgage stuff, and nothing's changed with the rate or any other info, that I can tell."

"That's definitely good," Kara added. "Wow, I still can't believe you did that—crazy!"

"Hey, he deserved it, as far as I believe," I asserted. "He was sexually lazy, and then wanted to hold my head down. It was starting to feel like it could go assault-ish; I don't like a guy to ever do something like holding me down unless I'm comfortable with him and I consent to allowing the situation. Holding a woman's head down like that during oral sex is disrespectful, you know?"

"Oh, I agree—he was definitely in the wrong on the sex. And, yeah, trying to push your head down is such a creep-loser thing to do," Hillary replied as she waved our waitress over, so we could have much-needed refills.

"I can't believe I never told you this insane story before," I said.

Hillary replied, "You didn't. I *know* I would have remembered it!"

"So, that's my worst date ever. Who's next with their worst date?" I asked, looking at both of them to cough up equally bizarre tales.

Kara raised her wine glass and started, "Let's see . . . my worst date. He picked me up, took me to a fancy restaurant. You know, the kind where they serve tiny plates of food that look like works of art and you're at the restaurant forever because of it? Well, it meant that the conversation had better be good, because you're sitting there a while. Unfortunately, the conversation with this guy wasn't all that. He was condescending and bossy. Seemed to love the sound of his voice more than caring whether I said anything at all."

"That sounds awkward," Hillary commented.

"Yeah, it does, but not awful," I added. "What made it your worst?"

"He had made a huge deal about how he was going to pay," Kara continued, "because he was a vice president and he was used to wining-and-dining people all the time. When the check came, he pulled out his AmEx Gold card, which was declined. So was his other credit card. Then, everyone looks at me like I'm supposed to pay. I was quite pissed. If it was up to *me* to pay, I wouldn't have picked this place. So we sat there and argued over who should pay. In the back of my mind, I was on the verge of standing up and running out of there!

"After about fifteen minutes, the manager comes over to us, and starts discussing payment with us. He ends up producing his debit card, but says he can only pay for his portion. So I look at the bill, announce I'm paying X dollars for *my* portion, and I go off to the bar to wait, because I don't want to be around this guy anymore.

"I pay just my part and tipped on my part, then get out my cellphone and call my sister to come pick me up. While I'm waiting, the bartender gives me two comped drinks, because she heard what had happened, and apparently I was the drama of the evening. The restaurant servers were all sympathetic to me, and laughing about my date behind his back. I could still hear him arguing with the manager as I had been walking towards the bar."

"Wow, what a weirdo," I said, then theorized "he probably wasn't a vice president."

"No," Kara confirmed, "I had actually googled him pre-date, since I knew his name. He did come up as a VP on LinkedIn, so that part was true. Either he was really bad at paying his bills, or he was spending too much to look like Mr. Bigshot."

"Crazy date!" Hillary added, then sipped some more wine.

"Oh, my story's not done!" Kara said, smiling at us. "My sis called me to let me know that she was outside the restaurant, so I went outside. I didn't know that my cheap-jerkwad date had followed me outside, where he started being nasty to me because I had refused to pay for his part of the dinner. I told him if he didn't stop it, I was going to call the cops, so then he backed off. He started yelling obscenities as I got into the car, and I was so happy when we were out of earshot, because he was getting nasty."

"Damn, what a nutjob!" I exclaimed, shaking my head.

"Yeah, really!" Hillary agreed. "Did you ever hear from him again?"

"Thankfully, no," Kara said gratefully. "And I haven't gone back to that restaurant either. The food was really good, but just too expensive for what it is!"

"Ok, Hillary, your turn for worst date!" I said, turning to her and gesturing for her to start entertaining us.

"My worst date, let's see . . ." she mused, "Thankfully it was long before I got married! We had met in a bar, and he wanted to take me out for dinner. He was a bit pushy, which bugged me, but I decided that he was still ok and I consented to dinner.

"We went out to a decent restaurant, and things were going good, until we were sharing dessert. He started talking about how women weren't equal to men and we should be happy we had even come as far as we did with regard to women's rights.

"So I'm sitting there, eating dessert and just stewing–" Hillary started.

"–So, why didn't you just cut the evening short after dessert? He sounds like a jerk," I interrupted.

"He does," Kara agreed.

"Don't worry, I was ready to! But I was really enjoying that chocolate cake! We went to that place downtown, the one with the organic gourmet food. The food was *so* good!" Hillary said, then drank some wine.

"Oh, yum!" Kara and I replied, in unison.

"Yeah, I wasn't turning down dessert," Hillary assured us, "even though he was a creep! He did pay the check, and then we left. It was around 9 p.m. at that point, and he had taken a break from being anti-female to ask me what we should do next. I was dying to say that I was tired and let's call it a night, but then I was stupid and suggested, 'How about if we go to the movies or something?' So, we get to the movie theater and anything decent is sold out, so that plan goes to crap. The mall was closing, and I really wasn't in the mood to do a bar, because I didn't want to see anyone I knew and have them think I'm really with this guy."

"I don't blame you," Kara said. "So he took you home?"

Hillary held her wine glass up and pointed at Kara to emphasize her point, "No, he said that he wanted to take me out to breakfast."

"Huh? That's odd. Explain, please!" I requested of her.

"I said that I wasn't following him, and he replied that he wanted me to go back to his place with him, and stay over," Hillary said, shaking her head. "That way, he can take me out for breakfast, then drop me off at home. He said he didn't want to have to drive out of his way to take me home."

"So, he wanted you to 'sleep over' to save some fossil fuels?" I said sarcastically. "Please, he's going skanky now!"

Hillary continued, "Yup, I said I wasn't really feeling ready for that, so if he wasn't comfortable with the drive, I'd call someone to pick me up, like my 6'2" brother."

"Nice threat!" Kara approved.

"I thought so," Hillary replied. "He changes his tune and says he'll just kill the planet and take me home, then. But also started a rant about how disappointed he was in me, because he really wanted for us to have sex. He was so whiny, talking about how it would have been awesome because every past lover he had had, told him how skilled he was at foreplay, and I was missing out on a major opportunity to be able to walk funny for a week, blah blah blah."

"Ewww, skanky. I bet he was the type to cry after he orgasms," I added, in a slightly bitchy tone of voice.

"Well, thankfully, I'll never know!" Hillary stated emphatically. "Anyway, he pulls up in front of my house, still reminding me that he's going to pick me up for breakfast. I said sorry, I actually have plans for brunch with some girlfriends. I was already using you girls as my excuse! And . . ."

"What? Tell us!" Kara exclaimed.

"He starts crying and whining how he spent all this money and he's not getting any return on his investment," Hillary continued, wrinkling her nose. "I was just stunned, but then I told him that he needs to not look at dating as an investment, that dating is like playing roulette, and that you could win or lose, but you won't get anywhere if you don't take a chance and play the game. He's still sitting there, quietly sobbing, and I'm about ready to get out of the car. And he asks me if he can come inside and talk some more. I said, sorry, no, I'm really tired, and I get out of the car lightning-fast to run into the house."

"That's crazy," I exclaimed, "but glad you escaped!"

"No, I didn't," Hillary said. "I was holding my keys, and dropped them somewhere in the grass. I ended up going over every fucking inch of my lawn and still not finding them. By that point, he had gotten out of the car and came over to see what was going on. Shittiest getaway attempt ever!"

"Oh no, that means he was closer to getting inside your house!" Kara gasped.

"Oh my God, no, there was no way that I was going to let his weepy, creepy ass in!!!" Hillary asserted.

"But," I interjected, "the keys?"

"I found the keys back by the curb," Hillary said, sipping some wine. "I was really worried that they were in the car, or that Don had picked them up and wouldn't give them back to me or something creepy was going to happen. After I found the keys, I got my house key ready and went right inside, yelling 'Good night and goodbye' at him on my way. I got the door shut and locked behind me, and went right upstairs to shower before going to bed."

"That's good," Kara replied. "You didn't listen to him trying the front door? You know he was trying that door multiple times, to attempt to get inside."

"Probably, but I didn't care," Hillary retorted.

"Wow, it's nuts how our worst experiences involve insanity or sex. It's a mix of insane guys and bad sex expectations. Honestly, it seems like you can't even date a guy unless sex is on the table," I summed up, in between sips of wine.

Both women nodded at me in agreement; it was much louder in Typesetters, since a music trio had started playing jazz, quite loudly.

"You're right. When the hell did it change?" Hillary asked, surprise in her voice.

"I don't know, even the decent guys seem to expect it now. So odd," I said.

I turned to Kara and leaned in to tell her, loud enough to be heard over the music, "I was telling Hillary earlier, before you showed up, that I'm burned out by bad dates, and probably just going to do a few hookups, just to give my emotions a break."

As I spoke-yelled the part about doing hookups, there was a break in the music. Of course, the four hot guys at the next table all turned and looked directly at me, because they had heard my comments about hookups. Oh shit! My face turned redder than my strawberry-blonde hair!

So, Kara leaned over and interfered, asking the guys, "So I guess you guys heard that about my lovely friend Cilla? Are any of you guys single and available? C'mon, help a very nice lady out!"

At that point, all of the guys came over to our table to meet all of us and talk. Two of the guys were married, one was in a relationship, and the fourth guy, Colin, was single and walked around the small table to meet me and shake hands with me. We started making small talk for a bit, and the other guys were talking, laughing, and enjoying the music with Hillary and Kara.

After twenty minutes, Hillary's cellphone pinged, and she said that we had to go. We got our check, and the guys insisted on paying our bill, even though we protested. As we were getting ready to leave, Colin asked me for my cellphone number, and he gave me his number and said I was definitely welcome to call him.

*   *   *

First order of business later that night, after I got back home from happy hour: I had a dating profile, but decided to revisit it, to see if I needed to edit it for casual dating, from its current "looking for a relationship" status. Of course, it was imperative that I take care of this right away; going on the Internet was always a great idea when someone was slightly tipsy!

I sat in front of the computer, sipping a huge glass of water, and looked at the basic info: my name, Priscilla Langford, nickname Cilla. The guys who pulled up my profile would only see my username, NBkitt3n, and my nickname. Age 40, height 5'4", strawberry blonde wavy hair, blue eyes, curvy/slightly overweight, but physically active. College degree, double major in IT and Communications, job as a software trainer. Loved to travel, watch movies, listen to music, ride my bike, eat healthy, all that kind of positive stuff that became your personal public relations profile that, on paper, seemed like a different person than you really were, even if it was "truthy."

As I stared at the screen, minutes ticked by while I read my profile over and over again, looking for spots that needed fixing. My eyes started to glaze over. This felt about as exciting as when I updated my resume, which I always struggled with. Found it difficult to promote myself properly in my resume. Probably the same reason I was drawing a blank on the profile updates.

I sighed and rubbed my eyes. Suddenly, just decided to tweak my "ideal first date" section of my profile, to say that I'd enjoy any activity on the first date, as long as we get to know each other. Maybe a spark would flare up between us, and the date would end in a kiss. It sounded ambiguous enough to stay with the original "relationship" intent, but suggestive enough to pique the interest of a guy who might want a quality hookup with a respectable woman, I figured. I finished typing in this update, read it for typos and clarity, then clicked the "post" button to save it into my profile. Exited the website and shut down the computer, then got ready for bed.

Saturday morning, I woke up around 9 a.m., and made breakfast while I contemplated my day, heck, my entire weekend. Holiday shopping was done, but I had to wrap and tag the mountain of gifts. I also had decorating to finish. Although I didn't hold many parties, friends did drop by in the evenings after Christmas Day, and we'd usually catch up over coffee and holiday cookies, and exchange presents.

I also had a lot of decorating projects going on in my condo. Although I had painted and updated the floors in my living room and kitchen before I had to quickly move in eight months ago, I had been unable to get anywhere else with fixing up the dated condo's décor in other rooms. I still had my bedroom, office, guest bedroom, and two bathrooms to finish up. I was going a bit slowly with fixing it up, but that was also due to all the expenses I had incurred over the past few months: new water heater, roof leak, and having to buy a new car.

After I finished my coffee and waffles, I decided that I'd paint my office, so that it felt like I was making some headway on the condo fix-up. I had already purchased the washed-coral-tinted paint, which was sitting in a corner of the room.

I got the furniture moved to the center of the room, covered with clear plastic tarps, and got the paint and rollers ready, and started painting. And thinking . . .

Dating really sucked. There, I admitted it to myself. It was like trying on pair of shoes after pair of shoes. Some looked ok, but the heel was all wrong. Or the finish was off (let's face it, you couldn't wear patent leather everywhere). Or some part of it wouldn't fit right, and wasn't fixable even though you bought it and tried to make it work, in vain.

Thought about what I had told Hillary last night, that I had been blown off by Adam, the latest guy I had dated. By text message.

I was still not completely sure why, but I think it had something to do with him cancelling a date night that was supposed to be special, as we had just decided to date exclusively. Instead of spending the evening together, he chose to do chores. Adam had said that he wanted me to be completely honest with him, so I told him that I was hurt that we weren't going to spend some time together. I had a feeling it was over, and the next day he texted me that it was "time to disconnect," which apparently meant break up, when someone was too cowardly to actually say the words. Or to even call and break it off like an adult. Well, we did agree on breaking up.

Ending that still sucked, even though I knew it was the right thing. A guy that couldn't see our decision to be exclusive as a reason to delay yard work a day or two and get together wasn't really part of the couple. Sad but true. However, because he made a choice that really went against what he seemed to want for us, I figured that my mourning period over him should be short. Still blew.

At least some of the guys who wanted a hookup were honest that it was a physical thing. Then I knew not to count on them for anything other than them being decent that evening.

Why would I seriously consider the hookup?, I contemplated as I painted. Being seduced was a bit of a rush when you knew how it could end up, and an ego boost that might be sorely needed. For physical needs, and because it was nice to feel close to someone for the moment. For that night, I was right there in the moment with someone, and it was reassuring that someone still desired me. After that, I would be sated, but back to being alone. Which, after the post-coital glow wore off, would still be a bit lousy.

Lately, I felt too jaded by too many of these dates that ended up not panning out. It seemed a bit sad to put effort into parading myself out there, only to find out that the guy had some odd flaw that showed me who he really was. Definitely disappointing, especially when they rejected me.

The more I thought about how my dating life had seemed to stagnate like a muddy pond, the more I thought about the benefits of hooking up. I had only done that twice over the years, and surprisingly, it had happened at the end of crappy dates.

The first time, it was with a guy who I seemed to have good rapport with in texts, but I could tell that long-term wouldn't work for us. Put tactfully, he wasn't as intellectual as I was—I couldn't see myself watching CNN with him and discussing the fiscal cliff, for instance. We could discuss the action films of Bruce Willis ad nausea (said nausea, for me, would occur about 30 minutes after the discussion started, and that would be after I had also balanced my checking account in my head). So it wasn't a lifelong match, but the sex was quite nice. He was younger, but was fantastic at kissing. Sweet but confident kisses, not too much tongue, really nice and passionate.

The second time was with a guy who was in town for a military assignment. We went out to dinner, which was awkward because he was a bit shy. Conversation was a bit stilted, but he was reasonably smart. After dinner, we ended up going back to his hotel room, watched a bit of TV, and then went from cuddling into sex. The sex was decent, but the foreplay was better. We decided to see each other the next night, and he texted me that next day to confirm, "Still getting together tonight?"

"Yes, after my haircut, remember?" I texted back to him, from the salon. My stylist, who was also on the dating circuit, was very interested in my online dating experiences, both the successes and the failures.

"Great, can't wait!" he replied. "Also, can I watch you pee?"

"WHAT???" I yelped, in the middle of the salon!

I showed my stylist, and she screamed, "Oh My God Oh My God! I cannot believe that!"

I was stunned; there was no precedent in anything we had texted, said, or done to each other to elicit that request from him. After a few minutes, while I listened to my stylist snipping my hair with the sharp scissors, I started to giggle, and she joined in. We couldn't stop, and she stopped cutting my hair, and was soon doubled over. I was gripping the chair's arms and think I cried, I giggled so much!

"I have to respond to this insanity!" I sputtered out, the first words I could form after the epic giggling attack. "What the hell do I say? There was *no* precedent for this," I continued.

I looked at my cellphone, which had been in my hand. A second message from him, "Or would you be able to pee on me instead?"

"*Holy shit,*" I exclaimed, then, "Sorry" to the salon's snooty general population, staring at me down their Princeton noses. I showed the latest message to my stylist.

"Cilla, this guy is nuts!" she managed before the giggles started up again.

I decided to reply, before he texted me a more kinky request than the previous ones. I texted him, "I'm going to have to decline, sorry."

"Decline what?" he responded.

"Decline seeing you tonight," I replied.

"But, I thought we had such a wonderfun time and you can give me a foot rub, too," he texted. Yes, he had said "wonderfun," and I didn't think it was a typo.

"Sorry, I don't think we're as compatible as I thought we were," I texted back, very quickly.

Then the begging and pleading texts from him started. "You don't have to pee for me, just come over and we'll have fun"; "Please come over and I'll pleasure you"; "Come on, you know you want me."

After the last one, he tried calling me a few times, but didn't leave messages. My phone was on silent, but the vibrating part of the notification messages was getting annoying. After twenty minutes of that, he texted again, "Can we please start over?"

I texted back, "Please lose my number, because we're done." The next day, I blocked him on the dating website. I kept his number on my phone, just so I knew to not engage him in any more communication. At least I was smart about it and he didn't have my address; I was quite sure that if he did have it, he would have shown up and it would have become quite awkward, especially when I would have called the cops on his stalker ass.

Even with that bizarre experience under my belt, I still felt dread at the thought of more dating—I didn't want any more awkward dinners out or making the same smalltalk ad infinitum. It had been about six months since I had even had sex after a date, and the prospect of just sex without the bad dates peaked my interest.

As I painted the final strokes on the wall, I seriously pondered just sticking to casual encounters/hook-ups for a few months. I would screen the guys better, of course, even though I was already quite selective. But, I'd try and see how that panned out—maybe it would give me a bit of practice in dealing with guys, without being emotionally invested in the outcome, the will he/won't he ever contact me again dilemma. Plus, maybe I could pick up some new sex techniques. And enjoy myself along the way.

By then, it was lunchtime. Made myself a sandwich, then ate it while I checked my inbox on the dating website using my cellphone. Saw that there were no new messages. I kept my phone on for about forty-five minutes, so that I was actively logged into the website. Whenever I was logged in, the site kept my profile more visible to others, which usually resulted in more interest from men.

After lunch, I started on laundry, alternating between that and wrapping presents in front of the TV, so that I was sufficiently entertained with random sitcoms.

Ordered a pizza for dinner, then I went back into the office to put on the final coat of paint. My thoughts kept straying back to the dating website, wondering if anyone had responded yet, but I didn't want to check it until the next morning. Didn't want to obsess and be stalker-ish over it, so after painting, I was done for the day. No fancy Saturday night out for me, which was fine.

The next morning, I woke up, and it was absolutely freezing when I left the bed! Was still groggy, but after walking around, I finally remembered opening up more windows to get the paint fumes out. And that I had turned the heat down last night. Must have been more exhausted from Saturday's errands than I realized.

Made breakfast and a lot of coffee, then I started on the holiday decorating. Luckily that was limited to the living room, so I was able to do some more TV time while I put up the tree and decorated it, strung some lights around the windows, and decorated the fireplace and mantle.

Around lunchtime, on a whim, I tried calling Colin, the nice guy I had met on Friday night. However, the number turned out to be a local drugstore. I asked if anyone named Colin worked there, in the pharmacy or regular employee. Nope, nobody by that name. Oh well, either he gave me the number wrong, or he was an ass who went out of his way to give me a fake number. At least I already had my hook-up plan formulated before I met him.

Checked the dating website on my phone again, but the dating site still showed an empty inbox. I stayed logged into it for about two hours, while I did some cleaning and bill-paying. More exciting stuff, but it felt nice to be a bit isolated, for once. Usually I wasn't crazy about feeling like that, but I was getting a lot done.

Sunday night, I decided to check the dating website again, only I logged into it from my laptop, in my very nice, light-coral-toned, though still slightly smelly, office at home. I looked at my inbox that was now flashing two messages. Clicked on the first one, from BigDan85, .and BigDan wanted to know my bra size. Ewww, that wasn't information that I would divulge to any stranger, so I deleted and blocked him.

The second message was from FooFooYea, who said,

"Hey,

The dating site matched us up! I think you're really pretty. Let me know if you want to chat sometime.

Todd"

Hmm, possibilities. I clicked on his username to go to his profile, and his picture came up—golden-to-medium brown tousled hair, brown eyes, tanned skin, 6' tall, with a camera around his neck and a really cute smile. Looked like a cross between a surfer and the sexy world traveler you'd have a fling with when you bumped into him in Prague. Very good-looking, and probably out of my league.

I read Todd's profile: his job was freelance photographer, who currently worked with mostly magazine and corporate photography. He loved 90s grunge music, his two rescue cats, and traveling. He was also a positive person, outgoing, looking for a woman who was also opinionated and who could be his intellectual equal. Preferred a college graduate, for more compatibility. Someone who he could kiss, to end any argument, as he said he enjoyed being affectionate. He didn't have too much more on his profile, but he sounded like a decent guy.

We had music and traveling in common, which was definitely nice; I always liked hearing about others' travels, where they had been, where they wanted to go, and why. And college degree.

His profile sounded interesting, and his pics were really great (as long as they really were him). Wait a minute. I checked his profile again.

His age was only 27. I sat back and let out a long breath. Oh, shit. Was I seriously thinking about replying to a 27-year-old man? I had turned 40 two months ago, and didn't want to be called a cougar at all. I hated that crappy "cougar" label with a passion, even though so many people joked about it.

I remembered a few years ago, a pretty coworker of ours was in her late 40s and turned "cougar." She showed up at our holiday party with her 22-year-old boyfriend. It had been a bit of a scandal at work, because she spent a lot of time at the party parading him around like a trophy, introducing him to all of us and dropping in on every conversation, to make sure we all noticed how witty she was. Previously she, had always been pretty and dressed quite classy, as if she was our boss and not our coworker. Never a hair out of place on her salon-perfect shoulder-length haircut; I always wondered if she wouldn't be better suited to read the news on the local TV station. Her performance at the holiday party was so out of character for her, we were just stunned. It was as if Santa had gifted our office with a very messed-up scandal.

After that, we called her "Midlife-Crisis Maeve" behind her back. She seemed a bit desperate and sad to me, and as if she was trying to relive her early 20s with that guy. Other coworkers wanted to start a betting pool to see how long it would last, but thankfully they abandoned that possible idea. It wasn't worth getting in trouble and possibly fired over, even if it could be legendary.

I thought about the comments we had all had over seeing Maeve with her young boyfriend: "She's so emotionally immature;" "Is she going to have babies with him? He's already a baby, compared to her;" "Do people call him her son when they're out on dates?" "He'll get tired of her, anyway, when his friends want him to go out drinking;" "When they go shopping, she goes to Nordstroms and he lives at Abercrombie & Fitch or the Gap;" "I wouldn't date him—he probably never does laundry. Oh wait, maybe he just brings it over Maeve's house for her to do?"

We had been secretly vicious with the comments, and it affected how we saw Maeve—she lost a lot of respect with most of us after that holiday party. We didn't include her in as many of the fun conversations at work, so when we had office lunches, she was out of the loop. She was changing, too—would go out in the evening at work, and show up for work the next morning in the previous day's outfit. I guess she was showing off how wasted she had been the previous evening? Or that she was over her boyfriend's house, but didn't plan to wear clean clothes the next day?

We weren't really sure what happened after that—we could only assume that management spoke to her about the clothes issues, or maybe it was a hygiene issue; she often smelled like the floor of a bar when she'd come in to work wearing the repeated outfits. I can't remember how long she lasted after it, but she was gone one day. No notice, and no time for us to throw a party wishing her happy times with her boyfriend and midlife crisis. We still wondered about Maeve every once in a while at work events. Nobody ever heard from her again, though.

I had dated other guys younger or older than me before, but not more than a decade, though. I had always thought that I was most compatible with a guy who was close in age to me, because of the similarity of life experiences. We would be going through the same life issues at the same time. I had always felt more comfortable with someone who saw me as an equal, though I had not made conscious choices to be with guys around my age; it had just always worked out that way.

Should I consider this guy or not? It was something I hadn't considered before, hooking up with someone who was significantly younger than me. I didn't know, maybe if conversation wasn't involved?

Because what the hell would we even talk about, beyond exchanging names, job info, discussing hobbies and anything else that was important to us? Well, it wasn't as if I was going to discuss the headlines on CNN with him, or with any hookup, for that matter. Maybe the less talking we did, the better. No, it would be nice to at least be able to respect the guy I'm having sex with. If he was reasonably intelligent, I'd at least meet someone that could be decent. Who knows what could happen with any guy?

Hmm, maybe I should be more open-minded and go for smart guys, rather than age? That guy Todd had said in his profile that he was a college graduate, which would great, as long as it was actually true. I had come across other guys on the website who said they were college graduates, who clearly weren't; possibly those guys had only attended college parties.

I knew I was making myself loopy by overanalyzing it, rather than just actually answering messages and starting a dialogue with some of the guys. Was I being too picky and elitist? Or just talking myself out of contacting them, so that I didn't have to exert any energy and take a chance on a guy who could turn out to be pretty decent? I knew I had to be more open-minded; it was only sex for an evening or two, not picking out a guy for my arranged marriage. That was the beauty of casual sex, no commitment and no issues. Just pleasure and fun. Like having a chocolate bar all to yourself.

But, if I ignored the age, and if he wrote his own profile, he seemed quite mature and together. And he didn't look 27 at all, he looked 34. And I knew I didn't look or act my age—oddly enough, I still got carded in restaurants and liquor stores, which baffled me. I could pass for 34-35ish, easily. Was this a good idea?

Had an out-of-body experience a few minutes later, screaming "What are you doing?!?!" in my head as I leaned forward in my office chair and moved the mouse to hit "reply," then typed,

"Hi Todd,

I checked your profile and you look nice and sound interesting . . . "

2

First Contact: Really, Is It Ever a Good Idea Between the Genders?

I went to work on Monday, and tried to put the dating website out of my mind entirely. I needed to concentrate on work, since I had trainings on Tuesday through Thursday. Definitely a busy week, and I would be away in Harrisburg, Pennsylvania for the Wednesday and Thursday trainings, so I'd have to deal with extra driving and staying overnight. Monday was a busy day of final preparation for my trainings, spending a lot of time yelling at our ancient, near-death copier as I copied handouts for the trainings.

In between my hectic moments, I did make a bit of time to check the dating website, and see Todd's replies, so that I could respond to them.

Todd's email reply:

"nice to meet you Cilla, do u mind the age difference? Have more pics?"

My next email:

"hi Todd, I don't think the age difference bugs me—
you seem more together than some guys my age! And I
don't "feel" my age anyway. I'll post some more pics
tonight, since they're on my home computer (I'm at
work). You going to send me more pics of you, too?"

His reply:

"thanks for the compliment! I rarely get my pic
taken, and I never think of getting copies of them, so
what's on the website are the most current pics of me.
It's ironic, since I'm a photographer by profession! I'll
check mail later for your updates!"

My reply:

"That is really funny about you not having more pics
of yourself! I've attached a few pics—had to sort thru a
bunch, because the friend who took them isn't good at
taking pics (most of them were very unflattering)."

His reply, about one hour after I had sent my message:

"U look very cute in those pics! So, whatcha looking
for in terms of dating?"

After reading his message, I thought about it for a bit, what
to say to him without sounding like I was blatantly soliciting
him for sex. Figured it was better to be a bit ambiguous in my
reply:

"Thanks! I think I'm a bit flexible on what I'm
looking for, only because I've dated and nothing's gone
past a few dates lately. Guess I just haven't found the
right guy in a while. It would be nice to meet someone
that I click with, but if that doesn't happen it's still a
decent experience. I'm guessing casual dating (dinner,
movie, hanging out at home and watching TV, going to
a concert or something), unless we mutually decide on
more? Are you on a similar page?"

His reply:

"Yeah, I think I'm most into the hanging out at home part right now—it would be nice to be low-key, since the holidays are already so hectic. Want someone to relax and be romantic with, so I'm not too alone during some of these cold winter nights."

We had emailed back and forth for a couple of days, and as I prepared to email Todd back on Tuesday evening, the chat window on the dating website popped up, and it was him, requesting a chat with me. I accepted it, and he started typing,

Todd: "Hey Cilla, how are u?"

Me: "I'm doing good, just relaxing and doing some computer stuff. How are you? "

Todd: "good good also relaxing"

Me: "yeah I know I should have finished final holiday shopping for family, but I needed tonight to myself! I was reading your last message . . . sounds nice about low key ☺"

Todd: "that's cool, im glad we're on the same page . . . not sure if w/the age difference we'd be the best relationship candidates lol but we could def have some fun and im enjoying getting to know u"

Me: "yeah, I wasn't sure about the age difference, but you're already more mature than any other guy that's messaged me ;) "

Todd: "thanks, pretty girl, that's really nice of you to say!"

Me: "you're welcome! So, did you want to plan to meet up later this week or over the weekend? Or is that too quick for you? "

Todd: "nah that's fine ☺ mutual attraction is mutual attraction"

Todd: "the thing is, my funds are tight thanks to the holidays otherwise id take u out on a decent date but im kind of limited for a while"

Me: "that's fine—less-expensive is good for now (since I'm fixing up my condo, $$ is a bit tight for me, too)! Coffee or something is fine! "

Todd: "that's cool thanks for understanding"

Todd: "u said it's been a while since uve dated?"

Me: "I was in a long-term relationship during my 20s. after that ended, I dated a bit and was in another relationship in my mid-30s, but that ended when I was 36. Since then, I've dated but nothing's panned out in a while, unfortunately! "

Todd: "ok, so I'm guessing its been a while since u had someone hold u and kiss u and all that ☺"

Me: "yeah, it's been a while—I definitely miss the kissing, etc! "

Todd: "well, we need to change all that ☺"

Todd: "and u got a young man too, you're not doing too bad for yourself lol"

Me: "#1-that sounds nice! #2-omg, too funny (though if you call me a cougar, that's instant trouble for you!!!) "

Todd: "lol I bet I could get away with it in certain settings while getting away with certain activities lol"

Todd: "youre like a junior cougar tho no worries"

Me: "omg you're still a brat! I need to figure out a nickname for you . . . "

Todd: "lol"

Me: "a question: u really ok with the age difference, even where affection is concerned? I've never been with any1 w/noticeable age diff"

Todd: "a lot of girls my age range are selfish when it comes to making love. I enjoy a woman with more experience and wisdom"

Todd: "so it's all good"

Todd: "ms. cilla ;) "

Me: "that's cool—selfish is lame! Intimacy should be about exploring/sharing/having fun ;)"

Todd: "yea definitely"

Todd: "there's something id like to say to ya, cilla, but I don't want to offend u…"

Me: "sure, say it, if it bugs me I'll let you know . . . "

Todd: "well I'll take my chances. I dig the fact its been like a while since uve experienced a different man and im kind of into the idea of raising the bar showing u what u been missing haha"

Me: "it does not bug me Todd, it sounds intriguing and kinda hot ;) plus, I'm glad you didn't go the dumb guy route and ask me bra size within 2 messages of initial contact!"

Todd: "haha no I dont need to ask questions about those kinds of things I like to find out for myself"

Todd: "do u text? Can I have yer phone #, so we can text instead?"

"Sure," I replied, then typed my phone number.

I got up from the computer desk and went into my bedroom to retrieve my cellphone; I had a feeling he was going to text me soon.

I set the phone down on the side of my computer desk and then it pinged.

"hey cilla, it's todd," he texted.

"Hey Todd, you got the number right! ;) Can I close the chat window now?" I texted back.

"Sure, we'll just text," he replied.

I closed the chat window and started closing my computer down.

"So, whatcha doin now?" he asked. "Anything fun?"

"Nah, turning computer off. Then, have to put more laundry in...so I have underwear for tomorrow!" I texted him.

"lol, just go free, that's what I do when I run out!" he suggested.

"Nooo," I texted quickly back. "I can't do that . . . the chafing...OMG NO!"

"LOL, chicken! wear a skirt or something," he texted back.

"Only if you wear a kilt!" I replied.

"Well, maybe you should come over now, and that solves the issue," he texted.

I paused.

I knew he and I were flirting and had blatantly discussed hooking up, but I hesitated to accept his invite. Why was I suddenly actually afraid of it? Was I worried he wasn't who he seemed to be? Was I afraid to end my dry spell? Or was I concerned that he would be who he seemed to be, and he'd be in a league above me, and I'd seem like some sad pathetic middle-aged creepy woman, compared to him being a cute, younger successful photographer? What the hell was wrong with me? I was overthinking something that I thought I wanted very much, yet I couldn't text him a reply that I was ready to go.

"u still there Cilla?" he asked. I didn't know what to say. I felt like a fraud because I was suddenly too scared to meet him. Didn't want to lead him, or anyone, on, though part of me did want to just have some semi-anonymous sex. Clearly I was conflicted and nuts. I scrambled for something credible to say.

"yeah, sorry, I was hanging up some clean laundry," I texted to him. "I think I'm getting tired tonight, maybe I can go over your place tomorrow instead?"

"you sure?" he texted. "we could have some fun tonight."

"yeah, I'm sure," I replied, feeling sad for being such an idiot. "tomorrow would be good."

"ok I'll text ya tomorrow, nite," he texted.

"nite Todd," I texted back.

But, he didn't text the next night. Or the night after that. After a few days, I figured that I had missed my window of opportunity with Todd, the hot 27-year-old, and he had obviously moved on. I did feel a little sad over it, because he had been very interested in me.

Christmas was on Tuesday, and I spent a quiet Christmas breakfast with my dad and his girlfriend, and exchanged presents with them. It was relaxing. Veronica made fruit salad and omelets, I made waffles, and my dad made cappuccinos on the espresso machine we had all chipped in to buy him for his Christmas gift.

By the time I went over my mother's in the afternoon, I was very wired from multiple test cappuccinos. I spent the afternoon at a very boisterous present-opening and dinner, which included my siblings and their sugar-infested adorable kids.

The day was fun, except for when my sister, Fiona, asked me in the middle of dinner, "How's your boyfriend prospects, little sis? Weren't you seeing someone? I half expected you to show up with a new guy on your arm."

Everyone turned to stare at me, and I stammered, "I was seeing someone, but we ended it. So, I'm single again. Can you please pass the biscuits?"

One of my nephews, who was six, chimed in, "Aunt Cilla, if you don't get married, what are you gonna do when you're really old?"

Fiona gasped, "Brandt, that is not a good thing to say to your aunt! We're having a serious talk when we get home!"

I looked at him, and knew I couldn't do anything nutty because of all the witnesses at the table, so instead I said, "Brandt, my honest answer is that I don't know. I just try to live my life and be happy and have lots of family and friends who love me. Also, Brandt, some people might think your question is a bit too blunt for Christmas dinner—a question like that might be better if you and I were alone, ok?"

"Ok, sorry Aunt Cilla," he apologized, clearly trying to head off future punishment from his mother on a holiday. Fear of not playing with his toys, probably.

I left after dinner, since I had to be at work the next morning. Emotionally, I was drained from the afternoon. I spent the evening sipping wine and watching some random TV, and not thinking.

*　　*　　*

The day after Christmas, I was at work and checked the dating site. A cute 46-year-old, Danny, had just started messaging me and seemed quite interested in meeting up with me that weekend.

If his info was true, he was tall, dark hair, thin but athletic, loved to snowboard the minute snow fell in the mountains of the northeast, and kept busy the rest of the year with his job as an IT manager at a testing company.

I felt a bit more comfortable about the 46-year-old, since he was closer to me in age and life experiences. Figured that he might be a good choice, and I'd see what happened with him. Assumed that we'd both be too mature to play games, which could mean that things could go well between us. From his emails and text messages, he was flirty and seemed interested in me. He also liked to travel, and was interested in museums and art, and spoke of doing a museum on our second date. So, he seemed great on paper, the more he messaged me.

Danny: "So, you liked my profile, huh? Or were you just interested in becoming part of my harem?"

Me: "Your profile was really funny—I loved the part about how your ideal first date is meeting in one of the parking lots at Newark Airport in the middle of the night, then asking if I had any money you could borrow."

Danny: "if I bring coffee to the first date and it tastes funny, will you still drink it? I'm not trying to drug you or anything!"

Me: "Hahaha! Um, you have to ask me out on a date before we can discuss the parameters of the date . . . "

Danny: "Oh, good point. So, what else do you like to do for fun "

Me: "Hang out with friends, go out to eat, movies, go to happy hour with friends, travel. How about you?"

Danny: "Similar activities. And stalk pretty strawberry blonde 40-year-olds, it's a newer hobby of mine."

Me: "Cute, real cute. Where's someplace you'd like to go, but haven't?"

Danny: "I try to be. Someplace I haven't been to...that newer art museum in Philly. It's supposed to have a great collection."

Me: "Oh that's really cool—I haven't been there either."

Danny: "Maybe that should be near the top of possible places for us to go together? ;) "

Me: "I'd like that."

Danny: "Cool, gotta go, talk to ya later, cutie!"

Later that day, he messaged me again:

Danny: "hey, how's it going?"

Me: "it's going good, I'm just going over some notes for a training I'm doing in early January. How are you?"

Danny: "I'm fine. Is that a work training?"

Me: "yes; it is. I run software trainings for a computer training company. That training is for some specific PowerPoint presentation skills at a private company."

Danny: "that's cool, sounds like an interesting job."

Me: "sometimes it is, other times it's a royal pain in the butt. Some people won't be helped with a few hours of training, so it's sometimes very frustrating."

Danny: "I bet. So, if I want PowerPoint advice, do I have to pay or is it free?"

Me: "You can ask me about the different features of it. I know all the tips and tricks on it; I can teach you its secrets. Of course, if you start asking me too much, I can send you a schedule for paying me per tip I teach you."

Danny: "God, yes, I'll ply you with wine as payment, and you can tell me your secrets. One secret per kiss!"

Me: "When?"

Danny: "This Saturday night?"

Me: "Sounds good to me!"

Danny: "Great, we can meet for drinks, and see what we want to do after that!"

I was excited to go on the date with Danny, and the next few days passed by in a blur.

Work was very slow and empty, since there was little work going on and many employees were on vacation. I spent time organizing my computer and email, and finishing all my expense reports.

Thursday evening, my girlfriend Mel, short for Melinda, and her husband and three kids came over for coffee/hot cocoa and holiday cookies, and to exchange presents. It was a long-standing tradition we had first enacted when we were about ten years old. She had been a professor, but was an English teacher at the local high school. I spent Friday night cleaning up the crumbs from Thursday night, but I had enjoyed Thursday night.

Saturday morning, Danny had messaged me about where we could meet that evening, but hadn't sent the time for us to get together. I sent him a message telling him that was fine, and asking him what time we should meet. However, by about dinnertime, I still hadn't received a reply from Danny.

I decided to get ready anyway—if he didn't contact me, maybe I'd call Hillary or one of my other girlfriends to get together. Carefully gathered up my long hair and used a hair clip to secure it on top of my head. After all, good hair days had to be preserved. Filled the tub with hot water and dropped in a bubble bath bar, and while the scent of fruity candy wafted around my bathroom, I perused my closet. Picked out a decent pair of jeans, then decided on my favorite blue v-neck sweater. Laid the clothes out on my bed, along with some lacy underwear, then I settled into the luxurious bubble bath. After the water started to cool, I stepped out of the tub, drained it and sprayed it with some chemical-laden smelly bathroom cleaner (always good to avoid a fatal slippery tub accident, because it would seriously suck to die right before having a hot date! That would definitely be my bad luck in life). Then I got dressed, took out the hair clip, finger-combed my wavy strawberry-blonde hair a bit, and put a bit of makeup on.

At that point, it was 8 p.m., and I realized that the guy was definitely not going to be contacting me about our date that night, which left me feeling slightly bummed. I called Hillary, but there was no answer, so I left a message, "Hey, just seeing what you're up to, since my date didn't pan out. Call me!"

I called Mel, who said she was busy picking up her kids from a birthday party. She said she'd call me back in a little bit, which usually meant that she was about one hour from passing out after a busy day with her family, and would call me tomorrow.

I hung up from chatting with her, and tossed my cellphone onto my sofa and plopped down onto it. Leaned over to the coffee table and grabbed the remote, and switched on the TV. Started flipping around for anything that would hold my rapidly declining mood. Finally settled on Titanic, even though I wasn't too fond of the bad dialogue in it. Although Leo was eye candy, the dialogue always ended up reminding me why I rooted for the ship, so that the movie could end. I ended up dozing while I imagined Leo drawing me, on my sofa . . .

3

Extra, Extra, the Heroine's
on the Prowl

Ping, ping . . . I jolted awake from the text message notification sound. Who was texting me at 10:15 on a Saturday night? I figured Hillary was getting back to me. Reached across the sofa to retrieve the phone and reply to. I looked at the screen and it showed that Todd had texted me.

Todd, the hot, young photographer from the dating website, had contacted me. Wow, maybe I hadn't blown it with him when I chickened out last week. I opened the text, "hey ms cilla!"

"Hey Todd, how's it going?" I responded. Was very curious now.

"it's going good, u doing anything important?" he replied, a minute or two after my message.

"just watching TV—I'm bored," I replied, hoping an invite was in the works.

"Come over Cilla, let's hang out," he texted. Yes! I thought, though I wanted to meet in public first. So I replied, "I'd like to, but can we meet at a diner 1st, just to see how we hit it off?"

"It's so cold! I'm a good guy, I promise!" he replied. I was a tad annoyed over that, and replied, "Omg, it's not that cold outside! I'll warm u up later on ☺"

I didn't get a response for a few minutes after that, and wondered if he didn't like my message. But, then another ping, ping and I read his text, "Lol, listen, u and I both seem to be down to hookup, I promise I'm a decent guy—I'll treat ya w/respect, so call and run your background check, ok Cilla?"

"Ok, I'll call in a min," I replied. Holy shit, what was I going to say? Oh yeah, his address, condoms, what else? I sat there, frantically thinking what else I needed to figure out. Suddenly my cellphone started ringing, and it was him.

"Hello?" I said a bit timidly. My mouth had gone dry, so I reached for the glass of water on my coffee table and held the phone away from my mouth while I drank. Didn't want to be gulping water in someone's ear.

He replied smoothly, "Hey, Cilla, it's Todd. I'm calling you, so ask me whatever you need to."

"Honestly, I have no idea what to ask you!" I exclaimed. "Tell me about yourself, Todd."

"Let's see, I'm single, 27, live in New Brunswick with my two cats. I spent the evening sending out a bunch of photos for my latest assignments, and right now I'm relaxing and waiting for you to come over so that my evening can really begin," he said. "What else would you like to know?"

"Um, I really have no idea what to ask," I laughed. He started laughing too.

"You're really not good at doing background checks, are you?" he teased me.

"Not at all," I admitted. "We should talk about some basics, though—are you ok with condoms?"

"Yes, not a problem, and I'm clean—no STDs or anything," he added.

I responded, "I'm clean too, no STDs. Do you have condoms or do you need me to bring some?"

"I have them, so you don't need to worry about it," he said. "So, would you like my address?"

"Yes, I do," I replied, reaching across my coffee table for a sticky note and a pen. "What is it?"

"It's 602 Emerson, at the Gateway Apartment complex off of Broad Street," he said. "Do you know where that is?"

"Yes, it's not too far away," I said.

"How long will it take you to get ready to come over?" he asked.

"Lucky for you, I'm actually ready," I answered. "I got stood up for a date tonight, so I can leave in a few minutes. I just have to stop for coffee on the way. I can be there in twenty minutes, if that works for ya?"

"That's awesome, Cilla," he said enthusiastically. "Wait, I meant that it's awesome you'll be here soon, not that you got stood up by some jerk. But I get to benefit from that, right?"

"Yeah," I chuckled.

"Call me when you're almost there, and I'll look for your car," he said. "See you soon!"

"Ok, I'll call you soon, bye!" I said before hanging up.

Put my phone on the coffee table slowly, then stood up and squealed. Yes, squealed! Possibly hot sex with a hot, seemingly decent guy was worth squealing over. I stood up, scurried around my apartment, gathering my stuff—purse, contact lens case and glasses (just in case I was staying over, though I assumed not), checked that I had a good lipstick in my purse, put my shoes and coat on, then got out my keys. Made it out to the car, and realized I forgot the sticky note with his address, so went back for that. Clearly the coffee was necessary.

I went to a convenience store on the way, and got my large coffee just the way I liked it, with a bit of vanilla creamer. Back in the car, I typed Todd's address into my car's GPS, and I was off, sipping the hot coffee while driving. Multitasking was important because I didn't want to delay meeting him.

After arguing with the GPS because it sometimes suggested a route I didn't like, I was close and pulled over to call Todd. "Hi, it's Cilla. I'm two minutes away," I told him.

"Ok, pull up near the front doors, not in the parking lot, and I'll show you where to go," he instructed.

"Ok, bye," I said and hung up.

I drank more of my coffee, and then got out my lipstick. Grabbed a napkin and wiped my mouth and teeth off, then popped in a breath mint from the depths of my car's glove compartment. Applied a bit of lipstick, then blotted it carefully so it looked less fresh. Didn't want to look like I was trying too hard.

I started the car and the GPS got me to the front of the building. As I reached to the console to turn the GPS off, I saw him walking towards my car. His face was shadowed, because the lights above the sidewalks didn't project enough light. Tall, lanky, and as he got closer I started feeling really nervous. He opened the car door, and got in.

"Hi, Cilla," he smiled at me. Oh my god, was all I could think. Every deity must have been watching over me and smiling down on me for bringing us together at this moment. He wasn't cute. He was devastatingly gorgeous. Model-hot.

He was so out of my league that I felt like a short freak next to him.

"Hi Todd," I parroted back to him.

We both looked at each other and laughed a bit nervously.

"Well, we both look like our pics, so that's good, right?" I asked.

"Yes, though you're even more beautiful than in your pictures," he said, still smiling.

"Thanks, you're really hot," I said, blushing because I wasn't good with receiving or giving compliments, especially since I figured he was being polite. "So, where do I go?"

"Thanks for the compliment, pretty girl! You'll go around the circle, then you'll take the first left to the parking lot," he pointed as I drove. He kept making small talk, and I responded. But I honestly had no idea what he was saying—I felt so distracted between driving and his presence. It was a bit surprising for me to act like this around a guy; I figured it was because it had been a while since I'd had sex, and I certainly hadn't been with anyone as hot as him.

I parked the car in the lot, and we got out. I locked it as he rounded the car to my side and held out his hand. I put my keys in my purse, then took his hand and we walked swiftly to his apartment. I was practically jogging, to keep pace with his long strides. He led me up the steps and opened the outside door with his key, then unlocked the inside door and held it open for me to go in before him. I squeezed past him and went inside.

"This is really nice," I said, looking around his studio apartment. There was a bit of clutter, but he had decent furniture, some looked like quality hand-me-downs and other pieces were from Ikea. It almost looked like a young professional lived there, except for the wires stretched along the tops of the walls everywhere, and the large photos binder-clipped to the wires. I felt as if I was in an art gallery that someone happened to live in.

"Thanks," he said. "Can I take your coat? Would you like something to drink?"

I shrugged out of my coat and handed it to him. "I'm done with my coffee, since I had to wake up. But I could use something cold. What do you have?"

Todd hung up my coat and his, and kicked out of his sneakers next to the door. I leaned down, unzipped my ankle boots, and stepped out of them, then followed him to the tiny galley kitchen off to the side of the main room.

"Let's see, I have iced tea, lemon-lime soda, water, milk, and whiskey," he said, looking into the fridge. "If you want whiskey, I can add ginger ale to it, if it's too strong for you."

"Sure, whiskey and the soda sounds good, with ice if you have it, please," I said, glancing back at his photos. "Are these your photos? They're amazing!"

"Thanks," he replied, as he made my drink. "I'm a photographer, as you know. Sometimes I have my favorites developed. These are extras from my portfolio. Plus, it's less effort than painting the walls or dealing with decorating."

Todd finished preparing our drinks, but then turned to me and looked at me.

"Can I kiss you?" he asked, as he reached to hold my hand.

"Yeah," I answered, mesmerized by how serious he suddenly looked. He leaned down and lightly touched his lips to mine, and then pulled away, letting go of my hand.

"Very nice," he said, "You really are beautiful."

He leaned down and kissed me again, and I clutched his arms. Todd brought his hands up to my waist and then deepened the kissing, as he slowly pulled me closer to him. We angled our mouths at the same time as we both opened them, and the kissing became deep French kisses quickly. He pressed me against the doorway of the kitchen, to steady us both, and the kisses seemed to engulf us with increasing passion as he held me tighter around my waist. His body was pressed into mine, and I was gripping his upper arms so I wouldn't slide to the ground in a puddle of passionate mush. After a few more minutes of kissing, he stopped, breathing heavily. I was breathing just as heavily.

"Did you enjoy that? Good chemistry, right?" he asked, looking directly into my eyes. I nodded, and found my voice.

"Yeah, that was great," I managed.

"How about if we sit down and chat for a bit? Maybe after that we can cuddle on the bed for a while? You've seemed a bit skittish in messages and in person, and I'd rather you were comfortable with me, ok?"

I nodded as he handed me my drink and we sat down in chairs next to his queen-size bed in the corner of the main room. I held up my drink.

"Cheers," I said as we clinked glasses.

"To the beginning of something very enjoyable," he said, looking quizzical. "I am enjoying getting to know you, but I do still think that we might not be the best candidates for a relationship. You're still in agreement?"

"I do agree with you, Todd. The age difference . . . it's something I can't really wrap my head around," I replied, not sure what to say, but he seemed to need reassurance that I wasn't going to cling to him or something. Unless he was interested, and trying to convince himself to keep his distance from me? I wasn't really sure, but I knew this was still just a hookup.

"I think we're in two different places with life experiences, so I'm fine with just a friendly hookup that could recur if we really want it to," I finished.

"Yes, exactly," he replied, as the quizzical look disappeared, and was replaced by enthusiasm. "I do feel as if we can really just be ourselves and have a really great time, without any tiptoeing around emotions or expectations."

I leaned back in my chair and put my feet up on the footstool that was between our two chairs. He did the same, putting his feet up outside of mine on the footstool. I smiled at him.

"So, tell me something," I said flippantly, just out of the blue.

"Like what?" Todd asked, making a funny face at me, since we both seemed to be in a goofy, awkward mood at the moment.

"I don't know," I wondered aloud. "Something that's not on your profile. Something unique about you."

He was silent for a few minutes, then finally replied, "Hmm, I've worn a Hello Kitty t-shirt, on purpose. How's that for a very secure guy?"

"Ok," I replied, laughing, "that's definitely unique. Let me see it!"

Todd got up, set his drink down on the dining room table, then went over to his closet on the other side of the room, dug around in the closet for a few minutes, and then produced a black Hello Kitty t-shirt, with a very weird gothic-design Hello Kitty on it.

"Where and how did you get that?" I asked, curious.

Todd retrieved his drink on the way back to his chair, and sat down, laying the t-shirt on his leg:

"I was in Tokyo on a college exchange semester," he replied, "and was friends with a bunch of different guys, all part of the exchange program. We usually went out together on the weekends. They dared me to do it, after a weird night of sushi and sake, so I bought it and wore it out on the streets. It probably doesn't even fit anymore; I was a lot skinnier six years ago."

"Wow, sounds like you had a lot of fun in Japan!" I exclaimed. "What college were you on the exchange program from?"

In the back of my head, I felt a weird sense of disappointment; even though I was older than him, he had had some very interesting experiences and seemed much more worldly than I did, because of his travels. I felt a bit inadequate next to him, and the sense of being out of his league returned.

"Yeah, it was a great experience, and I did learn a lot about photography," he said. "Oh, I went to Temple U. Graduated with a BFA in Photography. Need a transcript?"

"No," I laughed. "I was curious! I almost went there—I went to Rutgers instead."

"That's cool, I almost went to Rutgers!" he smiled back at me. "Now, something unique about you."

"I don't know," I replied, scrambling through my brain for something, wondering what the heck I could tell him. "I'm more suburban than you."

"Come on," Todd urged, "everyone has something unique and cool about them."

"Ok, fine," I sighed, then reluctantly told him, "I kissed Dave Grohl. You know, from the Foo Fighters?"

"Of course I know who he is, you goof. From our favorite band. Really?" he asked, looking impressed and very curious.

"I was in college, when Nirvana was starting to become famous. A girlfriend and I decided to go to Seattle during our fall break from college, and her cousin gave us concert tickets to a show he couldn't go to. We were in a small club the night before the concert, sitting at one of the tables. Didn't realize that Dave was standing right behind our table. He sat down at our table, started flirting with us, and bought our beers. My friend knew who he was, but she wasn't as into the new grunge scene as I was. As the evening went on, he and I kept getting more flirty with each other. When the club was closing, we all walked out together, and he escorted us back to where we were staying."

"Ok, then what happened?" Todd asked.

"My girlfriend was awesome. She knew he was more into me, so she went upstairs to her cousin's apartment. Dave and I just wandered around downtown and chatted randomly," I replied slowly, trying to remember since it had been quite a while ago.

"So, did you know who he was at the time?" Todd asked, entranced by my tale.

I replied slowly, "I figured it out in the club, but it was weird—nobody was approaching him, no fans or locals. It was odd, because that's when they had just released *Nevermind*, and the band was getting more famous by the day. But, at one point, we were talking and he looked at me, and was teasing, 'So, I'm wondering if you might have seen me somewhere else?'

"I replied to Dave, 'I'm guessing that you're a big deal around here? That's cool. Do you own the club we were at? Or are you a musician or something?'

"Dave seemed a bit surprised, but nice about it, and replied, 'Musician—drummer in a local band.'

" 'Oh, how cool!' I replied, then I broke down, laughing. 'I can't keep it up, sorry Dave, I know exactly who you are!'

"I was still laughing, and he grabbed me around my waist because I was drunk and swaying a bit.

"So Dave started laughing too, then said, 'Wow, you are sneaky!' At that point, we were looking at each other.

"We stood there, then he bent his head down and kissed me. We stood there for some time, just kissing. After a while, we stopped kissing and turned around and he walked me back to the apartment. I got chilly because it was the middle of the night, and he gave me his flannel shirt that he had on over his t-shirt.

"When we got back to the front of the apartment building, he asked me, 'Are you sure you want the night to end?'

"I said, 'I'm sure, but thanks for a really great evening.'

"He kissed me again, and said, 'I guess we'll see each other again sometime?'

"I smiled at him and replied, "When we're meant to, I'm thinking?'

"He wanted to give me tickets to his show the next night, but I told him that my friend and I already had tickets and were very excited to see the show. So, the next night, which was Halloween, we saw their concert, at some theater downtown. Amazing concert, but it was so crowded and hectic that I didn't see him at all that night.

"I forgot to give his flannel shirt back to him. I still have it. I did see him in concert in Philly a few years ago, but there's no way he'd remember me. It was a great concert!" I finished.

"Wow, cool story!" Todd said, leaning back in his chair.

"Yeah it is," I admitted, smiling. "I hadn't thought about that in ages!"

"So, do you have any Nirvana secrets?" he asked.

"No such luck," I told him. "He was there that night just to relax. We both talked about random stuff—I told him about my road trip. He told me about stress with his bandmates, and that he sometimes wrote his own songs just for fun."

"Oh my god," Todd exclaimed, "So he complained about Nirvana? Wow!"

"Well, if that's who's stressing you out at that moment, that's what you do!" I theorized.

"Yeah, you have a good point there," he agreed. "They did have a lot of fights and craziness in the band back then."

"Yeah, creative control, drugs, all that kind of stuff," I answered.

Todd nodded at me, and said, "Very cool story! So, tell me something else about you. What's your family like?"

"Let's see," I started answering, though I was surprised by Todd's question, and wasn't sure when flings ever asked about families. "My parents are divorced but it's very amicable. Neither of them have remarried, but both have long-term significant others, who are decent people and we all get along."

"That's really great of them. What do your parents do, for work?" he asked next.

"My mom is a professor of public health at a nearby college, and her boyfriend is also a professor, of communications," I explained. "My dad is a lawyer, and his girlfriend is a paralegal."

"Is that how they divorced—he cheated on your mom with his girlfriend?" he asked.

"He did, yes," I answered, "but I think they were just so busy that they drifted apart, emotionally. It was a bit rough for a while, but then we saw that my parents were amicable about the divorced and that kind of helped us to see that a new family dynamic could make us all a bit happier. Guess it helped us all to grow up a bit, too."

"Yeah, I know exactly what you mean about that," Todd said, with a small smile. "Any brothers or sisters?"

"Yes, I have one sister and one brother, who are twins and four years older than me. They're both married to great people and have two kids each. My siblings are a bit competitive that way. I'm the younger one, and they all see me as a free spirit who just doesn't have what it takes to 'compete' with them. But, since I'm an aunt, their kids think I'm awesome!

"I have some relatives in rural Indiana, and others in the suburbs around Chicago. Family reunions get crazy, but it's definitely nice—no creeps or any bizarre drama," I summed up. "How about your family?"

"My parents are divorced, too, and the divorce was rough on all of us," Todd explained. "Definitely not amicable, and still awkward, especially at holidays. I have one older sister, who's married and has a kid, and our parents still pull for both of us to go over their homes, and ignore the other parent. It's a mess at times."

"I bet," I replied, sympathizing with him. "That's really lame of them."

"It is," he agreed, "especially because of my niece. My sister and I try to be diplomatic, but it's a pain in the ass to deal with them when we would rather just ignore our parents and go somewhere else to celebrate the holidays: my sister, her husband, their daughter, and me.

"My mom nags me to find a wife and have kids, because apparently I'm not getting any younger. My dad nags me to just enjoy myself and not be tied down because I'm too young. I try to tune them both out and do what works for me."

"What is that?" I asked him, curiosity probably evident on my face. "I mean, is that what works for you?   Enjoying meeting new women, and seeing what you might be interested in, without any stress or pressure?"

"Definitely, at this point in my life. I'm not out to be mean and just "bang and run", but I think two people can have a decent time together in a casual encounter, and not regret anything," Todd explained, smiling at me. "Plus, it's not much different than dating. You still get to know a person's likes and dislikes, their preferences, and see if you and I might be right for each other or not. I think as long as I'm honest about it, then both of us can be fine with being casual."

"I agree," I smiled back at him in relief, because I hadn't been sure where his conversation had been leading. "That makes a lot of sense when people are honest about it. Then, it's not some cheap and regrettable experience, but a really pleasurable fling."

My last words hung in the air, and there was an awkward pause in the conversation. Todd looked at me with a question in his eyes.

"Want to join me on the bed, Cilla?" he asked, as he set his glass on the nightstand. He slung the Hello Kitty t-shirt on the chair as he stood up, then sat on the edge of his bed.

"Sure," I smiled at him as I stood up, then reminded him, "Don't forget the condoms, ok?"

"Oh, yeah, can't forget them, otherwise I don't get any action," he smiled, bounding off to his bathroom. "So you're not on the pill?"

"No, haven't been on it in a while. It started giving me allergic reactions about a decade ago, so I had to stop taking it and my doctors won't put me back on it ever again," I explained as I walked around his bed to the other side, put my mostly-empty glass on the nightstand, and stretched out on the surprisingly soft bed, enjoying how cloud-like it was. "So unfortunately condoms are the best option. I really appreciate you going along with it. Wow, your bed is soft!"

"Yeah, it's not my favorite thing but I can deal," Todd said as he returned, clutching a bunch of condom wrappers that he deposited on the nightstand. "Wait, condoms aren't my favorite, but my bed is! I love my bed! You can pull the covers down, you know. Get comfortable, relax."

He helped me pull the covers down, then sat down on the other side of the bed and grabbed the remote from the chair he had been sitting in. Found some random action movie to watch, then laid next to me, to take me in his arms so we could cuddle and watch the movie together.

"Feeling ok, Ms. Cilla?" he asked. "You're enjoying the affection, right?"

"Yeah, this is really nice, Todd," I answered. "I missed having someone to be affectionate with, so it's nice that you're into it tonight. And I'm really glad you texted me. I thought I blew it when I chickened out last week."

"Oh, no, you didn't blow it last week," he said, with surprise in his voice. "I could tell that you seemed nervous, and I started getting a bit tired, so I figured it wasn't our moment that night. I got involved in work as the week progressed, so I didn't really come up for air until today. I wanted to get some assignments out of the way, so that I could concentrate on relaxing over the next few weeks. You answered my text, so it's all good, baby."

"I guess I wasn't meant to go on that date tonight," I mused with a smile. "Guess this is where I'm meant to be tonight."

He looked down at me instead of the TV. "Was it a guy that you've been seeing, or a first date?" he asked.

"A first date, someone else from the website, a guy that was 46," I said as I snuggled a bit closer to him. "But clearly he's not that mature, if he's flaking out on a date with me."

"Clearly," Todd agreed with me.

"You're much more mature than him," I said, looking at him. "And cuter, and virile."

He slowly leaned down and kissed me, a slow, sweet kiss. We kissed for a few minutes, and then he pulled away to sit up and slowly pull my shirt up and off, tossing it on the floor. We kissed sitting up while I unbuttoned his flannel shirt, then stopped kissing to pull his off and toss it to join my shirt. Todd fell back on the bed and pulled me down so I was reclined on top of him, and told me, "You said you missed kissing, so kiss me as much as you want to."

I didn't reply, but just nodded as I leaned in to reclaim his lips. In the back of my mind, my thoughts swirled around: I had missed kissing a guy so much. That was my favorite part of being affectionate with a guy—the kissing. That's where you really learned what type of lover a man was. And Todd was already fantastic—caring, respectful, and passionate. Definitely passionate. I was very attracted to him, and the chemistry was powerful. I was French-kissing him, and his mouth matched mine with every kiss. I couldn't remember the last time I had kissed someone so passionately, if ever.

The kisses started to feel even deeper and more passionate, if that was possible. And more erotic, because my thoughts kept leaning towards wondering how skilled Todd was with his tongue, and what else he could do with that tongue on other parts of my body . . .

A few very sweaty and pleasant orgasms later, we got dressed and sat in the chairs next to his bed, as we had earlier in the evening. He was finishing his whiskey from earlier, but I was drinking water, so that I would be fine to drive.

I started the conversation this time, "So, what do you like to do for fun? This is where I test you and see if what you tell me matches up with your hobbies listed on your dating profile."

"Aren't you Ms. Funny Girl?! Let's see, what was on my profile?" Todd teased.

I grabbed a pillow and hit him in the head with it, and he wrenched the pillow from my hand to whack me back with it.

We both started laughing, and he answered me, "Music, TV, movies all help to relax me. I'm very lucky in that my career is my passion—I love photography. Capturing a specific moment really makes me feel fulfilled. And I'm surrounded by some of my favorite moments here, which also helps to relax me."

"Really?" I asked, a bit surprised. "It doesn't do the opposite, making you feel stressed that you need to try to top what you're already done?"

"No, it reminds me that I have been successful already, and that is probably a bit of ego showing, but it feels good," Todd admitted, looking right into my eyes. "It also reminds me where I've been, and that work can take me places I haven't even conceived of yet."

"That's pretty cool!" I approved, looking around at his walls. "I love how you have these photos all over your apartment—it feels like you live in a gallery, not a regular apartment."

"Thanks, I love it, too! It does feel like my sanctuary that I escape to, I guess," he replied. "And the ladies seem to like it, too!"

"Oh, there it is!" I teased him. "You're a sexy show-off, and turned your apartment into a babe lair!"

"No, that's not it," Todd replied, laughing at my comment. "I decorated my apartment for *me*, not because I feel I need to impress anyone. I've had some women look down on me for what I do."

"Really? Why?" I asked him, surprised.

"A few women said I was a drifter or a freelance loser. Rude, huh?" he asked, with a little bitterness creeping into his voice.

"Yeah, that's really rude and mean," I agreed. "Maybe they were just interested in whatever prestige you had, or whether you had money that they could glom on to."

"Yeah, that was my sense, too," Todd replied, with a surprised look on his face. "You actually get it. It's as if you really understand me. But, I do have to ask: are you one of these women?"

"No way!" I shuddered. "I like to think that I'm successful in work, maybe successful in my personal life. I own my own home. It's all on my terms!"

"Well, that sounds like success to me," he replied. "It's interesting how people do define their own success. You speak of how to not define it, but don't necessarily address what you think it is."

"Actually, yes, I do," I corrected him. "It's doing stuff on my own terms."

Todd yawned, then admitted, "Ok, my bad, you're right!"

"How do you define your own success?" I asked him, trying not to yawn, either.

"Well, I have a lot of work, and people are starting to recognize my work," he replied, in between sipping his drink. "I pay my own rent, I'm self-sufficient, and I'm happy."

"That's a good measure of success," I smiled at him.

"So, you know all about my job," he said, steering the conversation around, "but you never told me about yours! You're a trainer, if I remember, right?"

"Yes," I confirmed, in case Todd was quizzing me on my dating profile. "I'm a software trainer at a computer training company."

"Which means what?" Todd asked, gesturing for me to explain.

"It means that I train groups of people in different software programs," I explained. "If your company needs training on how to create PDFs, for example, I come to your company and train a group of people on the ins and outs of it.

"Sometimes, we also run public training sessions at hotels, that people can pay for. When I'm not out in the field, training, I'm back at my office, planning custom training sessions, or *actually* learning the software. Sometimes, a company will send me a document to troubleshoot, and I'll base a training session off of that document's issues."

"Ok, that's interesting," he approved. "So it's a mix of being in front of people, and being on your own and preparing trainings? Cool."

"It's exactly that mix," I replied. "It's interesting at times, but at other times it can be frustrating. Troubleshooting documents is probably the easiest part of what I do, which might seem strange."

"Yeah, that sounds odd," Todd replied. "Why is that easier?"

"Because I'm sitting in my office, just focused on that one task," I explained. "When I'm leading a training session, I'm busy presenting material, reacting to questions and issues, and trying to help people understand the material. But, when I'm troubleshooting a document, it's basically solving a puzzle with a piece in the wrong spot—it's more satisfying to me because the answers are right in front of me. I'd rather solve the puzzle than stand in front of a room of fifty people any day; sometimes the public training sessions are an exercise in futility, because some people just aren't as qualified for the material as they think they are.

"I do like doing the corporate trainings, because they're customized to the company's needs. It's not some cookie-cutter software presentation, so the employees are more dialed-in than other audiences might be. I wish I just did those trainings and none of the public sessions, but all of us trainers have to split the public sessions equally."

"Spreading the pain, I guess? Your job does sound interesting, and not boring," he commented.

"It has its moments of excitement and moments of boredom," I clarified. "So, how about your job—exciting or boring? Or a mix of both?"

"Definitely a mix of both, since I have to spend time doing networking and advertising. I hate that part of it, and making sure that I charge clients enough, and that my prices are still competitive. Generally, a pain in the ass.

"So, what kinds of software are you doing trainings on currently?" Todd asked, curious. "I'm trying to see if there are any hot new programs I need to learn, and if I can get any free training out of it!"

"Oh, really?" I inquired, sweetly.

"I kid, I kid, sweetie," Todd teased me. "I'd pay you in orgasms, of course!"

"Hmm," I replied seriously, "that form of currency isn't accepted at my job, but I could freelance on the side. That just might be the right price!"

"I knew you'd like the idea, but you know I'm kidding, right?" he smiled at me, then leaned forward in his chair and kissed me. "I wouldn't treat you like a ho."

"I knew you were teasing. And, you seem to be a gentleman, which is definitely good," I approved. "Well, currently, I've been doing a lot of trainings on PowerPoint presentations, especially with using the multimedia features. Same thing with using PDF software programs—people want to learn how to use the more advanced software features, but they don't always understand *why* they want to use that feature, meaning what to convey or emphasize, using that particular feature. So, we're also teaching the purpose of the design, I guess. It's a bit more advanced, but it's a challenge to train to others, because of the level of analytic skill involved."

"Wow, that sounds really tricky," he replied.

"Yeah, sometimes I want to stab myself in the brain in mid-training," I admitted. "At times, people just don't get it, and ask questions that come out of left field, and it makes my job more difficult than it should be. I try to break the concepts down into small chunks that are easily understood, but sometimes the material is beyond a person's capacity. Companies want people to learn new skills, but sometimes it's the person, not their skills. Sometimes, there's that one person in the training session who's outgoing but just doesn't understand what I'm trying to teach, unfortunately. The person who holds up the entire session for everyone else, and just isn't helping, every time they open their mouth. I spend that time just screaming inside my head!

"Enough about my crazy work stuff, Todd, tell me some of your work stuff!"

"Ok, one of my easier jobs is a yearly gig, advising a local high school's yearbook club on doing their photos," he explained. "You know, what to take, how to set up the shots that are posed, how to work on taking good candid shots, how to use the camera, if they need it, that kind of stuff. Also, have to choose the best photos, when you have twenty shots of the same scene. It pays well, and the students are great. They're into it and they're very appreciative and friendly. It's a lot more rewarding than doing stock photo shoots with egotistical or slightly high models."

"Working with the students sounds really great," I commented. "So the models are all messes, huh?"

Todd continued, "Some are, and they don't have a clue what the hell's going on, so trying to give them directions is like trying to herd ten kittens. Fantastic, right?"

"Sounds like fun!" I replied sarcastically. "So . . . what to chat about now?"

I tapped my index finger against my mouth, thinking of what topic to discuss next.

"So," Todd started, then paused to think, "did you ever have any great loves in your life?"

"Uh, that's a pretty random question to ask! Um," I hedged, not sure if I really wanted to answer that question.

Todd urged me, "Come on, you must have had something by this time in your life, right?"

"Well, there was Dave!" I said, laughing.

"Oh, come on," Todd insisted, "if there was something, you would have added it to the story you told me earlier. What? Just answer the question!"

I paused, because part of me didn't want to share it with Todd. It seemed too personal to share with someone who I wasn't going to be getting closer to. Why would he be interested in my relationship history?

"Ok, ok, stop nagging me," I sighed, then reluctantly started. "His name was Jeremy, and we started dating in college, and it got serious during our twenties. The problem was that he was stringing me along; he said that he wanted the happy ending of marriage and family with me.

"When I would have 'the talk' with him about marriage, he'd lecture me on how pressured he felt, and I just ended up feeling awful about him feeling awful. It took me a long time to realize how manipulative he really was, and that he just didn't want the same things as me, after all. It was so unfair to me, and I finally ended that relationship when I was 28. After that, I dated a bit, had another serious relationship with another guy when I was 33."

Todd interrupted me, "What happened there?"

"Let me speak, and you'll find out!" I admonished Todd. "I reconnected with an old friend that I had known from summers when we were kids, and it turned serious. We moved in together, and everything seemed perfect. Until he came to me, one day, completely out of the blue, and said he just wasn't in love with me anymore. That was it, just 'it's over'. Three years, down the drain, just like that."

"Oh my god, that must have really sucked!" Todd replied, surprised. "He had no other explanation? There wasn't anyone else?"

"It turned out that there *was* someone else he was in love with," I confirmed. "She wasn't me, and I couldn't make someone love me when he had ended the relationship. I fell into a depression after that for some months, and had to go to the doctor to help deal with that. Since recovering, I've just dated on and off, but there's been nobody special."

He reached over and held my hand, while he said, "Well, tonight is pretty special, right? You get to feel really good, with me. That's gotta count for something, right?"

I smiled back at him, "Of course it counts for something! But I wouldn't put it in the relationship category unless we decided to do that!"

"Yeah, you do have a valid point there!" he smiled at me as he squeezed my hand.

"So, I told you about my relationship history, but I have yet to hear about yours," I reminded him. "Come on, Todd, cough up some info for me!"

"When the hell did you get to be so bossy?" he laughed. "I have no problems telling you. Ok, I had a serious relationship with my high school sweetheart, but things went to crap after we had a surprise pregnancy when we were twenty."

"That sounds like a rough time," I commented.

"It was. We were too young, but I did still work hard to try to make it work out between us. Unfortunately, Denise ended things between us," he said, looking very serious.

"Do you still wish you were with Denise, or is that a nosy question that I shouldn't ask?" I ventured.

"No, it's fine for you to ask," he said, sipping his drink, then continuing, "I don't want to be with her again. Actually, the last I heard, from a friend, was that she was engaged to someone from her college. Oh well. Since then, I've just dated casually or hooked up with women. I should stress, though, that I'm very selective; I don't just go with anyone."

"I get that; I'm choosy, too!" I replied, then paused before asking, "I'm just curious. You mentioned the pregnancy, so what happened to the baby?"

"That's definitely the sad part," Todd answered, clearly uncomfortable with discussing that part of his past. "She had a miscarriage at eighteen weeks, and we were both devastated. After a few months, I suggested we try again, to have another baby. I really wanted one then, and was ready for it. I was still in college, but I actually had it all figured out: I planned to transfer to a local college, rent an apartment, and get a job. Denise wanted none of that scenario, though. She wanted to go back to college, live a typical college student's dorm life, and being around me was a reminder of the miscarriage, I guess. She ended up transferring to a different college, in Michigan, far away from me. That really hurt, too—her rejection.

"But, I eventually got over it and moved on. Graduated, worked on my career and being self-sufficient, and doing whatever I wanted to. Whatever made me happy."

"I'm really sorry to hear about the baby," I said seriously. "Sounds like you found a way to make it work. Do you still want a family of your own?"

"Yes, I do, when the right woman comes along, I guess," he shrugged. "Haven't thought about it much lately. Work's been occupying my brain, since I've had a lot of assignments coming at me."

"Like what? Traveling to anywhere exotic?" I asked, leaning back in my chair.

"I'm flying to a resort in Mexico in two months to do a photo shoot, since they remodeled and need new photos of everything," he said, leaning back in his chair also. "And, I get to relax there for a few days, on the house, besides getting paid well, so you can imagine I'm looking forward to that part!!"

"Lucky you," I gasped, "that sounds so awesome!"

"I know, right?" Todd smiled at me. "After that, I'm doing a corporate photos job in Houston, and then I'm doing a shoot in Virginia of some nature shots for someone's book on the Shenandoah Valley National Park, and finally return home."

"Wow, that's all on one trip?" I asked. "Sounds exciting and hectic!"

"Hectic doesn't even begin to cover it!" he said, scrunching up his face in disgust. "It takes a lot of planning to get trips like that together, to make sure I have all the equipment I need, lug it all on the trip, and to make sure I don't lose anything. And, I always have to double-check that the assignment is the same as what's in the contract *and* that the payment is taken care of as specified in the contracts, so that I don't have any problems with the clients. And making sure I'm tracking my expenses carefully, and that there are no flight delays. It's crazy, right?"

"Even with all that hassle of logistics issues, it sounds like you love it, or you wouldn't even be in that career, right?" I wondered.

"Very true, I wouldn't necessarily do this for the money, though after a few years of really pushing myself, the money is starting to pay off. I don't have to choose between paying a bill or buying a much-needed camera lens, for example."

"That's great!" I replied. "So do you use digital or manual cameras?"

"Mostly digital, since it really makes turning in the assignments so easy," he explained. "Manual sometimes, if it's a more artistic photo that's needed, or if I just feel like using it. But it's more work to deal with, logistically."

"Ah, interesting," I commented, then sipped more of my water.

Todd burst out laughing at me, "Oh please, you don't care about digital versus manual cameras!"

"Maybe not," I blushed as I admitted it, "but I am enjoying our stream-of-consciousness conversations. You're not going to make fun of me over that, are you?"

"Nah, it's cute," he smiled at me. "You're really nice, you know that?"

"Thanks, that's sweet of you to say," I replied, smiling back at him.

Neither of us spoke at that point; we just looked at each other, not wanting the evening to end yet.

"Want some more water?" Todd suddenly asked me, glancing at my empty glass.

"Yes, please," I nodded at him. "I'm still not perfect to drive."

Todd stood up, retrieved my glass and went into the kitchen to refill it.

"That's ok, I wouldn't send you out into the cold all drunk," he called from the kitchen.

"That's good, you just got elevated to nice status, too," I grinned at him.

Todd returned with my water, and his drink.

"You drinking water, or on something else now?" I asked, being a bit nosy.

"I switched to water," he replied, with an eyebrow raised. "I agreed to teach an acquaintance some camera tips around lunchtime, so I want to be reasonably coherent."

"Is this a good thing or a bad thing, offering up some tips? Or are you getting paid for this lesson?" I asked, curious.

"I'm not getting paid, but she did happen to book me for two jobs for her ad agency, and there is the possibility of more work. I'm spending five minutes giving her tips on taking her vacation pictures, and she said if all goes well on her vacation, she wants me to do her engagement shoot, and wedding photos!"

"Wow, that's cool too!" I smiled at him. "Have you ever shot weddings before?"

"I have, and it's a lot of directing people into the formal shots," he said. "Sometimes a pain, but also sometimes fun. I do prefer candid shots, though, and that's what Mary really likes. So this could be an interesting project, and I'm always up for a challenge.

"You know, I've been talking about myself way too much tonight! Tell me more about you—something, anything to keep me from taking over the conversation!"

"Honestly, that's fine," I tried to reassure him. "Sometimes I'm a little shy at first, so I'm not mad at you for conversation-hogging. Let me see . . . I bought a townhouse eight months ago."

"That's great, congrats on being a homeowner!" he said, smiling at me. "Now I'm jealous. You have your own space to do anything with."

"Thanks. Of course, I've learned that my home actually owns me! Actually, there are a good number of condo community restrictions on what I can and can't do, but I read those rules carefully before signing anything. So, at least the rules are ones I can live with. They're not too confining for my preferences."

"That's good. Where is it?" he asked.

"It's at Fresh Pines development, one of the stone buildings," I told him proudly. "I had to fight for it, but I have an end unit. The crazy thing is that I ended up with a better price because the owner was dropping the price *during* the deal. They were doing anything possible to make it sell quicker because they needed the money from the sale, otherwise they were going to have even worse financial problems."

"How much of a deal did you get?" he asked, curious.

"It was $225 thousand when I first submitted the bid," I recalled. "When I signed the closing papers, it was down to $170 thousand. Good deal, right?"

"Are you sure it's not haunted or something?" Todd seemed to be thinking deeply. "That seems too good to be true!"

"No, it's not haunted!" I exclaimed, indignant. "Now I'm annoyed at you for suggesting that! The seller was in dire straits, and needed the money to pay off a lot of medical bills acquired when she had no health insurance. Initially, I was very concerned. But, after the home inspection came out decent and my mortgage was in place, I was fine with moving up the closing and having the price go down. Moving out of my apartment was a pain in the ass, but I survived it."

"Sounds like a great situation—I'm definitely jealous!" he replied, smiling at me.

"It is. The only thing is that I didn't have a chance to paint or fix up anything before my moving day," I explained. "So, it's been an ordeal to work around the stuff I had in the rooms already. There were things still in boxes for a while after I moved in, so I actually ended up getting rid of some junk and clutter post-move."

"That makes sense," he mused. "If you don't use it within months, what are you holding onto the boxed items for?"

"Exactly. It just made it a bit easier for me to pare down certain items. And, what I have, I really appreciate and have spaces for it all," I said. "It feels great to have my own home, and I can entertain friends sometimes."

"That sounds great, maybe I'll see it sometime!" Todd said.

"Maybe, that would be fun. I'm sorry, Todd, I'm getting tired so I think I need to go home and get my beauty sleep," I said, standing up.

"No problem, Cilla," he said, also standing up. "I'll walk you out to your car."

"Thanks, I appreciate it," I replied, as I grabbed my boots and sat on his sofa to put them on.

"It's the least I can do, since you drove over here," he said. "And when you get home, text me so I know you got home safe, ok?"

"Ok," I said nonchalantly, but inside I thought, wow, that was really sweet of him; guys just didn't say things like that.

That seemed like a relationship move, not a hookup move. And very respectable to care about someone else like that, when he didn't really have to.

I stood up, and he handed me my coat. I put it on, and he put his sneakers and coat on, grabbed his keys and opened the door. We went outside the second door, and he reached for my hand as we went down the steps. His pace was very slow now, unlike our mad dash earlier in the evening in the opposite direction. We were both quiet as we walked in the moonlight to my car in the parking lot. Finally reached the car, and he stopped right in front of the door, blocking me from opening it. He brought his hands up to the back of my waist, and I raised mine to rest on his arms.

"So, if I texted you again, would you be interested in another evening together?" he asked.

"Yes, I would," I replied, smiling. "I really had a great time tonight, thanks Todd."

"I'm glad, Cilla, I did too," he said, then pulled me closer as he kissed me softly. We kissed for a few minutes, then he carefully set me back from him a bit, still holding me around the waist.

"I better get inside, otherwise I'm dragging you back in there!" he smiled.

"Yeah, I have to get home since my coffee is wearing off and I'm getting tired," I said, playfully shoving him away from blocking my car door. I opened the door, got inside and started it. He knocked on the window, and I pressed the button to roll it down. He leaned in to kiss me, then reminded me, "Text me when you get home, ok?"

"I will, night, Todd," I said.

"Night, Ms. Cilla," he replied. I rolled up the window and backed the car out and then forward. As I pulled away, I slightly glanced in the rearview mirror and he looked so gorgeous in the moonlight, with bedhead hair that looked sexy from our passionate encounter. I couldn't tell if he was looking at my car or not, but he hadn't moved since he kissed me through the car window.

I made it home about 20 minutes later, fueled by adrenaline from the evening and from my car satellite radio's alternative 90s station. I texted Todd from the car after pulling into a parking spot at my apartment complex, "Made it home safe. Tonight was awesome, can't wait for more fun w/ya!"

I went inside and locked the door behind me. Dropped my purse on the floor near the bed, went into the bathroom and took out my contact lenses, then went back into the bedroom and stripped naked, fell on the bed, feeling unbelievably exhausted. Leaned over the edge of the bed and grabbed my cellphone, then put it on the bed as though it was my bed partner that night. Don't know why I slept naked that night—I was never one to do that. But it just felt like the thing to do.

Woke up late that Sunday morning, from weird dreams that had me walking through an art gallery, searching for something. In the dream, anytime someone asked me what I was searching for, I didn't know. All I could do was hand them an ice cube and shrug my shoulders, and keep walking through different sections of the art gallery. What the hell was the ice cube all about? That was weird.

Roused myself from bed to the sounds of hail against the windows. It felt soothing because I didn't have anywhere to go that day; I just had to clean and get ready for the week, since Christmas was later that week. I still didn't want to leave the bed, though. Started thinking about last night, replaying it in my head.

The kissing . . . the way we held each other . . . the kissing . . . I still couldn't stop thinking about the kissing. The best part about last night? He made me feel desired, in a way I hadn't felt in so long. He made me feel alive.

Todd was definitely a skilled lover. I did worry that I was too shy for him in bed. It had been too long for me since I had last had sex, so I felt self-conscious when I was pleasuring him and not being as adventurous as he was suggesting. After last night, though, I felt more empowered by my own desires being rejuvenated, so I thought I would be less shy if there was a next time. Plus, maybe next time I'd request some fantastic oral pleasure, too.

I was glad that Todd turned out to be honest, ambitious, secure in who he was. He was a very interesting guy, ambitious and justifiably proud of it, which was a refreshing change from the previous dates I had had the misfortune of being on. Remembered thinking on the drive to his place that I wouldn't do anything with him or anyone unless I liked him and respected him. Even for a casual evening, I had to give a shit about the other person. I had been more than a bit worried that he'd turn out to be a jerk that I'd have to be mean to or escape from. Or that me insisting on condoms would be a huge problem. But the logistics were all fine.

He had talked a lot more than I did last night—maybe it was because he was a bit drunk, since he wasn't driving last night. Or maybe it was just because he was more outgoing than I was. It was definitely nice conversing with him, but I wasn't sure how much talking was too much, when we were being casual. There were moments that he seemed to be a bit more personal. Asking me about my family, for instance. Was the conversation too date-like? That made me pause. If we were to stay casual, I didn't want to know too much about him. I didn't want him to know that much about my business, either. It made me feel vulnerable to know there was a random guy out there, who know all this stuff about me, even if he didn't really care that he knew my secrets. I was a private person, besides being a little shy or reserved. It made me uncomfortable to put myself out there. That was how people got closer, and we had vowed to keep our evenings together just casual. Did guys usually ask those types of questions when it was a casual hookup? Not sure if I was overthinking it.

Saturday night was quite enjoyable with my young stud; being spontaneous paid off in a good way. Maybe we would get together again. Maybe not, since there was no guarantee that I'd even hear from him again. I had to be realistic about that, since he might have had second thoughts the morning after.

With that thought, I finally got out of bed and into the shower, to wash off last night and Todd's slightly spicy-citrus scent that seemed like a pheromone, as it was embedded in my hair. After a very refreshing shower, I walked back into my bedroom and saw my phone was flashing a message: text from Todd. Grabbed my phone off the bed to read his message.

"Sorry I fell asleep last nite—glad u got home safe!" he had texted.

"Yeah, glad I'm home—it's sleeting outside now," I replied.

"I know . . . I have to go out in it soon for work ☹," he texted.

"oh, that sux. Be careful," I replied.

"yea it does. I'll text ya soon Cilla," he ended the conversation.

*   *   *

Monday found me going to the office, instead of being out in the field conducting a training. I also had a very important luncheon scheduled—catching up with Hillary and Kim, which was as vital as payday. I rushed through as much of my workload as possible during the morning, so that we could have a leisurely lunch.

Kim and I got to the restaurant first, and Hillary joined us a few minutes later. After we ordered, I said, "I have news."

"What?" Kim gasped. "It's guy stuff, isn't it?" Hillary said, slyly.

"Yes, ladies, and not at all what you think!" I replied. "Well, that date with the 46-year-old didn't happen."

"Oh," Kim's face fell. "That sucks, he sounded nice."

"Yeah, I know," I replied. "But, then I got a text that changed the evening completely . . ."

My voice trailed off while my friends waited expectantly.

"Stop dragging this shit out and *tell us!*" Hillary implored me.

"That guy that I was texting last week, that I thought didn't pan out," I paused, "he texted me, and I went over his place—"

"—Whoa, you did what???" Kim interrupted. "Do you know how stupid that was? What could have happened? You should have met him in public, *always always always* meet him in public first. You don't know what their deal is."

"Yes, I know," I replied. "But, he turned out to be exactly who he said he was, an honest, decent guy. He has a successful job, his own place, and takes good care of his cats. And, yes, he used condoms."

"Go Cilla, you Happy Ho!" Hillary exclaimed, as other restaurant customers looked over at us. At least they didn't work with us, so I felt slightly less embarrassed by her outburst.

"How many condoms?" Kim asked slowly.

"How many condoms did he own, or did we go through?" I asked, just to rile her up.

"That you guys used. Don't be all coy with us now!" she replied.

Suddenly, I didn't feel like telling them too many details. For once, it felt too personal for girl-talk. I just looked at them with a small smile on my face, while Hillary tapped her fork on her napkin expectantly. Kim just stared at me, willing me to give up the information.

"Two or three," I finally admitted, thinking how nice it had felt with Todd. "And, he's great, he's got some skills."

"Yay, you're definitely a Super Slut!" Kim teased, dropping her fork on the table and high-fiving me, then Hillary also high-fived us. We broke into serious giggles after that. Loved my friends for keeping things real.

Our giggles subsided after a few minutes, when our lunches were brought out. We ate and discussed work gossip and caught up in discussing our other weekend recap and plans. When we were mostly finished, I cleared my throat.

"There is one other thing about this guy, Todd," I said, slowly.

"Can we see his picture again?" Kim interrupted. "He was the really hot guy, right?"

"Yeah, he's even more gorgeous in person, if you can believe it," I had a goofy smile on my face as I pulled my cellphone out from my purse, then found his pic to show them.

"Wow, you had *him* on top of you, all sweaty?" Hillary teased me.

"Shhh! Yeah, I was there!" I teasingly confirmed. "The only thing is, um . . . he's 27."

Kim and Hillary looked at each other, then at me. "You're sexing a young hottie, and that's a problem?" Kim asked, smiling.

"That's not the problem, oh maybe I'm just being neurotic and obsessing about it," I sighed. "It just . . . the age difference . . . it seemed really cool when we were together. But thinking about it after the fact, it just seems too unreal that I really did that.

Plus, I'm worried that it's a bit like Midlife-Crisis Maeve . . ." I trailed off, feeling more than a bit vulnerable and unsure of their reactions.

"OMG, don't even worry about that," Kim exclaimed, waving my words away with her hand. "She wasn't discreetly conducting her sex life in private; she was practically parading her vagina around, at the office party. She was an unprofessional mess!"

"Yeah," Hillary chimed in, "you shouldn't compare yourself to her. That woman turned herself into a caricature of a public whore and melted down. You've been part of our ongoing debates, whether it was just for attention, which seems sad enough, or if she ended up with some mental illness."

"True," I mused. "She really did have some serious issues going on. Wonder whatever happened to her? I guess I shouldn't think of her in reference to what I did on Saturday night, then. I do still seem to be slightly sane, and so was the guy."

"You're both consenting adults, and you said it was a really great evening, right?" Hillary asked.

"Yeah, it was great, I'm definitely pleasantly stunned. He's *so* hot, it just seems like he's too out of my league or something," I shrugged, feeling really uncomfortable to admit that I felt a bit insecure about his looks. "He could be with any woman, so why with me?"

"Maybe he didn't want something shallow? Maybe he wanted to be with a woman who wasn't some flaky visually-perfect-but-selfish silicone-boobed clone?" Kim suggested. "Have you considered that he might be into you? Not just for a one-night stand?"

"No," I waved her off. "We both agreed to just keep it casual, so that's not it. Besides, there's always a chance that he might never contact me again."

"If that's the case, Cilla," Hillary said, leaning back from her now-finished lunch, "why are you so worried about his age? Just accept that you had a fantastic time with him, and think of the memory with happy thoughts. You know what I mean?"

"Yeah, I think I do," I said slowly. "I do need to unclench and just accept last Saturday night for what it was—really hot sex with someone that I might never have met otherwise."

"Exactly!" Hillary agreed with me.

"Besides," Kim added, "you might come across an even better guy soon, or at least an older version of this guy."

"I'm ready for this imaginary guy!" I smiled at them. "Except we have to get back to work now."

*   *   *

During the week, I did get a few messages from guys on the dating website, when I checked the website in the evenings. I checked their profiles, and decided not to reply to any of them, because I could tell that they just wouldn't be compatible with me. Two of them said they were heavy smokers, and since I was anti-smoking, I just couldn't fathom kissing a guy who tasted of cigarettes. The third guy was older, didn't want kids, and looked like he had spent decades partying too hard. Even after clearly making the effort to take decent pics for his dating profile, his ragged hair looked so greasy I thought he was part seal.

Since I was thinking that Todd and I had left the door open for another fun evening, I didn't want to expend effort contacting any other guys on the website to arrange for a hookup. And, I could afford to be a bit picky, since I didn't seem to have any trouble at the moment attracting some good-looking men. I felt a bit lucky, in that respect. Though I didn't take it for granted, there was no guarantee that this would always be the case with any guy. There was always the possibility that the guys might not be truthful about who they were, or their profile pictures might not be current. At least I knew I was telling the truth with my profile and pictures.

I was glad that Todd had been honest, and it was nice to know that there was the possibility of seeing him soon. It took away the pressure I had felt, to find someone for a fling. Definitely a reassuring feeling, and exciting, if it would even be a repeat of last weekend's pleasure.

4

The Dry Spell Is Really Over!

The next Saturday, I was out to dinner with Mel, at a new seafood restaurant. We were leaving the restaurant around 9:30 p.m., about to say goodbye and go to our separate cars, when my phone pinged.

"Who's that?" Mel asked. "Is that the guy you were telling me about?"

"Yes, it is," I confirmed, looking at the screen.

"Hey," Todd texted.

"hey, what's up?" I asked.

"I'm bored, need your mouth . . . and the rest of u," he texted.

"Lol, I could bring my mouth by . . . I could use some fun too ;) ," I replied.

"Awesome," he replied. "How long till u come over?"

"about 20 min," I texted.

"k, call when u are close, cilla," he replied.

"So, he texts and you jump?" she asked.

"No, it's not like that," I told her, defending him, "we agreed that this would be casual and he could text me, so we could get together again if we both wanted to."

"It's still on his terms, though," she said decisively. "You lose the upper hand in interactions when you allow him to decide the contact. He dictates when you get together, and I'm betting he decides just what you do."

"You're being a bit critical, for someone who hasn't dated in about fifteen years," I protested, a bit annoyed that she would judge me. "This is what guys do now—they text. Dating is so much different than when you were on the market–"

"–but you're not dating; you're having really hot sex with a guy. I get it—you're amusing yourself with this guy. Cilla, all I'm saying is that you might feel better about this, or any sex arrangement with a guy, if you set the terms, rather than leave the terms to the guy's whim. This way, he chases you, he asks you to be his girlfriend, and you know that he's really into you for all the right reasons," she lectured, looking directly at me. "And yeah, maybe it started as just sex, but you can always try to get a guy interested in the real you, if you want more from him."

"Mel, why would you think that I'm interested in something more with him? And why are you concerned that I don't feel good about my current arrangement with Todd? For now, casual sex is working out very well for me. This guy is skilled, really nice, respectful, and respectable," I countered. "Plus, he's 27."

She paused at my last statement, and just stared me down, finally saying, "So what about his age? That sounds like a lame excuse. It's in your expression, just talking about it. You're uncomfortable with this hookup arrangement.

"Cilla, I'm not saying any of this to be critical or mean. I *am* surprised you're hooking up at all—I didn't think you had it in you to be so bold and spontaneous like this, so *yay* on that!" Mel said, raising her arms to cheer me on to victory. She continued, "Guess I just want you to be happy on *your* terms, not on any guy's terms. You know I'm only looking out for you; we've done that for each other since high school. Just think about what you really want, to make you happy, ok?"

"I'll definitely think about what you're saying. Hold back a bit, so that he pursues me and has to ask me?" I asked, knowing that Mel and I had very different perspectives on the dating world, and not wanting to delay the evening with Todd by another second.

She nodded and confirmed, "Exactly. Let him pursue you, and you'll be empowered enough to get what you want out of him."

"Ok, thanks for a great evening, Mel, but I'm going to go now," I replied as I hugged her.

"Good night, Cilla, this was great!" she replied, hugging me back. "Keep me posted on this guy, especially in case something good pans out with him!"

We got into our separate cars, and I drove towards Todd's apartment. Stopped at a different convenience store along the way, to get my Saturday night coffee fuel.

I started to allow myself to think of what Mel had said. Making sure I was keeping the facts of the situation in mind, and also thinking of her advice. She did mean well, but in the past she had always been the pretty one that the guys would compete over, to date her, while I was usually the sidekick that the guys would ask for advice on concerning dating her. I didn't think she had a clue what it meant to not be the prettiest girl or woman that every guy was after. Guys just didn't chase after me. Occasionally, someone might approach me. So, I never had that many options, even out of the potentially viable online choices.

I didn't think that I'd ever have the upper hand with Todd, if he did use his looks for personal gain. He was still too mysterious; I hadn't known him long enough to figure him out, and I probably wouldn't be acquainted with him for much longer. I knew that Mel meant well, but she was trying to push me towards a relationship with someone that I wasn't supposed to even think about more than in a passing fashion.

With that thought, I realized that I was a few minutes from his apartment, so I pulled the car over to the side of the street and called Todd.

"Hey," he greeted me."

"Todd, it's Cilla. I'm two minutes from ya," I told him.

"Ok, I'll be on the lookout, bye!" he said, then hung up.

Hung up my phone, and pulled my car back out onto the road. Made it to his apartment a few minutes, later, and he was pacing on his front steps. He jogged down the path, and got into my car.

"Hey beautiful," he greeted me, then leaned over and kissed me.

I broke the kiss after a minute, replying with a small smile, "Hi, guess you really did miss my mouth?"

"Cilla, I told you I did," he reminded me, keeping his face close to mine.

"Well, I missed all of you, my young hottie!" I said, pulling back from him and preparing to drive, with a big smile on my face. Out of the corner of my eye, I saw him grinning at me.

I pulled the car around the turn and into the parking lot behind the apartment buildings, then parked the car. We exited the car, then he walked around to my side and reached for my hand. We walked to his apartment, as swiftly as we had last weekend. Either he always walked-ran, or he was cold. I followed him up the steps and into his apartment, which looked the same as it had the previous week. It almost seemed like a routine, taking off our shoes, Todd reaching for my coat and hanging it up next to his, then Todd going to his kitchen to prepare drinks, while I followed him.

"Same poison as last week?" he inquired, holding the bottle of whiskey.

"Yes, please," I answered him, leaning against the door frame and watching him pour. He finished and gestured to me to sit on the sofa across the room. I walked over and he followed me, carrying our drinks.

"So, how was your week?" he asked, handing me my drink as we both got comfortable on his sofa. I sipped my drink, then leaned forward and set my drink on his coffee table. I started telling him about my week, including my usual job drama. I sat back and he dropped his arm from the sofa to my shoulders, pulling me close to him so that I leaned on him.

"Do you like your job?" he asked.

I thought about it for a minute, then answered, "I do and I don't. Love the paycheck and the benefits; I get tired of some of the training sessions, where I've been training for two hours and all I see are blank faces out there. People who can't even find the 'on' button for the computer sometimes attend my trainings, and it's frustrating as hell at times."

I reached to the coffee table for my drink, and asked him, "What's the best and worst parts of your job?"

"Best is the freedom and the travel. I get to go to so many different places that I'd never see, otherwise. It's eye-opening to see so many different parts of real life, in every corner of the globe," he said, as I finished my drink, then snuggled back into him on the sofa.

"That's so cool," I murmured, "I'm jealous of all those stamps in your passport. I want to travel to some of those places."

"Well, it's not all glamorous life, Cilla. The flip side is that I don't always get the fancy international assignments. I have to hustle for what I do, even though I've been at this for four years. I've busted my ass to get many assignments, and there were times I was almost broke. My parents are only proud of me when I'm doing something worthwhile that they feel I've accomplished, because then it's something that they can brag over. Otherwise, they harass me to find a 'real job.' So, my relationship with them isn't as good as it used to be, even with me becoming more successful every year I've been at this."

He took a final sip of his drink, set it on the coffee table, then continued, "Sometimes deadlines have conflicted, and it's been difficult because I don't want to lose any clients. Or I get new clients, and they don't want to pay the fair rates for my services. They want something for barely any money, which is an insult when I need to at least make enough to live on. So, I'd say that being self-employed is both a dream and a nightmare, in different moments."

"Are you happy?" I asked him, softly, looking up at him.

"Do you mean tonight, or in general?" Todd asked, as he glanced down at me, his expression unreadable.

"In general. I wasn't fishing for anything, so you don't have to be paranoid!" I teased him.

"Yes, I'm happy. Sometimes stressed, obviously, but content," he replied. "How about you?"

"Not always," I admitted, out loud, for probably the first time.

"Seriously, how come?" Todd asked, looking at me with concern on his face.

"I'm definitely tired of my job—that's part of it. Think it's also because I haven't had a relationship in a while, about four years. So tired of the awkward dates and guys disappointing me, usually by not being who they start out impressing me as. I do want to find someone to love and be in a relationship with, and hopefully have a future with," I finished.

A silence hung between us after I finished talking.

"Cilla, are you sure you're still interested in our terms that we've decided on?" he asked, slowly.

I looked up at him, surprised. "I didn't say that to try to manipulate you into falling for me. I'm fine with tonight and our terms. I was just talking to you as a friend, you know, venting. Same as you're doing with me. And, for your info, I'm still looking on the dating website."

"Oh, that's cool, then," Todd said. I felt a bit surprised by him still needing to be reassured that I didn't have designs on his heart, which seemed a bit odd and insecure for someone who seemed quite confident and secure in every other aspect of his life. It was a strange contrast, since he did generally seem in control of his life.

I wondered if Todd did still secretly have feelings for Denise, the woman from his past. If he hoped to reunite with her, and start the family that he seemed to have wanted very much. He had impressed me with how mature he had been at age twenty, figuring out how to make his new family happen, while not losing sight of his own career and dreams. Not many twenty-year-olds, including me, would have volunteered for that type of responsibility, especially when so focused on college and trying to hold onto the carefree aspects of being a student.

Or maybe he was mistrustful because his parents were divorced, and he felt that relationships weren't as permanent as he wished, and he'd only want to be in a relationship if it was on his terms, if he was falling for someone who he could pursue. He wouldn't want to be swept up by a surprise passion, I was sure of it.

And, it made me think that I needed to get it in my brain that Todd, while a great catch for many women, wasn't the catch for me. He was too concerned with being in control of any situation; I was more of a free spirit who was fine with enjoying the romance, being swept up by a great passion. So, Mel's advice to me earlier that evening just wasn't applicable to this situation with Todd. I enjoyed the passion, and wanted to be with someone who would be romantic and affectionate when I wanted it, not just when he wanted some sex.

I'd never be able to control him, not that I was ever out to control any guy. I wasn't sure that I'd be able to be on equal footing with him, because he'd still want to navigate the relationship on his terms. I couldn't really fathom having a relationship with someone who might not want to conduct it on equal terms.

Todd looked down at his glass, and as I watched him, I also sensed that underneath it all, he seemed a bit lonely. Melancholy and lonely, and hated to be vulnerable by being caught by surprise. I looked away, since I got the feeling he didn't want me looking at him, seeing that vulnerability in his expression. Just glanced around at some of his pictures on the walls of his apartment. Realized that it was strange how he had hung up some of these photos of real life, people being vulnerable every day, but he couldn't be like that, even in his home. Odd.

Our conversation hadn't restarted, and we looked at each other.

"Is this the awkward pause that we fill with kisses?" I asked him, smiling up at him.

"Maybe," he confirmed, bringing his mouth down onto mine. Kissed for a while, then I gently pushed him down to lay across the sofa, so that I could lie down on top of him. Resumed kissing, and we started caressing each other. He caressed my butt, and kept pushing me closer and closer into him, with our legs entwined.

After a while, he pulled his face back from kissing me.

"We should go over to the bed," he said quietly.

"Sounds good," I said. His arms supported me as I got off of him and the sofa, and we both walked towards the bed, splitting off to the different sides. We smiled at each other across the bed, and I removed my shirt, then he removed his.

"This, I like—us on opposite sides of the bed, watching each other strip," Todd said, staring at me with a hot, intense gaze. "Makes me think of the beginning of a porn flick."

"For real? How much porn do you watch?" I asked, pondering our scenario. "Guess it is kind of hot. We can see each other, but we're just out of reach."

"None of your business, Lady Cilla," he teased. "You'd better continue stripping before your mouth gets you into more trouble! Just wait until I can reach you!"

"Well, maybe we need some porn movie music to go with this, our very own soundtrack?" I giggled. I had no idea what kind of music would be played, but hopefully it wasn't something creepy. My fingers played with the waist of my jeans, then I slowly unzipped them and removed them, bending a bit more than was necessary.

"I'll put something on," he said, conveniently before his jeans came off. He grabbed his cellphone, and then started playing some Foo Fighters, at low-medium volume. Then his jeans came off, and he stood there in boxers, and I was across the room in bra and undies.

"You next," he challenged as if it was a poker game, grinning at me.

"No, you!" I countered.

Then, his boxers came off and he stood there, watching me, raising an eyebrow. I took off my bra and flung it at him, completely missing him. It fell in the living room, right near his cats, who started acting like it was the motherlode of string games. I dissolved into a fit of giggles while he rescued my slightly-mangled bra from his pets, and put it on his table. He looked at me, trying to be annoyed, but then started laughing too!

I was giggling so much I ended up collapsing on the bed, and he sat on the bed and dragged me over to him, still laughing also.

"Maybe I need to silence you, for getting my cats all riled up!" he shook his head at me.

"I dare you," I managed, giggles tapering off finally.

Todd leaned over me and kissed me. I couldn't care about funny after that, when passion quickly took over. There was a good amount of kissing, and then his mouth started moving everywhere on my body. His mouth on my breasts was making me beyond insane—I could have climaxed from just his mouth, it was so pleasurable. Then followed by lots of oral sex, and wow, his fingers on my clitoris were so amazing. The kissing was so intense after that, so deep and passionate. I reciprocated after that with some oral for him. He had wanted to climax in my mouth, and I was fine with that. But, we both ended up wanting him inside me too much.

"Cilla, do you want to switch position so you're on top?" Todd asked in a low voice, breathing hard.

I shook my head no, and he asked again, "You sure? I think you'd look very sexy from that angle, and it could feel very good for you."

"Not tonight, maybe another time," I said, then leaned up and kissed him hard, hoping he'd drop the idea. I didn't want to think about the last time I had been on top of a guy during sex . . .

It was in college, and we were both drunk. That's how the best and the worst instances in college always started, right? I was hanging out with a friend in his dorm room, drinking beer and watching a Jackie Chan movie on a Saturday night. Fun choice for a movie, action and comedy, but definitely not romantic. Jason was the kind of friend who I'd hang with, but didn't feel a spark with. It was comfortable, but we both knew we didn't want more from each other. No complications, which made life easier since we were also study partners. But, that night, we were destressing following a big exam.

After a short time of us sitting on his bed next to each other, I was cuddling against Jason, then he turned to kiss me and it got kind of hot after that; the movie was definitely forgotten.

We made out for a while, then clothes started coming off. After some decent oral pleasure, he put the condom on and wanted me to be on top of him. I straddled his hips and we started, and it felt good, even though my head was a bit cloudy from being drunk. Jason changed the angle we were joined at, and things suddenly felt different, but I couldn't figure it out. After a while, he started touching my clitoris, and then we both climaxed. I collapsed on top of him and we both laid there, breathing heavily, so it wasn't too awkward. Except when I stood up and realized that when Jason had previously moved, we had had anal sex instead. Put as delicately as I could (because I was a lady, of course), the evidence was on the condom.

My head started to spin, as I felt worse by the minute. Jason stood up then, too, and then I walked, stiffly, clumsily, to the sink in his dorm room.

Jason asked me, "Are you ok?"

I shook my head, then leaned in to throw up into the small sink. After about a few minutes, I was done and rinsed out my mouth, then splashed some water on my face. I sunk to the floor nearby, and Jason cleaned himself up at the sink, then helped me up and into his bed. It was awkward, but we were both more drunk and uncoordinated than we had realized. Jason was very apologetic and embarrassed, but I wasn't mad at him, instead I was just stunned. And extremely sore.

We were in a few classes together, both being computer science majors, but we got along well. Were still friends after that incident, as if nothing more than a burp had happened between us. Definitely a decent outcome, considering either of us could have been a jerk about it.

After that, I learned to not drink that much again. And that I wasn't into that type of sex, at all. And, I was rarely in that position, on top of a guy, without thinking of that experience— for me, it was a sex drive-killer. Didn't know that I wanted to really tell any guy that story, in case someone ever asked why I didn't care for that sex position!

"So, why won't you be on top? Come on, it'll be fun," the guy would whine.

"Because when I was in bed with a guy in college, we were both too drunk to realize that he ended up doing surprise anal sex to me while I was on top. You know, the wrong hole," I'd say flippantly, acting much more confident than I'd feel.

"After that, I saw poo remnants on the condom, then I barfed in his sink. So, I don't want to be on top of ya, sorry!" I'd smile and apologize, hoping he'd shut up about it.

No thanks, I could see that being an instant mood-killer for the guy, too. Like instant abstinence . . . maybe they should scare kids in high school with stories like this? I could also regale them with tales of my bad dates. Do the lack-of-decent-dates lecture, in case I ever lost my current job.

* * *

Back to Todd, who was staring down at me.

"You ok? You looked like you zoned out," he asked.

"Yeah," I replied, realizing I did *not* want to tell him what had flashed through my brain, "I was just lost in the kissing, because it felt so good!"

"Still making up for lost time with the kissing, huh?" he smiled down at me. "You are really good at it, but you should spend some more time practicing, I think!"

"Oh, that sounds very nice," I smiled up at him, weaving my fingers through his hair, so I could pull his head down to do as he suggested . . .

After a lot more kissing, followed by some fantastic sex, we sat on the bed, clutching each other, both of us breathing heavily as we calmed down from our intense shared orgasm.

"I think this was even better than last week, and last week was so great," he said with a smile.

"I agree—somehow it got even better. Wow!" I agreed with him.

"Well, the chemistry is really great, so maybe that's why?" he theorized. "Or maybe because you do whatever I tell you to!"

"Oh no, that can't be it—no guy bosses me around!" I teased back. We just relaxed and listened to the music still playing for a bit. Then we both got up and I started to get dressed.

"Did you want to hang out some more?" he asked.

"For a little bit," I replied, "I do have family stuff going on tomorrow, well actually later today! So I do have to get some beauty sleep soon."

"Oh please, you probably look adorable in the morning," he smiled, getting up to get dressed too.

"Yeah, the dark shadows under my eyes are extra-sexy," I was sarcastic.

"Along with your nice hair and your pretty smile, it'll look cute!" he replied. I figured he was sweet and delusional.

I smiled at him, and we just looked at each other, then I scrambled around for my pants.

"So, do you want some water or something?" Todd asked.

"Sure, that sounds perfect," I replied.

Todd retrieved my glass from the nightstand and went into the kitchen to pour the water for me. I finished getting all my clothes on and put my purse and shoes near me as I sat on the sofa across the room.

"Oh, you're over there," he said, a little surprised, as he came over to the sofa, holding our drinks. "Let me put some clothes on, since I'm getting cold now."

He set our drinks on his coffee table, and I watched his cute butt disappear as he put on boxer shorts, then jeans and a t-shirt. He came back to the sofa and sat down.

"So, you mentioned you have family stuff going on this week? What family stuff is that?" he asked, sipping his water.

"I have a family dinner over my mother's house, for my sister and brother's birthday. So, I can't miss it, otherwise I'd be in deep trouble with my family!" I said, smiling.

Todd smiled back. "I can imagine, they'd really disown you!"

"Exactly," I said, then drank some more of my water.

"Do you have anything else going on, besides the party and work?" Todd asked.

"No," I replied, "but that's plenty of stuff going on for me to deal with. I mean, I could work on some more projects around the house, but with the holidays, forget it."

"Very true," Todd answered, sipping his water. "I don't have many assignments going on at the moment, but I am lining up a bunch of them for January and February. It'll be good for then, but has me a bit bored lately."

"Bored?" I asked, surprised. "I'd love to be bored right now. Can I give you a few hundred tasks to do?"

"Like what, anything good?" he asked, teasingly.

"Keeping up with cleaning, especially dishes, since I've had friends over in the evenings after the holiday, just catching up and eating cookies. Oh, and laundry, because I'm just about out of clean clothes again!"

"Yeah, none of that sounds fun, I'll pass," he smiled at me.

"Thanks, then I refuse to listen to you whine about being bored, ya brat!" I teased him back.

"Fine," he said emphatically.

"Fine," I parroted back to him, then glanced at his alarm clock. "Crap, it's 3 a.m., I really have to get going!"

"Ok, I'll walk you out," Todd said, standing up slowly and stretching.

He put on his sneakers, then retrieved our coats and we put them on. He scooped up his keys from the coffee table, and opened the door and we walked into the hallway. Todd locked the door behind us, then opened the outside door, and we quietly walked outside to the still, frozen night. He held my hand as he led me swiftly to my car.

"Sorry we're walking so fast, but it's fucking freezing out here!" he said to me, quietly.

"It is ridiculously artic chilly," I whispered back to him. It felt so cold that nobody should have been outside at that moment; I would have given anything to have gone to sleep on his nice, soft, warm bed, instead of leaving his apartment.

"So, do you think you'd be up for another evening together, sometime soon?" Todd asked, as we reached my car and stood next to the driver's side door.

"Sure, I do know that next week I have my holiday party, but it should be over early enough," I replied.

"That sounds good, then you can come over and we'll have a very exciting party here!" Todd said, grinning at me. "We can see what kind of stamina you have then."

"Funny, especially after an evening of eating and schmoozing. I'll be ready to scream or something," I replied wryly.

"Of course, you can come over all bored, and I can rock your world!" Todd said confidently.

"Ok," I laughed, "text me and I will. We're going to be pre-frostbitten if we stay out here much longer, so I really have to go! Night, I had an awesome time," I said quickly, then leaned up to kiss him. It was a very chilly kiss, but we did try to warm each other up.

"Night," Todd said, when the kiss ended. "Have a safe drive home, and text me when you get in, ok?"

"Ok, I will, night," I said, getting into my car and shutting the door. Started it and waved to him as I backed out of the parking spot. As I drove away, I saw him in the rearview mirror as he jogged back to his apartment.

I arrived home rather quickly, or maybe it just seemed that way because I was getting a bit sleepy.

Texted him, "Got home safe. Tonight was FUN, seeya soon Todd!"

Barely got my contact lenses out before my head was ready to hit the pillow.

Woke up to the pinging of my cellphone, a text message from Todd: "glad u safe @ home. i'll text ya soon, cutie!"

I smiled, because it was sweet of him to compliment me. Didn't need to reply, since it was up to him to contact me. It was 7:30 a.m., so I went back to sleep for a while.

Ten minutes later, my cell rang. Damn, guess sleep was futile, I thought, looking at the display and seeing that it was my mom.

"Hello?" I croaked out my first word of the day, after answering the cellphone.

"Morning, dear," my mom said crisply. "What time are you coming over, to help me decorate and set up?"

"Mom, it's 7:30," I sleepily protested. "I think I said 10:30 a.m., last time we spoke."

"That was before I added ten people to the guest list. Wait, no, twelve people," she continued, oblivious to my need for more beauty sleep.

"Oh god, who else is coming?" I sat up and felt more sober by the minute; all traces of my post-coital glow dissipating, unfortunately.

"My brother and his family, your sister's friend and family, and two friends of your brother's," she continued. "And, make sure you bring a nice dress to change into, after you finish setting up. Be here at 9:30 instead, ok? Thanks, darling!"

"Mom, huh? Hello?" I asked, but she had already hung up on me. Which meant that she was plotting something, maybe trying to set me up with one of my brother's "friends," if they were even his friends and not just students of my mother's, who owed her favors. It wouldn't be the first time she had pulled this setting me up with someone crap.

I mumbled some choice curse words and got out of bed, then went to the bathroom to insert my contact lenses. Wished for a moment that I was taking Todd, my younger fling, to today's party, just to shock everyone into silence. Nah, I reconsidered, that would be really mean to use him like that. Not cool.

Although it would be funny to render my very proper mother speechless, for once!

I showered, ate a quick breakfast, and drove over to my mother's house to help her set up for the party, grumbling to her at one point that she could have hired a caterer to do this. But, apparently my mother preferred the "personal touch" from family.

By lunchtime, the party was in full swing, and quite chaotic. Although I had been introduced to the two single guys, who were actually my brother's friends from work, they didn't seem to be any more interested in me than I was interested in them. I ended up in a corner, catching up with Fiona.

"So, what's going on with you?" Fiona whispered. "You seem pretty happy today, despite Mom bossing you around. Normally, you'd be ready to walk out of here while shooting fire out of your eyes."

"Um," I whispered back. "I kind of met someone, and we're hooking up."

"Ok, I know I'm out of the loop, but that's just sex, right?"

I nodded, and she continued, "That's cool! Is that what you were going for with this guy?"

"Yeah, it is. He's completely gorgeous and really nice. Has his life together," I explained in a whisper.

"Wow, that's cool. He sounds great! Will you see him again?" Fiona asked.

"I think so, since we've really enjoyed ourselves," I whispered back.

"Oooo, great sex, huh? I'm so jealous of you right now!" she smiled at me as she whispered.

"Fi, it's the best sex I've ever had; even I'm really surprised how great it is with this guy. I never expected this," I whisper-admitted.

"Cilla, do you think it has potential to develop into something more than just lovers?" she asked.

"I don't know, but I'm leaning towards probably not. He's younger than me, and we decided that we weren't going to pursue a relationship," I told her, quietly.

"How much younger?"

"27."

"Damn."

"Exactly," I whispered back. "He's too young. We wouldn't have anything in common, and we're at different experience points in our lives. There wouldn't be any shared experiences, to help build a relationship on."

"What do you mean?" Fiona asked me, looking perplexed.

"You know, that we've both gone through experiences, and can share our perspectives on those experiences," I replied.

"Shared experiences means what you and this guy would experience together—do things together, and that is what you guys can share. You don't have to be too similar to someone in order to be able to get along. Have some shared values, and talk to each other to see where you might be compatible, and complement each other," she explained. "Sometimes it's our differences that might make us the most exciting match with someone else."

"Huh, I never thought of it that way. Sounds interesting," I commented, as our conversation was broken up by my mother bringing out the birthday cake and motioning for me to help her yet again.

During the week, I met Mel at the local mall, after work. I had to buy a dress for my work party that weekend, and needed Mel to keep me from buying something awful. I had only realized the day before that I had donated any fancy dresses I owned right before I had moved into my condo. For once, it was a dress crisis!

We went to three different department stores in the mall before I found a decent dress option. Then to two more stores to find shoes and a purse.

I was getting ready for the party on Saturday, and I started thinking, "I hope Todd does text me tonight, so he can see me looking all girly!"

5

Third Time's a Charm, Right?

That evening, I was at my work holiday party, when I heard my cellphone receive a text message.

Ten of us occupied the table, chatting about marriage and relationships, and the talk turned to dating.

My boss, Kevin, turned towards me and asked, "Any prospects lately, Cilla? You haven't mentioned any new guys in a little while."

"Thanks, Kevin," I replied, thinking quickly on what to say, to be professional and keep Mr. Nosy off my back. "I am seeing someone, but it's just casual and new. We're not at the stage of going to work shindigs together, yet."

"Oh, that's fantastic," Kevin said enthusiastically. "What does he do?"

"He's a photographer, doing magazine and corporate work, mostly," I replied, hoping the conversation was done, and I could just relax. Thankfully, Hillary saved me at that moment.

"Oh, my sister and I were talking over the holiday, about the best pickup lines. So, let's see who has the best!" she said, smiling as she glanced around the table. "Who wants to start?"

Kevin waved his hand, saying, "This sounds great. Ok, here's mine: I go up to a beautiful woman and ask 'Do you have any Italian in you?' If she says 'no', I reply with 'Well, beautiful, would you like one in you?' They're either intrigued or repulsed, but usually intrigued."

Dead silence followed Kevin's pickup line. I furtively glanced around the table, and others seemed as horrified as me, or just stunned at his idiocy.

Hillary's husband, Doug, was brave enough to ask, "So, Kevin, what do you say if the lady tells you she is part Italian? Doesn't that blow your line to hell?"

"Good point, but I can usually find something else to add to it. I'm quick on my feet," Kevin smiled.

Doug, Hillary's husband, went next.

"I don't go in for all those elaborate stories. I've walked across the room and simply told the woman that I think she's pretty or beautiful, and ask her what her name is. If she's not interested, she'll tell me."

"Does that work?" Kim asked, curious.

"It worked for Hillary," he replied proudly.

"No, it didn't," Hillary chimed in. "We didn't meet that way, so you can't say it worked on me.

"We met at the Motor Vehicles agency. I cut in front of him by mistake, and he chewed me out over it. After I let him in front of me, he felt bad and started apologizing to me," she explained. "After I was done, I was walking outside to my car, and he ran over to ask me for my phone number!"

We all looked at Doug, who could only say, "Ok, guess I remembered that wrong. I'm in the doghouse now!"

Tyler jumped in next, "Mine's awesome: I walk over to her and say, 'You're so pretty, I completely forgot the pickup line I was going to say!'"

We agreed, not bad!

His girlfriend, Emmie, said, "This isn't my line but a guy used this on me once: 'Did you sit in a pile of sugar? Cause you have a pretty sweet ass.'"

We started laughing, and she added, "I did slap him over it, because he was older and I wasn't even eighteen yet!"

"My best pickup line is really a hook," Kim offered. "I ask the guy his top three favorite movies, and out of those, I can usually find some random moment in one of the movies to mention as a moment that made me so emotional that I couldn't control myself the first time I saw it."

"How do you know what movie to go with? Or that you even saw those three movies?" I asked, very curious.

"I'll admit that this became easier because of movie database websites—if I really didn't know, I'd check with a website and pick a specific scene," she admitted. "It works because the guy thinks I have a lot in common with him, enjoying the same movies and that I'm all deep and emotional."

Kim looked at me, and said, "Your turn!"

I shrugged my shoulders and started, "This was a former line I used to throw out, when I previously worked for a software developer. On a date, we'd talk for a while, then when he would ask about my job, I'd let it slip that I had a security clearance. It was like guy catnip!"

Doug nodded at me. "Cilla wins, so far!"

"We're not done here yet," Kevin protested, holding off Doug with his hand. "And I don't see how her line works."

"Well, it was the way I said it, and the way I said I couldn't ever elaborate on it. Made them think I worked for the CIA or something. Or maybe they were imagining some James Bond fantasy scenario. Whatever it was, guys looked at me differently when I mentioned it," I explained.

"Huh," was Kevin's response. I figured he was jealous that he hadn't thought of something so clever, and a lot more classy than his line.

"Was it the truth?" Doug asked me. "Your security clearance?"

"Yes, I had one, but for a completely different government agency," I replied, unable to keep the grin off of my face. "Only because our work involved a very boring medical database!"

Everyone at the table burst out laughing, and I finally had a chance to open my purse to look at my cellphone.

"hey, cilla," Todd had texted.

"hey todd, how's it going?" I texted back.

"it's going good," he replied. "how are u, beautiful?"

The conversation flowed around me at the table, but I didn't do more than nod when asked a question. I was busy.

"I'm good," I texted back, "almost done with my work holiday party."

"Do you have after-party plans?" he asked.

"Not yet—are you planning an after-party?" I asked in return.

"Yes, but it's a party for just us," he texted.

"Cool, I'm in!" I replied, smiling so much that Kim whispered to her boyfriend, "Guess who's planning to get some tonight?"

"Shhh," I admonished her. "I'm being totally respectable. I'm simply being propositioned by my gentleman caller."

"For what position?" Hillary asked.

Everyone at the table cracked up.

"Bitch, shush!" I exclaimed. "Let me respond to him, then I'll smack ya!"

Looked at my phone, which had just pinged again, to check Todd's reply.

"How soon can u come over?" he had texted.

"I'll leave now, grab some clothes, then be over in 30 min, ok?" I confirmed. "Oh, can u help me out of my fancy dress?"

"OMG yeah! Can't wait to help w/that!" he texted.

I stood up, told my friends I was leaving, and started hugging them and saying my goodbyes. After I got through the table, Hillary walked me out to the lobby and I retrieved my coat. We walked to the main door of the hotel, still chatting about random topics.

Then, she broke in with, "Don't forget to use condoms, ok?"

"Yeah, because I'd forget that!" I said dryly. "You know I'm too logical and in control to ever forget the basics."

"Hey, in the moment, anything can happen, right? Especially since you're not too sure about him," she teased gently, elbowing me.

"I'm not sure about him because I know this is just casual. I told you, we decided against a relationship," I reminded her.

"Except that sometimes, the more you see someone, the more you think of them, the more you care for them, the more you do them . . ." Hillary's voice trailed off as she looked pointedly at me.

"Girlfriend, you're drunk!" I deflected her and laughed as we hugged our goodbyes.

"Oh, I stole this from the bar on our way out. Take it with you," she said, suddenly producing a bottle of top-shelf aged whiskey. "It'll go over well with your young hottie."

"Thanks, klepto, bye!" I smiled, taking the bottle from her as we hugged again. Then I waved backwards, as I walked outside to my car, as fast as I could in 3-inch heeled sandals.

Drove home, grabbed another outfit and shoes to change into later on, and shoved it into a bag. In the car, I put the whiskey bottle into the bag, not wanting to forget that item. Then drove to the convenience store for my required coffee. Also bought a maple granola bar to help absorb the alcohol, as I was slightly tipsy, but not too far gone to drive. I had a silly smile plastered on my face while I prepared my coffee. Paid for my purchases, then sat in my car and ate the granola bar. After that, drove to Todd's while I sipped the coffee.

Parked the car in his complex's parking lot, then grabbed my bag of clothes, my small fancy purse, and the coffee, and walked swiftly to his front door. Then, I juggled the items I was holding, to dig my phone out of my purse to text him.

"Open the door, please!" I managed to text, without dropping anything.

Two minutes later, he opened the inside door to his apartment, then opened the outside door, smiling down at me.

"Hey, no phone call! I would have escorted you to the door, but here, let me take your stuff," he said, taking my bag from me.

"Thanks, it's been a hectic evening," I said, following him into the apartment. "I totally forgot to call ya—too much running around tonight!"

He set the bag of clothes and whiskey down on the sofa, and I tossed my small dressy purse on top of it. I drank the rest of my coffee while he locked the door, then he just leaned back against the door, staring at me expectantly.

"Can I take your coat, Cilla?" he asked, not moving. "You staying, or just here to show off your dress?"

I stopped drinking the little bit of coffee that was left, put my coffee cup down on his coffee table, then went over to my bag. Didn't answer him because he clearly had my outfit on his mind, but had a slight smile on my face.

"My girlfriend stole a bottle of whiskey from the party, so you're welcome to crack it open, if you want," I said, producing the bottle from the bag, and holding it outstretched towards him.

Todd walked over to me, took the bottle, and watched me as I shrugged out of my fancy wool coat.

"Damn, you look amazing!" he gasped, clearly checking me out in my navy blue silk dress and silver high-heeled sandals.

"Thanks," I replied, feeling very self-conscious. He took my coat and hung it up, then walked over to the kitchen. I sat on the sofa and took off my shoes, putting them close to the door. He returned from the kitchen with whiskey and ice cubes in two glasses, and sat down next to me. Handed me one of the glasses.

"You look like a holiday present I need to unwrap soon," he winked at me, "so tonight I toast to you."

He clinked glasses with me, then we sipped the whiskey.

"Wow, this is strong," I sputtered, since I had sipped too much of the strong liquor. I put the glass down on his coffee table, moved my bag of clothes and purse to the floor, and leaned back on his sofa. He sipped his drink, then put his glass on the coffee table next to mine, and leaned back next to me on the sofa.

"So, good party?"

"Yeah, for a work party, it was good. Tasty food, very short speeches, and I had a lot of fun catching up with my girlfriends," I told him, smiling.

"That sounds nice," he replied.

"What's going on with you? Did you have a good week?" I asked him.

"Let's see, I was busy sending out invoices, getting paid for some jobs, and taking care of bills. Not as exciting, but I feel better when I get everything taken care of," he explained.

"That's good, less to stress over when you take care of the paperwork and bills, right?" I asked, in between sips of my drink.

"Exactly," he confirmed. "So, how was your week?"

"It was decent. I had one training, which wasn't too bad. I think people were in the mood to learn, so it was pretty uneventful. Then, on Wednesday I realized I didn't have anything to wear to the party, so I dragged one of my girlfriends all over the mall to help me pick out a dress."

"Well, your girlfriend definitely did a good job helping you pick the perfect dress," he grinned at me.

"I'll tell her you approve—" my words were cut off by him kissing me. We kissed for a little while, then decided we were done with sitting on the sofa, and both stood up. I walked around to the other side of the bed, and set my drink down on the nightstand, next to the pile of condoms.

"I see that you haven't cleaned lately," I teased him, and then ducked as he threw a small pillow at my head. "How many condoms are left? Eight or so."

"Wait—are you keeping tabs on how many we've used, or checking to see who else I've been with in your absence?" Todd asked slowly, looking astonished. I couldn't tell if he was faking surprise or secretly pissed at me, so I guess I had to play it cool.

"I'm teasing you. I don't know what else you're doing during the week, but we haven't decided on anything exclusive," I answered.

His eyes narrowed. "Before you, I told you my last partner was eight months ago. And, no, I'm not currently fucking anyone else but you," he said bluntly, while looking annoyed. I had the distinct feeling that he was ready to be a jerk about this, if he wanted to be. "Are you currently fucking anyone else?"

"No, I'm not! I haven't ever had more than one lover at a time. I told you it's been much longer since my last partner than it was for you," I quickly answered, wondering why he was acting like we were exclusive, suddenly. We hadn't had any conversation about exclusivity. I'd definitely analyze it when I was alone, but for now I wanted to get back to our sexy, playful anticipation.

"Todd, are we ok? I didn't mean to mess things up; I was just teasing about the condom-counting," I said, just looking at him, while my fingers reached for the side zipper on my dress.

His expression slowly softened while he looked at me from head to toe. "Yeah, we're cool. Come back over here so I can get you out of that dress. And, please, don't open your mouth before it gets you into more trouble!"

"I thought you liked my mouth? Especially what it does to you?" I flirted as I slowly walked back around the bed and stood in front of him.

"Yeah, Cilla, it's all I thought about today," he grinned. "What your mouth does to me. And what I want to do to you."

Todd walked around me then, unexpectedly. He went to his dresser and started lighting candles, about five or six of them, then he turned off the lights. That was something he hadn't done before; I couldn't remember if I had even noticed the top of his dresser, let alone what was on it. He walked back over to me and embraced me from behind, resting his chin on my head.

"This feels so good, Todd," I sighed, leaning back into him. "The most relaxing moment of a very busy Saturday."

"Good," he replied. "I've been waiting for this all week, relaxing and having fun with you."

He paused while we just stood there, enjoying the moment. "That whiskey is some really strong shit!" he said suddenly. "It's really hitting me!"

"Me too!" I agreed. "And I had a fair amount of wine at the party."

"You can't leave my place if you aren't sober—don't do anything dangerous, ok?" he asked. "In fact, maybe you should have said something before you even drove over here."

"I was fine to drive," I protested, looking up at him. "I would have said something if there was a problem, I swear!"

"Cilla," he said really softly, glancing down at me, "don't put yourself in danger just to come over here, ok? Promise me?"

"Ok, I promise," I answered him.

After that, his hands moved to my right side, to start pulling my dress's zipper down. I put my arms up, and he slid the dress up and over my head, then walked over to his kitchen table to lay the dress nicely over one of the chairs. He walked back over to me with a serious expression on his face, and I started to remove his shirt, then his jeans. Both of us finished undressing each other slowly, quietly, then we both peeled the sheets back and climbed into the bed. We laid facing each other, but just looked at each other.

"So, what do you want to do?" I asked him, lightly touching his stomach with my fingers.

"I don't think I want to talk anymore tonight," he replied slowly. "Just go with me on this, ok?"

"Ok," I said slowly, not sure what he had in mind for us that evening.

He moved his arms around me, and pulled me close, and my arms went around his neck. We started to kiss and press our bodies closer together. Legs twined together, arms pulling each other even closer together.

During our two previous evenings, I was never sure that he was as into the kissing as much as I was. I had felt a bit insecure that he was just humoring me with all the kissing (how much kissing was really standard for a hook-up, anyway?), but at this point, the kissing was so different. It felt as if he wasn't holding back tonight—he was right there with me on every kiss, and it felt incredible. And I never knew what I had been missing from his kisses the two previous evenings. It was so intensely passionate, as our lips met again and again, kissing deeper as our arms kept caressing each other.

I felt his heart beating faster, and I'm sure he felt mine, too. The kisses kept increasing in passion; it felt as if the air was charged with some kind of current. My lips felt like they were on fire from his passion and we could barely breathe from our intimate marathon. He broke off the kissing suddenly, and rolled me gently onto my back. Then Todd released his embrace and trailed his hands down my torso, his heated glance following his hands.

He leaned in to gently kiss me, then slowly trailed kisses down my body to pleasure me at my center with his tongue. He slid his arms under my legs to anchor me, while I gasped and moaned with increasing frequency. Eventually, I cried out and was sated, and he kissed a trail back up to my mouth, and we kissed again, as the kisses became increasingly passionate yet again.

Until I broke off the kisses, to caress down his torso, then caressed his large penis with my hand. Lightly massaged his thighs after a bit, to tease him. Then, I leaned down to touch the tip with my tongue, and started sucking him into my mouth. Until Todd gasped, "Damn, Cilla, I need to be inside you now!"

I sat up and he followed me, then I grabbed a condom from the nightstand to hand to him. He put it on, then put a hand on my butt to lightly push me back to the bed. Todd kneeled between my thighs, as he had on the previous evenings. But instead of plunging forward, he caressed my legs while he just looked at me, a slow, sexy look.

"You ok, Todd?" I whispered, wondering what was going on.

"Yeah Cilla, you just look so beautiful," he replied. "I want to take a pic of you right now, but I also don't want to move from the bed."

"Oh my god, no pictures of me right now!" I gasped. "You can't do that!"

"It's ok, I'm not gonna grab my camera, unless you want to get it. It's on my desk, in that black case. I'm not moving," he grinned. "Well, maybe I'll move some," he said as he moved his hips closer to my body, almost inside me.

I sighed. "You're teasing me now, aren't you? Checking how much I really want you...I want you, Todd, you're sexy and amazing," I managed to say, not believing that I said all that, when I was so focused on the passion he was teasing me with.

He leaned forward to kiss me once, a long, slow, deep kiss. Then pulled back slightly.

"Cilla, you are so beautiful, inside and outside. I want you so much," he whispered.

I leaned up to press my lips to his, and he entered me. After that, we both let passion carry us away, until we both found our release.

Afterwards, we laid there in the semi-darkness, just recovering and relaxing. Enjoying holding each other. I lightly stroked his shoulder with one hand, lazily; he held me and rested both palms at the small of my back.

Todd kissed my forehead, then asked, "You ok? Need anything?"

"Feels so good right now, I don't want to move," I replied, content to snuggle into his chest a little more. His hair was damp but cool, and I moved my hand up from his shoulder to smooth his hair back from his face.

"Mmm, that's nice, thanks," he said as we smiled at each other.

"I like just going with what you want; we may have to try that again soon!" I grinned at Todd.

"Let me recover a bit, first, ok?" he teased, kissing me on my nose.

"Of course, I know you're old and all," I teased back.

"Not cool, baby cougar!" he spanked me lightly on my butt, then I leaned over and spanked him back. After that . . . well, another round of fantastic sex ensued, with a bit more spanking during it. Definitely a feisty time!

After that climax, we both collapsed, and then Todd asked me if I was thirsty.

"I'm parched," I squeaked out, as I had almost lost my voice over the vigorous round of sex!

"Ok, I'll get us some more whiskey," he said.

"Wait, Todd," I called out, on my way to the bathroom. "I won't be able to drive home for a while if I have any more, possibly even until morning."

"That's ok, I promise I won't let you leave until you're safe to drive, ok?" he said.

"Sounds good," I said, feeling a bit surprised. So I wasn't being evicted after the usual two to three hours of fun? Huh, maybe he was more drunk than usual. Or maybe it was something else, I surmised. My dress had cast a spell over him, rendering him my sex slave. I liked that theory!

Or a similar theory: he was becoming as addicted as I was to the intensely pleasurable sex? That made sense to me; he was very skilled, and we really did seem to connect and have great chemistry together. Even hanging out before and after the sex was a lot of fun, with interesting conversations and lots of flirty banter. He was definitely the perfect lover for me, because I had never had sex that was so much fun. It was like going to an amusement park, and he was the ride. Less screaming, though probably only because he had neighbors so close by!

I used the bathroom and looked into the mirror at my tangled hair and messy makeup. Took out my contact lenses and put them in their case. Used a bit of toilet paper to get rid of smudges and blend out whatever makeup was left, so I didn't look like Vogue's idea of heroin chic. Then, I took a different piece of toilet paper to blot the slightly-greasy roots of my hair, and then finger-combed the tangles out of it. Threw away all the toilet paper, then walked back into the living room.

Todd was reclined on the sofa, drinking another whiskey. He whistled at me, then reached out his hand and grabbed my butt, pulling me over to him. I put his whiskey down on the table, and he pulled me down on top of him, so that we were cuddling.

"You ok?" he asked, kissing my cheeks.

"Definitely, I feel refreshed. Oh, can I have my drink, please?" I asked, moving so that I was laying on my side.

"Just a sec, let me grab this blanket," he said, straining to reach a blanket behind him in the laundry basket.

"Lucky for us that you have your clutter strategically placed all around your apartment," I teased him.

"Oh shush, I didn't see you getting back up to get the blanket, either!" he managed as his fingers finally made contact with the blanket, which he then threw onto my face and our bodies. I worked on getting it untangled and straightened out, while he leaned over to the coffee table and picked up my drink. As soon as the blanket covered us, untangled, I took the glass from him. We both sipped our drinks slowly in the semi-darkness, facing towards the candles on his dresser.

"Were they always there, or are they new?" I asked him, nodding towards the candles.

"Wait, what are you asking about, Cilla?" he seemed confused, or maybe a bit drunk, from all the whiskey.

"The candles, on your dresser," I clarified. "Are they new or were they there last week?"

"New. I saw them on clearance when I was at the store last week. I thought you'd like them, for mood lighting and all that. Some are vanilla, others are citrus. Nice, huh?"

"Very nice! I like a little bit of light, so that you don't grab the wrong thing by mistake in the moment," I giggled. "Otherwise that could be a big mess!"

"What the hell do you do in bed that I don't know about? You're a bit of a wild one, imagine that!" he teased me. "It's like you can't get enough of me!"

"Well, you are incredibly handsome, with or without clothes," I said, smiling behind my glass. "And you're a very skilled lover, and a fascinating man. We have fun together, right?"

"Yeah, this is great, Cilla, you make me feel very good inside," he said slowly, then smiled, holding me closer to him. "You chase away all my demons."

"What demons are those?" I asked in surprise, glancing up at him. He was drinking, and I wondered how drunk he was. I also wondered how drunk I was getting, since I could feel my sips of the whiskey hitting me again.

Todd finally put his drink down on the coffee table, and spoke slowly, "My demons are self-doubt. When I doubt my talent and ability to deliver on assignments. I guess it's an artist thing."

"That makes sense, you do put a lot of pressure on yourself to succeed," I said, in support of him.

"Thanks, Cilla. I'm not finished," he said overly emphatic. Clearly he was drunk. Goody. Hopefully he wouldn't be a pain in the ass type.

"My other demon is loneliness. Sometimes I'm so busy and get too involved in what I'm doing that I forget I need to be more social. I forget that I need to be in my head less sometimes, so that I'm not egotistical or selfish, ya know? I need to be told when I'm an ass. I need to be with someone who makes my heart happy. I need to be with you," he finished, looking at me with a dopey grin.

"Cool," was all I could manage.

"And we can get married one day, and have babies together. I could see us with two, that would be fun, right?" He slightly slurred his declaration of his plans for us, with the grin still on his face.

"Todd, you're shocking me," I said, giggling as I lightly spanked his hip. He was saying things that were sheer lunacy, but he looked so cute while he said them.

Then, he looked at me, quite seriously, and said, "Cilla, I mean what I'm saying. Truth is, I want you. Only you."

After that statement, I had no idea what to say, so I kissed Todd on the cheek. His arms tightened around my waist, and after a few minutes, his breathing evened out and he was asleep. I was glad, because I was still stumped. Figured his comments were just pillow talk or the whiskey, after our serious euphoria of all the sex.

*   *   *

We woke up around 9 a.m. that morning, tangled together on the sofa, with a blanket over us. Todd and I sat up, and I yawned repeatedly. He slowly stood up and stretched, muttering about being too tall for sleeping there. Todd looked the same way I felt, as if a truck had run over us during the night.

"Do you mind if I use the bathroom first?" I asked, still groggy.

"No, go ahead. Use whatever you want to," he smiled at me, still stretching.

I went into the bathroom and freshened up, and reinserted my contact lenses. Put my hair up with a clip, then came back out into the living room and got dressed. Meanwhile, Todd had gotten dressed, and was in the kitchen.

"I'm going to put some tea on and make breakfast," he called to me. "How does that sound?"

"That sounds great, thanks!" I exclaimed, walking over to the kitchen, to lean in the doorway and watch him. "What are you making?"

"I have some cinnamon muffins, with orange marmalade or butter," he said, as he put two muffins in the microwave to warm up. "Go sit down, and I'll bring them out."

"Thanks, breakfast sounds really good!" I smiled as I left to do as he ordered.

I sat at the dining room table and looked around while I waited, then I got up and retrieved my cellphone. Made a list of the tasks I was going to do that day, such as grocery shopping and taking down my Christmas tree.

Todd started bringing in the tea and milk, sugar, and honey for it. "Wasn't sure what you wanted in your tea, so you have options," he explained as he went back to the kitchen.

"This is perfect, I usually use milk and sugar," I told him as he returned with the muffins, marmalade, and butter.

"That's good. I usually don't have anything this good for breakfast, but I got some muffins yesterday. They're really good," Todd said as he put honey in his tea.

"You're right, these muffins are great," I smiled at him over my mug. "It's a good way to wake up."

"Definitely," he agreed with me. "So, doing anything special today?"

"I was just making my list," I told him. "Have to do grocery shopping, and I'm taking down the Christmas tree, while I'm motivated. Otherwise it'll be Valentine's Day and the tree will still be up. How about you?"

"Working on bills, answering work emails, that kind of crap. I don't always get a break from the job," he replied, wrinkling his nose.

"Awww, poor baby," I smiled at him.

"I might actually do a vacation this summer, though," he said suddenly, smiling back at me. "I might go visit a friend in Vegas. If I do, we'll go to the Grand Canyon."

"That sounds like fun! I bet you'll take lots of pictures, right?" I asked him.

"Of course, but I'll do other things, too," he said. "I do have a life, you know."

"I never said you didn't," I replied. "I haven't even thought about vacation. I didn't do one last year because of buying my home. Not sure if I have enough money to do one this year."

"Not even a small road trip?" he asked.

"I'm not sure," I answered honestly. "I want to finish fixing up the rest of the rooms, including the two ugly bathrooms I have, so it depends how much money it will take to make the ugly go away."

"That makes sense, especially since you see those every day. You'll probably be really happy once the fixes are done, I bet," Todd said.

"You're right, it'll make a huge difference in the future. Currently, though, it still feels like I'm in an ugly rental," I complained.

"I'm still jealous that you own your own home," he said, standing up and starting to clear away the breakfast debris.

"Don't be," I told him. "Every month, I feel nauseous when I pay my mortgage."

He chuckled from the kitchen, then returned to the table.

"Sit, I'll take care of this," he said as I tried to gather plates, to help him.

"Are you sure?" I asked.

"I insist," he ordered. "Relax, I'll be done in a minute."

I sat in the chair while he finished cleaning up, smiling at his bossiness. It was sweet of him. Picked up my phone, and started going through some emails.

"Ok, stand up," Todd ordered me again, from right behind me.

I stood up, pushed my chair in, and turned around. I wasn't prepared for the passionate expression on his face, or him suddenly kissing me, but I didn't mind it at all. The kisses became deeper, and Todd moved us back to the bed. He sat down and pulled me on top of him, and we just kissed for a while. I had no idea how long we were entangled, but time seemed to stand still. It felt perfectly delicious, until I had to sneeze.

I pulled back, and turned my head away to sneeze, at the same time Todd asked, "What's wrong?"

I kept sneezing, so we both sat up, and he reached over to the nightstand to hand me some tissues. I nodded, still sneezing. Finally, the sneezing subsided, and he asked, "Are you ok?"

"Yeah, that was odd. Sorry I ruined the mood," I muttered from behind a tissue.

"It's ok, it was fun until your nose went insane!"

"Thanks," I said. "I should get going, unfortunately, since we both have stuff to do."

Todd insisted on walking me out to my car, even though it was broad daylight. I actually appreciated it, since the weather had turned cold and a bit icy, due to a bit of sleet falling.

"Text me when you're home safe?" he asked, in between goodbye kisses at my car.

"Of course," I sighed. "I have to go, but my lips don't want to leave your lips!"

"Mine either," he smiled.

"Ok, I'm gonna go now," I pouted as I got into my car.

He tapped on the window, and I rolled it down. He kissed me again, then said, "Bye, have a good week!"

"You too, Todd. I'll text you in a little bit," I said, then rolled the window up and backed the car out of the parking spot. He waved as I left, and I waved back.

On the way home, I started thinking about the elephant that had stampeded through our cuddling on his sofa: I was still a bit in shock about what he had said. I never really addressed his comments last night, or earlier; I had no idea what to say to Todd about it. I didn't want to decide to be committed to a future with someone through a drunken conversation, though. Maybe I was romantic or a bit immature, but I wanted it to be memorable, something I'd always remember in a sweet and nostalgic way.

The insane thought I had was that I could easily see myself with him in that light. Being a couple, married, having the kids. And it sounded like fun with him; he'd be a great husband and father. Telling me during a drunk conversation, unfortunately, left a bad taste in my mouth. It bothered me, and I didn't know if I could or even if I should bring it up to him later.

I made it home safe, then texted Todd, "got home safe, 3x satisfied (yum!) ;-) "

About an hour later, he texted back, "great, later Cilla ;) "

6

Another Fun Saturday . . . or Is It?

The next Saturday night, I had no plans, but it was fine. I figured Todd would text me later on. I got Chinese takeout for dinner, then did a bubble bath and got ready. It was relaxing, doing my nails while I sang along with Prince. Was glad I was alone, so nobody could hear me butchering his songs! By the time I was all ready and looked good, it was 9 p.m. I went downstairs and decided to just flip around on the television. Watched some sitcoms, then realized it was about 10:30 p.m., figured he'd be texting any minute. Went back to flipping channels and settled on a drama, even though I had the movie on DVD, too. Became engrossed in the story . . .

Woke up the next morning, quite groggy, and couldn't remember where I was. Took a while to fully awaken, only to realize that I was still in my apartment, on the sofa, with my contacts fused to my eyeballs. Fantastic, because that meant I would have to use half a bottle of saline to separate them from my eyes. Total pain in the ass, I grumbled to myself as I slowly went up the stairs to my bathroom.

As I squirted saline into each eye and carefully moved the contacts around, I realized what had, or rather, hadn't happened. Last night, I was reminded that casual meant casual. No expectations and no explanations were needed. In other words, Todd didn't text me last night about going over to his apartment.

Maybe he was done with the idyllic holidays and was sated, and ready to be busy with work. Or maybe it was my last text message, which hadn't left the invitation blatantly open as in previous texts. Who knew.

Or maybe it was about what he said before he fell asleep, about wanting to be with me, have babies with me. I thought it was just him being possessed by the top-shelf whiskey, not that it was a truth serum in his case. Maybe he was too embarrassed to ever want to see me again, after saying what he did.

Maybe our paths would cross again, since we lived in the same town, though at opposite ends of it.

Part of me was a bit relieved that he didn't text me, though. I was actually not in the mood for some really hot sex (gasp!). Must have been the impending PMS. Or my overpacked work schedule for the next few weeks—hopefully it wouldn't snow and I wouldn't lose my voice. Or maybe I was just a bit overwhelmed by how surprisingly great those evenings with Todd were? It didn't seem completely real that I had spent those evenings with him. He was too sexy, too interesting, too virile and confident. Not like any guy I had ever been with.

The other part of me was disappointed, though. I was used to the mini-routine of going over his place late Saturday nights. It was something fun to look forward to, and I had enjoyed myself. I liked hanging out with Todd—that was fine to admit. It wasn't as if I was being clingy or secretly buying bridal magazines and calling caterers. Seeing him was an easy way to supplement my social life, without much effort.

And, I knew that he had been very into me, too. Maybe he was afraid of being dependent on me. Or maybe he had found a younger model, or preferred a variety of women, so that we had no chance of being even remotely clingy. But, he really shared himself with me, though, by talking about family stuff and asking me so many questions about my life. That's the action that didn't sit so well with me; it kept creeping into my mind at odd moments.

It bothered me, our conversations had been quite interesting. Him not contacting me made me think, in one moment, that he was turning his back on our great rapport. Chemistry wasn't something that happened every day, and we definitely had it, quite intense at times.

Wondered if he had had similar thoughts, or if he just didn't care; he was on his "casual only" agenda and that I just wasn't part of his schedule now.

Maybe I just needed to be smart and forget him. Accept that we had enjoyed the fling, but it had been flung, and move on. Besides, if we did date, people would think that he was my son or a young relative. Thirteen years' difference in our ages. Not something to easily deal with. We were at completely different spots in our lives. I wanted a family of my own; his idea of family was probably just seeing his parents and sibling at the holidays, as an obligation. See? Different spots.

And, yeah, part of me still longed to roam free, as he did when he traveled on his freelance assignments. But, I needed most of my money for my mortgage; my home was my main destination now.

Completely different priorities—the other week, he had shown me the fancy $1,000 camera lens he had bought. Meanwhile, I had splurged on a fancy wrinkle cream, which apparently cost three times as much in the United States as it had when I had purchased it in Paris last year. At least the cream had seemed to work miracles—it got me Todd, right? Maybe it could help me to snag the older version of him. Hmm, wondered if he had a cousin?

I thought of this and more, while sitting at a local café, staring at the lunch menu on Sunday.

"Hey, table for one!" a voice said, towering over me like a shadow.

I looked up, and saw that it was Dan, a former coworker, who had moved on to a different job a few years ago.

"How are you?" I exclaimed, standing up and hugging him. "You here alone? Join me!"

"I will, thanks," he said, sitting, as a waiter brought another menu over. "Let's order, then catch up."

We did, and then he started on our catch-up and gossip session: his job was ok, but similar gossip and drama as where I worked, he was happy, and I was happy.

"I'm single," he said, in the middle of our spring rolls appetizer. "About a year ago, I found Liza cheating on me–"

"–No, that's awful!" I exclaimed, surprised. They had seemed very happy together; I had figured he was married to her, but just hadn't mentioned it yet in our meandering conversation.

"It was," he said slowly, in between bites of his spring roll. "She was chatting with an old friend from high school, who we had actually double-dated with. I didn't know it, but they became closer over time, and I found their 'I have feelings for you' texts by accident. Everything was over after that."

"Wow, that's awful. I'm so sorry for you," I said, sympathetically. "Did you suspect anything before the texts, or was the relationship going downhill before then?"

I had no problem being in his business, as we had always been close, going out to lunch in our tight-knit group—Hillary, Kim, Dan, and me.

"I think, deep down, I knew something was going wrong. She had been distant, we were fighting. But, I never expected a betrayal like that from her. It was devastating," he finished, shrugging.

"Yeah, I bet. You guys had that really nice house, too. What happened to that?" I asked.

"I kept the house—she didn't have enough money to pay the mortgage on her own, but I was fine with my finances. So, I did a bit of repainting and it looks like it's all mine," he replied with satisfaction.

"Oh no, you redecorated in 'bachelor style'?" I said, in mock horror. "It was fine before!"

"Hey, I'm completely offended by that," Dan replied, "I had to repaint, so I could clear out the cheating karma. It was bothering me to look around my house and see the same decor as when we lived together. I needed the changes for my mental health, otherwise it was going to make me crazy."

"All kidding is gone," I sympathized. "That does make perfect sense."

"What the hell is "bachelor style', anyway?" he asked me, seeming genuinely surprised.

"The pairing of a ridiculously huge flat-screen TV, navy blue and hunter green ugly squishy sofas, black squishy leather chairs, and ugly oak accent tables in the living room. And posters of sports stuff in thin black or gold cheap poster frames. The kitchen table is really a pub table with bar-height chairs. The bedroom is always either black furniture or 1980s oak furniture, either way it's outdated. Maybe the bed has a headboard, maybe not. But, the bedspread is always either black, blue, or green, or some combination of those colors. And, either blindingly-bright halogen lamps to spotlight all that beauty, or hand-me-down tacky 1980s gold lamps with plaid lampshades," I answered, picturing the apartments of some of my past dates.

It was an easy explanation, because I had hated such décor. It was as if they had all shopped at the same store, "Single Man's Sanctuary."

"Holy shit," he replied slowly, looking a little scared. "Not sure if I can invite you over my place now. You might hate it."

"Eh, I'm teasing a little. I wouldn't criticize anyone's home I visited; that would be very rude of me!" I was trying to back away from my "male house decor" rant, hoping I didn't sound all snobby.

"Well, there is only one way to test that, you know," Dan suggested, smiling at me.

"You're having a party?" I blurted out. "That would be a lot of fun, so our old lunch gang can catch up! Work isn't as much fun as it used to be; our lunches were crazy at times! Hillary and Kim will be so excited to see you!"

"Yeah, I'll have a party," he replied, his voice sounding a little hollow, for some reason. I wasn't sure why he was reacting that way; a party reuniting our lunch gang would be a lot of fun.

"I promise I'll be very nice and respectful, and I'll even bring something sweet for all of us to eat," I smiled at him.

Dan sat up straighter in his chair, and said, "Ok, it's a party. You're right, it'll be good to catch up. I need to be more social—think I've gotten too wrapped up in making sure I've moved on, that I haven't spent enough time just kicking back and relaxing. I let work consume me sometimes, which I know isn't good. At least I exercise, to get out the stress and the rage, right?"

"That is good," I agreed with him. "Otherwise the stress multiplies, then it eats at you."

He leaned forward and slowly asked, "Enough about me, what else is going on with you? Are you still renting? Are you single? How's your family?"

"Not renting anymore, yay! I bought a house about eight months ago, and it's been keeping me busy, between things breaking down, things I wanted to improve, and things I'm trying to decide between unpacking or donating to charity."

"Oh, nice, congratulations," he said, smiling at me. "That is an ordeal, but it's worth it."

"Next question, family: the family's doing good. As crazy as ever. Nothing really exciting on that front. Final question, am I single? The answer is yes. I was seeing someone for the past few weeks, but it's over," I finished.

"That's good about the family; I guess it's good that nobody's sick or has drama," he commented. "And sorry that it didn't work out with this guy, but I'm sure there's someone better out there for you."

I wondered why he had a little smile on his face when he said that, and maybe part of me wondered if he was considering asking me out. No, Dan was my friend, and his ex Liza had been absolutely gorgeous; she had been in a league above me, always perfectly polished and coiffed. I was usually running late, so I employed as many beauty shortcuts as possible, and it was probably obvious I wasn't as girly as some other women. I'd be very surprised if Dan was actually attracted to someone like me; I didn't seem to be his type at all.

"Thanks, Dan, I really appreciate it," I answered him slowly. I wasn't sure what to say to him, but maybe I could use a guy's perspective. "I'm not heartbroken. We weren't really dating."

"Oh, really? What were you doing?" he asked, curiosity evident in his expression.

"Um, kind of hooking up," I said, feeling my face turn very pink at my confession.

"Go Cilla! Wow, I would have never guessed that you would ever do that. You've always been so, so . . ." his voice trailed off.

"Oh god, please don't sit there and judge me, ok?" I asked, feeling a bit freaked out. It was one thing to tell my closest girlfriends, but an entirely different thing to talk about a guy to another guy. I was wondering what he was thinking.

"So . . . in control. That's it. And traditional. I guess that's the word I'm looking for. It just doesn't seem like you. You're the kind of woman a guy dates and pampers," he finished, slowly.

"Yeah, I'll agree that it's not the usual way I conduct my love life. But, I wanted to try something new. This guy was actually decent, though. It wasn't some creepy bang-and-run. We hung out and talked for a while, and I spent a few nice evenings with him," I explained, hoping he didn't judge me to be a slut. I didn't think I was a slut, but an empowered and modern woman.

"So, what happened; how did it end?" Dan asked, smiling at me. "Or am I getting too nosy? You can tell me to shut up if I am. After all, you were always good at saying that to me!"

"All that really happened is that he didn't text me, after our third evening together," I explained, my face still as pink as I'd ever felt it, without it being from a sunburn. When we had been coworkers, Dan and I had discussed a myriad of subjects, but never specifics on our sex lives. And definitely not anything pertaining to casual sex.

"So, it just faded away?" he asked, no more humor on his face. "That stinks, but some guys do that, unfortunately."

"Yeah, I guess so," I said, feeling quite awkward. "I guess it might have been easier if it had just been a one-night stand, then. After the third evening, I was kind of expecting him to text me for a fourth evening. And, because we also talked and got to know each other, it felt like we were getting a little too close too quickly. He was a nice guy, though. So, it does feel a bit disappointing, you know?"

"Yeah, I get that—it almost seemed like an affair of convenience, and you did sort of expect the text, right?" Dan commented.

I felt myself relaxing slightly as I nodded at him. Maybe he wasn't judging me as much as I worried he was.

"I did expect it, and it was him initiating the contact for each evening, so I didn't think it was really my place to text him. You know, hookup protocol and all that," I smiled at him, hoping I sounded more sophisticated than desperate.

As if I had men just constantly contacting me, who I had to sift through for the best offer. Ha!

"Ah, yes, protocols for hookups." he teased. "Maybe you'll have to inform me of all that, in case I go that route!"

"Have you dated since Liza?" I asked him, curious.

"No, I just haven't looked at women that way. Guess I'm having a bit of a dry spell, too, now that I think about it," he said, looking a bit surprised that he had admitted it to me.

"I don't blame you," I offered. "She definitely betrayed you, so you needed time to heal and move on. It's a good thing you can be more social now. Have this party, and it'll be your kick back into having fun, dating, whatever you want to do."

He smiled at me, "That does sound like a great idea. Listen, I do have to go because I have to meet my brother, but we'll be in touch very soon, ok?"

"Sure, that sounds great. You remember our office emails, right?" I checked.

He waved the waiter over, and as the waiter came over with the check, Dan quickly glanced at it, then handed his credit card to the waiter before I could grab for my purse or even lodge a verbal protest.

"Wow, you're sneaky! I have money; what's my half?" I asked, surprised at how sneaky he had been with the check.

"No, it's my treat, so don't open up that wallet!" he insisted.

After the waiter brought his card back, he paid the tip also, then we both stood up.

"Sorry, didn't realize I'm now late," he said, hugging me quickly. "Talk to ya soon, Cilla, this was a lot of fun!"

"I agree, bye Dan!" I waved as he rushed away from the table.

After Dan and I parted from our impromptu cafe lunch, I wandered around the scenic downtown for a little while, just thinking. Was Dan interested in me? Why did I tell him about Todd? It was good to hear Dan's perspective; he had always been a good guy to talk to. However, I wondered whether his reaction would have been entirely different if I had told him about the age of my recent lover. Would Dan have judged me differently? Would he have had advice for me to forget him and stick to guys around my age?

I also ruminated on the idea of Dan, since he was clearly back on the dating market, or would be at his "welcome back to social life" party. Would I consider dating Dan, and forgetting about Todd? I pondered everything while I walked past the cute storefronts, until I circled back to find my car, barely warm in the bright sun of a lazy Sunday.

Of course I would tell Kim and Hillary that I had seen Dan, and all that we had chatted about. Would they think it was a good idea for me to throw Dan a hint that I was interested? Was I even interested?

That was the bigger question. When I had been with Todd, I felt the butterflies. My expression always seemed to border on lovestruck goofball when I was in his presence, so maybe that's why he hadn't texted me again? "Cilla's a weirdo," he had probably thought!

I had just spent two respectable hours in Dan's perfectly pleasant company, and . . . nothing. No spark of chemistry seemed to flare up between us. I didn't glance at Dan's lips during our lunch and consider kissing him once; when I had been with Todd, I couldn't get enough kisses because the passion seemed insatiable.

But, I had been focused on the conversations with Dan, so I hadn't been thinking whether I wanted him for more as a friend. I had only just found out that he was even available; he had been with his girlfriend for so long that I was actually surprised that he hadn't been engaged or married.

I worried that I had been sending him mixed messages by encouraging him to have that party. Oh well, maybe it was just all talk between former work acquaintances, and he'd end up forgetting about it.

At that point, I reached my car and concentrated on getting home without incident, shutting the uncertainty of his possible interest in me out of my head.

The next day, I got up, got ready for work. Another week on the hamster wheel.

On the way to work, found myself singing along to a Foo Fighters song, "Miracle." The sentimental ballad put Todd back into the forefront of my mind, just like flipping a switch. Definitely frustrating, when I had been working on forgetting him. It was 8 a.m. on Monday, and I was stuck in traffic. Picked up my cellphone from the beverage holder, and found his name in my contacts. My hand hovered over it, but then I dropped my phone back into the beverage holder as the traffic light turned green. Traffic started to move, and I was mercifully saved from my stupid insane impulse to text him.

What the hell was I thinking about texting him for? Especially on a Monday morning—that's never when you text a former hookup! Either I was sleep-deprived, therefore rendering rational thought insanely useless, or I was having a bit of trouble shaking this Todd thing. Maybe I did have a bit of a crush on him; who could blame me, since he was a great guy? Best to keep myself busy, I thought, then I pressed the satellite radio button for the 1980s alternative rock channel. At least then I wouldn't hear music that would remind me of Todd, since that genre of music was from when Todd was a child. Oh fuck, that was a sobering thought.

Made it to work a bit early, and then to my desk. Turned on my computer and started sorting through my emails, to get my day organized. Wow, there was an email from Dan. Holy shit, there were two emails from him, actually!

The first one was addressed to me, Kim, Hillary, and about ten other people, including a few other coworkers who were younger or partiers, part of our "cool people" former lunch clique.

We were invited to Dan's house in two weeks for a "Survive the Winter" party. Cute theme, I said to myself, in between sips of my morning coffee. The invite said we were welcome to bring our significant/insignificant others, of course.

I figured I'd have to explain to the work people, especially Hillary and Kim, how the party had come about, so I sent out a quick email:

> "Hey guys,
>
> Just FYI—I saw Dan when I was out yesterday. We ended up having lunch at Moonshine Café, and I suggested he have a party to catch up with everyone. So, guess he really loved that idea! You guys thinking of going?
>
> Cilla"

The second email from Dan was addressed to only me.

> "Cilla,
>
> I'm glad we ran into each other yesterday. Lunch was great, as was the conversation—catching up on our lives was interesting, as always. As you can tell, I took your advice and I'm having a party. You should feel flattered; usually when people give advice, the recipient doesn't take it, and keeps on being a miserable ass down their toxic path that's strewn with crap.

But not me! I'm taking your advice, and this could be a life-changing event! Right? At the very least, I get to show off the new décor in my home . . . and you're welcome to judge away at my 'bachelor' decorating style. This means that you really don't have any excuse for not showing up, unless you have prior plans.

Anyway, talk to ya soon, Cilla!

Dan"

Funny email, I mused, as I started getting some materials together for my slides on a big training I had on Wednesday and Thursday.

Just then, Kim emailed, "can I come by? have updates!"

"Sure, anytime is good," I replied. Waiting for a gossip session would only keep me from fully concentrating on work, so it was best to get that priority task taken care of first.

Three minutes later, Kim was there, knocking on my open door.

"Hey, good morning," I greeted her, my smile turning to interest as she came in and shut the door behind her.

"Morning, Cilla," she greeted me, with a huge grin on her face.

"So, spill, what's going on?" I asked, very curious.

"You won't believe who called me yesterday, around dinner time," she said, practically ready to explode, as she sat down on the extra chair in my office.

"Um, is it work-related?" I asked.

"Yes and no," she replied.

"Is it related to your life or mine?" my second question.

"Actually, more your life," she replied, clearly dying for me to guess.

"Oh, is it related to Dan?" I suddenly realized that she had probably read the emails.

"Yes, *finally* you guessed right!" Kim exclaimed! "He called me yesterday, talking about you and having a party. Oh, and did I hear correctly that you did *not* receive a text message on Saturday night? And you actually told Dan that? Oh my god, girlfriend, I want details on everything!"

"Um, wow, he called you and told you all that? So you're just here for my confirmations and denials."

"No, Cilla, I'm here for the details, so spill it all!" Kim pleaded.

"Ok, first of all, Todd never texted me. I guess it's over, though it seems so odd and unfinished," I started, realizing how sad it made me to just speak of him. Odd.

"That stinks, it sounded like he was really into you," she sympathized, getting up from the chair and coming over to give me a hug. "Are you upset about it? Do you think you should have texted him?"

"No, this was all on his terms, so I didn't feel that it was my place to contact him," I said. "It does feel really weird, though. I felt like he was really into me, but maybe that's just how he is. Like it was a micro-romance or something."

I paused, not sure what to say next. Then continued, "It just feels really strange, though, having someone just blow me off like that. He seemed really into me, and I was getting into him. He was just really nice, and I had a great time with him."

"He sucks, but maybe he was just more shallow than you realize. Or this romance had a shelf life, and you were dazzled by him and didn't notice?" Kim theorized.

"Maybe, or maybe he just couldn't deal with possibly falling for me, given the age difference?" I wondered aloud.

"I bet it wasn't the age difference. It's probably him, not you," she said, clearly dying to switch to a more positive topic. "So . . ."

"Ok, you tell me what Dan said to you, and I'll tell you about yesterday. Oh, I take it you got an email this morning, with your party invite? I also received a second email from Dan," I added casually.

Kim gasped, "What did he say? Tell me!"

I ignored her, and started telling her how he saw me at the café yesterday, and we started talking.

"Cilla, I know all of this already. What does the email say?" she pleaded.

"Can you believe he and Liza broke up? I was really surprised," I commented.

"Come on, now you're just toying with me," she begged. "Tell me about the email!"

"He invited all of us to a party—no, I can't torture you any more, you might implode," I finally gave in. I pulled up his email that he had sent only to me, on my computer and turned around my monitor so that Kim could read it. A few minutes passed while she read it, then she sat back in her chair and looked at me.

"So, explain it," she said, tapping her fingers on the arms of the chair.

"What? He's being casual and breezy. On purpose, I think," I replied, hoping I was correct.

"That's exactly it. I think he's into you. Especially since he's single and you're single. He took your advice about trying to be more social, and made a point of giving you credit for it— that's cute. And that you have to go to his party. He's being flirty, without being obvious. Classy and subtle of him," she concluded.

"Kim," I hesitated, "I'm just not sure I feel that way about him. I don't know if it's because of Todd, or because I've always seen Dan as someone who was off-limits because he wasn't single before. It just seems awkward to think of getting involved with Dan, even if he does ask me out or make a move."

"Nobody's suggesting you marry him, just see what happens," Kim said. "You've wanted to do different things to meet men, so maybe this is one of those things you should do. Just keep an open mind. Not everybody has that instant spark at the first meeting. Sometimes it's like a slow burn."

"Other times, it's a wildfire," I countered with a smirk.

"You're right," she laughed. "Who's that?"

"Who the hell knows?–"

We were interrupted by a knock on my office door, and Kevin, stuck his head in.

"–Team meeting in fifteen, kids," he said, acting businesslike even though we both knew he had probably stumbled out of some woman's bed this morning and barely made it to work on time.

"Guess our session's over," Kim sighed.

"Yeah, but at least you got the info you needed, correct?" I smiled at her. "Oh wait," I suddenly remembered, as Kim stood up and turned to leave.

"What is it? Hurry up," she nagged me.

"I'll walk with ya," I said, scooping up a notebook, my calendar, a pen, and my coffee. "One thing I just thought of. You said Dan told you about me not receiving a text?"

"Yes, he did tell me about it, and also asked me my take on the situation," she said.

"So, what did he say?" I asked-whispered, since we were hurrying through the hall to her office, two annoyingly long hallways over from my office.

"He said that the guy didn't text you, and he kind of figured it was over between you guys, since you said it was casual. He was really surprised that you would be in that type of situation, but asked if you did that often," she whispered back.

"What did you tell him?" I asked.

"First, I told him that it was a very rare situation for you to be in, so you're welcome for that. Next, I told him he shouldn't judge you, because women have a right to have a fling on our terms, too!" she said, retrieving a notebook, pen, and her bottled water from her desk.

"Oh, he also asked if you were into that guy or hung up on him, and if I knew what he was like," she suddenly remembered.

"For real?" I stopped walking. Damn, did he already have a bit of a crush on me?

"Come on, we have to get there, to get a seat in the back of the room," Kim reminded me. "Otherwise, we're right in front of Mr. Slut-Spitter."

"I'm going," I replied, and started walking again. We made it to the conference room, and grabbed the last two seats at the back of the room.

"Happy now?" I whispered, then waved to acknowledge a few others; they had been on Dan's invite list for the party.

"Yes, and eternally grateful," she replied. "Oh, to answer you, I told him that I honestly wasn't sure, but that I'd have to dig and find out. His reply was interesting, though. He said 'be subtle, don't let her know I'm asking, ok?' Pretty interesting, right?"

I didn't get a chance to answer Kim, because Kevin bounded into the conference room and we all fell silent.

"Ok people, let's discuss some new software trainings," he said, a little too enthusiastically for Monday morning . . .

After the extremely long snooze-meeting, I went back to my office and decided to reply to Dan's message.

First draft:

> "hey Dan, that's cool that you didn't waste any time being inspired on the party front! I'm honored you took my advice; nobody ever listens to me (which you should remember from all of our work lunches)! I checked my calendar and have no prior plans, so I can go that night. I even wrote it on my calendar in pen—that's quite a commitment, hahahaha!"

Second draft:

> "I checked my calendar and had to turn down 3 different invitations. People cried and mourned, but I'll be attending your party."

Neither draft seemed to work; I was either trying too hard to be breezy, or being a bit pretentious and egotistical. Why was I getting writer's block? What did I even want to say to him? Looked at the clock on the computer monitor and realized it was lunch, so I went off to the lunchroom to retrieve my lunch and clear my head.

After lunch, I walked quickly back to my office, then shut the door behind me and was alone with my thoughts. And my stack of notes to go through, but I ignored them. Instead, I slowly sat down in my office chair, and started spinning it around. Every time I slowed down, I put my foot down to push, to keep the chair spinning again.

Suddenly, there was a knock on my door. I stopped the spinning by grabbing my desk edge with my hands, called out, "Come in," and stood up unsteadily, banging my legs against my desk.

"Hey, how are you?" Hillary asked, walking in and shutting the door behind her.

I hissed in pain, in response, "Dizzy," I muttered.

She grinned, "What the hell were you doing?"

"Spinning around on the chair," I replied, smiling while I pictured myself as a cartoon character with squiggly lines above my head. Even my friends probably thought I was nuts.

We looked at each other and just cracked up. After about five minutes of laughing, we regained our composure.

"So, Dan?" she asked.

"Yup, Dan," I confirmed. Sometimes it was good that we didn't need to mince words—we didn't have as much time at work to catch up as we wished.

"I already caught up with Kim, but I had to find out from you. So, does it seem like he's into you?" she went right to the serious dirt.

"It seems possible, from what Kim was saying. I wondered, but wasn't really sure. Frankly, I'm very surprised that he and Liza aren't an item anymore. It seems odd to think of him without her, since they were a couple the entire time he worked here," I mentioned.

"It's true, we only know him from being part of a couple. That's not necessarily a bad thing. You know how he treats others. He's great to talk to, even as a friend. Not a cheater or a skanky creep, right? Kim said you're hesitant, in case Dan does make a move. Why?" she asked, mirroring Kim asking that question earlier that day.

"Hillary, I'm not sure. I'm still really surprised how quickly things change sometimes: I was involved in this fling with Todd, which seems to be over since he didn't text me. I still don't know if I have feelings for Todd or not, even though we had both decided not to fall for each other. He's a great guy, but the more I think of it, it really sucks that he didn't text me.

"And then Dan randomly appears, we have a long lunch and lots of great conversation catching up, and now it feels like you guys are pairing me up with him. It's like switching TV channels, and I no longer have access to the previous channel. Everything's moving too fast for me to process it, and I'm not sure what my emotions even are," I answered her thoughtfully, realizing that it was the truth.

"Ok, I get that. Maybe we do all need to chill and see how things go at his party, anyway. It is two weeks away; a lot can happen between now and then, I guess," she responded, shrugging her shoulders.

"That's true, some other guy could show up and demand my love. Or Dan goes insane and I suddenly need a restraining order from him," I laughed. "I do have to work on some notes for tomorrow's presentation, though. And I'll RSVP that I'm going to Dan's party. Will that make you ladies happy?" I grinned at Hillary.

"Yes, especially Kim. She couldn't believe Dan called her last night, asking her to be subtle about asking you if you'd be interested, or if you were still into Todd and the details of what Todd was like. I think she might have peed herself from excitement after hanging up the phone with him!" Hillary said, raising her eyebrows to tease.

"Just like a hyperactive puppy, right?" I sighed, rubbing the middle of my forehead slowly. "I get Dan asking about my possible interest in him, and asking whether I'm hung up on Todd even though that seems to be over. But, why would he ask what Todd was like?"

"Probably because he sees Todd as your competition. Todd was the object of your affections, and he wants to know what kind of guys you're interested in. It makes perfect sense to me, especially if he is considering asking you out. He wants to know how you'd perceive him, compared to your previous fling. You said he told you he hasn't been dating or anything since his relationship ended, so it's been quite a while since he's been on the market. Most likely, he wants to know all the info, in case he does go for you," Hillary said, looking at her cellphone for the time.

"Crap, I have to get back to my desk. We'll talk again very soon, I'm sorry about Todd flaking out, but not sorry you saw Dan. I have to check with Doug, but I'm sure we'll be there. Bye!" Hillary stood up, rushed over and hugged me, and then practically ran out of my office. I waved as she left, leaving the door to slowly close from her momentum.

I sighed. Had a lot to think about, with all of the developments just from having a long lunch with Dan yesterday. And because Todd did flake out, or ignore me, or abandon me. It was definitely lame, even though I knew that I had gone into it with him with fling-only intentions. Had he become a friend along the way? Or was I already missing the hot sex?

I glanced down at my desk and my stack of materials. Hadn't started anything for Wednesday and Thursday's training sessions, so I started to spread the stack of materials out on my desk, in a slightly logical order, to create my presentation slides. I stared at them, trying to force my brain to concentrate, but doing work felt so futile when my brain was already occupied with my personal life. This wasn't good; I needed to get some work done today.

I grabbed the small yellow pad from the edge of my desk, and searched for a pen. Couldn't find one, so I started patting the piles of materials. Finally felt my pen under a pile, so I retrieved it and wrote on the pad:

"To Do list:

RSVP to Dan's party invite

Reply to Dan's other email

Ignore Todd, since he hasn't texted me

Do work

Clean home (vacuum, laundry)

Figure out what to wear to Dan's party, and go shopping as necessary (note to self: I'd do this whether I was interested in him or not)"

I could focus on the list, since it simplified the stress hanging over me. Decided to see what I could cross off the list—I'd RSVP to Dan's party.

Dashed off the reply to that email,

"Hi Dan,

I checked my calendar, and since I know of nothing going on that evening, I'm RSVPing yes to your invite. I even wrote it on my calendar in blue gel pen, which is quite a commitment since it's not erasable! I'll bring a dessert, probably something from the grocery store that I'll transfer onto my serving plate, thereby passing it off as a homemade treat!

Talk to ya soon,

Cilla"

Crossed one thing off the list, and realized I'd take care of another item. Pulled up Dan's other email and hit Reply, to start my third draft of that reply.

"Hey Dan,

I agree, yesterday was a lot of fun—good conversations and good company! I'm definitely pleased you took my advice on re-entering the social scene with your party; nobody ever listens to me (which you should remember from all of our work lunches)!

At the very least, it gives you a chance to clean your house and get it ready for guests, especially the judge-y ones like me! I tease, I'm not going to be all snotty if you have leather furniture; I'll let you in on a little secret: I have 2 gray leather chairs in my living room. But, they are a unique style, kind of upscale hotel-ish. Not bachelor style. ☺

I'll talk to you soon—have to do some work today. I've spent most of today in meetings and discussions, and have to work on a presentation. You remember how much fun those were, right? Nothing changes, it's still crunch time when they completely change the objectives of a training a few days before it, and we have to completely revamp our presentation slides. At least I don't have the training until Wednesday.

Cilla"

Pressed Send, and crossed another item off my to-do list. At least I wouldn't obsess over what reply to send to Dan, and it was more "me" because I didn't overthink it.

A few days later, I arrived at work, exhausted, but relieved that it was finally Friday. Sat at my desk and sipped my large coffee, while my computer slowly came to life. Felt blah, because the weekend was almost here and I had zero plans for it. I wanted to do something . . . or maybe someone? Funny! Perhaps my sex drive was a bit more intense than usual, due to the past weekends with Todd. But, the chances of him contacting me were slim to none. And, I didn't see any other prospects pending at the moment.

Thinking that I might as well go on the dating website and look for another victim/guy to hook up with. After all, it seemed to have been successful so far; I had met one really decent guy that way, so maybe there were other great guys out there who were honest and interested in the same thing. Added it to my mental to-do list; maybe that would keep me busy at lunchtime.

I sipped my coffee, but still felt groggy from the past few days of intense trainings. At least I knew today would be a slow day, just evaluating what had and hadn't worked in the trainings. I alternated between eating my croissant and checking my work emails.

Cool, an email from Dan, buried in the lineup from yesterday, was in my inbox.

"Hey Cilla,

How's it going? Surviving your work week? I am, barely. Had a lot of computer issues to deal with at work, but thankfully no fires to put out. And, I even started on cleaning up my house for the party, imagine that! In fact, that's probably all I'm doing this weekend, unless someone has a better idea about what I should do this weekend! ;-)

Dan"

Interesting, that I received an email from him, while I was planning to go back onto the dating website to hunt down another hookup candidate. Was he subconsciously saving me from looking for someone else? Was he someone I should be pursuing? I wondered whether I was encouraging him, especially if Dan and Kim were conspiring to set him and me up.

Or was the universe conspiring to throw Dan and I towards each other? That was an interesting thought, if he and I were destined to be together. I was likely jumping the gun even thinking about that. But, wasn't I usually logical and over-thought everything anyway? I drove even myself crazy with my brain sometimes!

He was directly hinting that we should get together. I wondered if I should take the bait and suggest something. Dan was nice, a really great guy, and I would have more great conversation and laughs with him. Or did I want a weekend filled with carnal pleasure from a sexy hookup, possibly from another younger guy?

I grabbed my purse from my lower left desk drawer and fished around in it for my lavender leather wallet. I found it and fished around for a coin, producing a nickel.

The coin toss had me perplexed—Jefferson's head on the face, and some Lewis and Clark explorer shit on the back. Was that tails? What was I supposed to assign to heads—seeing Dan? And tails equaled hooking up with someone from the website?

I flipped the coin into the air, and it ricocheted on the edge of the desk, then ended up landing somewhere in the small air vent on the floor in front of my desk.

"Dumb fucking luck," I muttered aloud, then sighed. "If there ever was a sign . . ."

Someone knocked on my door, and I quickly tossed my wallet back into the desk drawer, and opened Word to cover up my emails, in case someone did peek at the screen. One of my best work skills was making myself look quite busy even if I hadn't actually done anything work-related in a while, often thinking of it as my "prolific illusion."

"Come in," I called, wincing because the coffee hadn't gone to my brain yet. It was too early for loud noises or even talking. Kevin came in and sat down.

"How's it going, Langford?" he asked, then sipped his coffee.

"It's persisting, Bauer," I replied, wondering if he was here to discuss work or if he was going to regale me with tales of his Penthouse-like exploits.

"How was your training yesterday? Any issues with training the latest version of the software?" Kevin asked next.

"Eh, it was a little tricky at first, but I think the day ended up well. I got a few good questions that I told them I'd research and email out the answers, so I'll add those to the database soon," I replied, glad that my coffee seemed to be kicking in.

"That sounds good. Hiccups will happen, but you always handle those fine, so I wasn't really worried," Kevin complimented me.

"Thanks, Kevin, I appreciate that!" I replied with a smile. "So, what else brings you to my neck of the woods? Anything exciting going on with you?"

I figured since he seemed to be in a really good mood, I could spend some time just chatting with him. Especially since I didn't want to do any work today.

"Nothing too much going on, probably hanging with Tara, my current ladyfriend, tonight," he replied, looking very happy.

"Sounds great," I commented. "Is she someone new?"

"No, I've seen her on and off over the past few months. Her new tattoo was healing, so she was out of commission for a little while. But, tonight I get to see it, when she comes over."

"Cool," I managed, hoping he would swing the conversation away from his amour d'jour to anything else. Although we were all friends at work and did sometimes discuss crazy topics, it was too early in the morning for me to hear tales from Kevin's bed. And, we usually discussed the crazier topics in groups, not one-on-one.

"So, she said she got some heart design tattoo, but didn't specifically tell me where it was. Just said that it was sore, so she couldn't have sex until it was healed. I'm trying to figure out where the tattoo is," he commented, clearly expecting my input.

"Um, I'm guessing it's probably in the area where a female would get a Brazilian wax?" I ventured. "And that's probably all I should know about that."

"You're probably right," he agreed, wisely switching topics. "So, what's on deck for you this weekend? You seeing that photographer that you skipped out on the end of the party for?"

"Maybe, but I think that might have run its course," I replied, keeping the sudden sadness out of my voice. "I'm not sure what I'm doing this weekend. Maybe a movie or something with a friend."

"That stinks about the guy. I'm sorry to hear that," Kevin replied, genuinely sympathetic. "You should see that new action comedy that's out. My friend said it's hysterical."

"Oh, yeah? That sounds like a good option," I mused, drinking more of my coffee.

Kevin asked, "So, which friend are you taking to the movies?"

"Wow, you're a nosy thing today," I stated, half-teasing him. "Actually, I was probably thinking of asking a friend who used to work here, named Dan. He left the company about four months before you started."

"That's cool," he replied. "Yeah, I'm being nosy, but I also heard Jonathan and Tyler chatting about Dan's party invite, and mentioning you. So, of course I was just interested whether you were doing ok, and if there was a possible newer guy involved."

"Ah, now we get down to the reason your ass is planted in my office," I laughed. "If you want to know something, or want an invite, you could have come out with it a bit earlier, you know."

"Oh, no, I'm not fishing for an invite, or planning to crash this guy's party. That's not it," he reassured me. "I was just curious whether you were ok, that's all."

"Oh," I said, taken aback. "That's nice of you to be concerned, Kevin. I'm fine, though. I figure there's seven billion people on this planet, so someone out there is a good match for me, right? I'm sure he and I will find each other soon."

"Statistically, yes," he said, "but will you really want to settle down with them? There's so much life and fun out there, do you really want to settle for one guy for the rest of your life?"

"I think so," I smiled at him. "I happen to like being in a relationship, and enjoying becoming emotionally closer to that one person I'd love. Sharing experiences together and all that good stuff."

Kevin just looked mock-horrified at my statements, and I laughed.

"You ok, Kevin?" I asked. "Did I scare you too much with meaningful comments on monogamy?"

"Yes, you did! I can't restrict myself to one woman for the rest of my life!" he said, still slightly horrified.

"Ok, now that I've scared you with my suburban ways, maybe we need to go do work and recover?" I suggested.

"You're right, Langford, I do need to recover from your statements!" he said, standing up.

In the doorway, he paused and turned, saying, "I'm sorry it didn't work out for you with the photographer. You did seem a bit different when I asked you about him. Definitely happy, but it was different than I've seen you. I do hope you're happy, because you are my friend and I want my friends to be happy."

"Kevin, thanks," I replied, genuinely surprised at his honesty. "That means a lot to me. And I hope you have fun this weekend with Tara. Just, you can skip telling us the tattoo details on Monday!"

We both laughed and he left my office. I decided to email Dan:

"Dan,

Let it never be said that I can't take a direct hint. I could pencil you in to go to the movies sometime this weekend, if you want a break from cleaning your home? Notice I'm not offering to help you clean your home. ;-) There's an action comedy out that's supposed to be pretty good.

Cilla"

I got some work done, and about two hours later, Dan replied:

"Cilla,

Hey, so sorry I didn't reply but I was on a conference call. A work crisis, of course, and it might actually take ALL F'IN weekend for me to help fix. I'm sorry, but chances are I won't be available to go to the movies this weekend. I really wish, though—it would be a lot of fun.

What's your phone number, in case I need to cry to someone this weekend because I'm overworked and cranky?

Sad Dan"

I replied:

"Dan,

Don't worry, I understand about work pain. Sure, you can call or text me, at 555-6771. What's your number, so I know to not screen out your calls? ;-)

Cilla"

For me, it ended up being a boring weekend. I was going to go to the movies by myself, but ended up just wandering around the local mall for an hour on Saturday afternoon. Didn't buy anything, but I saw a guy that looked suspiciously like Todd from the back. I would only admit to myself that I followed said guy around the mall, until he turned around and it was clearly a different, less handsome, man. I felt embarrassed and awkward for having done that, and left the mall.

Sunday was even more uneventful and boring. Dan didn't call or text, so I assumed that he had been swept up by his work crisis. He did email me briefly in the beginning of the week, just to say hi and make sure I was still coming to his party. I replied that I was, and bringing a homemade dessert.

I was busy with work during the week, but managed to drag Mel out with me on Wednesday night for a quick shopping trip, since I wanted to buy a new sweater for the party, and she needed a dress for a school banquet.

The entire time we shopped, I was about to tell her about the end of my fling, and the possibility that I might be starting something with Dan, but I bit my tongue on it all. Maybe because it felt too complicated for me to say out loud? Or maybe because part of me felt a bit rejected that Todd hadn't texted me for a fourth evening together, and I didn't want to face that rejection along with Mel's reaction and subsequent well-meaning lecture?

Friday afternoon, Dan sent me an email:

"Cilla,

Hey, sorry I've been MIA. Between work, cleaning my house and getting ready for the party, AND preparing for that blizzard we're supposed to get on Monday, I've been going nuts! Rather squirrelly, in fact.

How are you doing? Want to come over earlier tomorrow, to catch up in person, before the party's in full swing?

Dan"

7

Another Guy on the Horizon?

I looked at the sticky note that I had written Dan's address on, and programmed it into my car's GPS. It was Saturday afternoon, and I was going to Dan's house early. Twenty minutes later, I pulled up in front of his house and parallel-parked right in front of it, leaving room for another car behind me. I turned my car off and was reaching down to get my purse and its spilled contents off the floor, and spent a while just fishing everything off the floor and shoving it into my purse without rhyme or reason.

I glanced at the passenger seat, which held my carefully packed dessert of mini cheesecakes, then glanced at the driver's side window and screamed at the creepy face pressed against the glass!

"What the hell?!?!" I yelled, then realized the person was laughing. Dan had had his face pressed against the glass, but now he was doubled over, laughing at me.

"You are such an ass!" I yelled, as I opened the car door, which pushed against his hysterical form.

I stepped out of the car, then shut the door and walked around to the passenger side and opened that door. He started to calm down and stood up, looking at me. I glared back at him and reached down to retrieve the tray of cheesecakes from the seat.

"So, if you're done scaring and mocking me, you could hold the doors open," I told him.

"Sorry, I couldn't resist," he said, looking sheepish as he walked over to the open car door. "Did you get everything you need out of here?"

"Yes, I did, so you can close it, thanks," I replied, balancing the tray.

Dan walked ahead of me and opened the front door of his house, holding it for me to pass by him. I looked around at his living room in surprise.

"Wow, Dan, this is really nice," I said, forgetting my crankiness. "Where can I put this tray before you give me the tour?"

"Hmm, on the counter or in the fridge?" he asked. "Do you think it should go in the fridge for a while?"

"Do you even have room in there?" I asked, looking at his fridge and wondering if the oversize glass tray would even fit in there.

"I don't think I do," he mused. "Would it work if I put the tray on my back porch? It's cold and it'll be protected. We can put it on top of the cooler there, and it won't be forgotten."

"That sounds perfect," I replied. "Lead the way, and I can set the tray down."

"Ok," Dan said as he opened the back door, then motioned me through.

I walked onto the chilly porch and set the tray down, then turned and walked back into the kitchen.

"Give me your coat, and I'll hang it up," Dan said, from right behind me. I set my purse down on the kitchen counter, then took off my coat and handed it to him.

"Thanks," I said, "now I'm ready for the tour!"

"Do you want anything to drink, first?" he called from the living room.

"No thanks, I'm fine!" I smiled at him.

"Wait, let me put some music on," he called.

After a few minutes, the sound of U2 filled the downstairs.

"Wow, great stereo system," I said, as he came back into the kitchen.

"Thanks," he smiled at me. "So, this is the kitchen. I do actually use it, not just to store beer!"

"I figured you had a skill or two, since you always seemed to understand when we discussed recipes at work," I shot back at him. "So if I peek in your fridge, it's not just meat and mustard in there?"

"Go look," Dan challenged me.

"Ok," I replied, slowly opening it. "Although if I see anything like they saw in *Ghostbusters*, I'll be highly displeased!"

"*Ghostbusters*, huh?" he looked confused for a minute, then it registered and he laughed. "No, monsters aren't taking over my fridge!"

"Yeah, your fridge looks pretty normal," I confirmed. "Nothing to mock you over here, so let's move on to the next room."

I wandered through the rest of the downstairs, telling him, "I'm officially apologizing to you; this is nice!"

"Not bachelor décor, hmm?" he asked, standing right behind me.

"Definitely not," I replied, smiling at him over my shoulder. Dan smiled back.

I walked over to the staircase at the side of his living room and looked around.

"Spill," I said, "how did you figure out to decorate so well?"

I was honestly curious, since his house was already really nice, being a historic Colonial farmhouse style, that he had kept as close to original as possible. Things like not painting over the brick fireplace and the wood mantle, or messing with the brick wall or the ceiling beams in the kitchen.

"Because the house is historic, I can't change anything major without submitting plans to the town committee. All I can really do is basic cosmetic stuff, which I did. I had the plans and original house information when we bought it, so I went through it and figured out paint colors for each room based on the plans. Then I poured through some websites until I found looks that seemed to fit, and bought whatever I needed."

"So this is the original paint color, this blue color?" I asked, looking at it.

"Yes, though I didn't get the exact shade from the plans. I looked at it, but decided to get a very similar tone that looked more modern. Didn't want the house to look like a Colonial museum!"

I smiled, and started up the steps to the second floor.

"Creaky steps," I remarked, as Dan followed me upstairs.

"Yeah, haven't gotten around to fixing those yet. I figured my time lately has been better spent getting rid of some snake holes I found in the basement," he replied.

"Eww, snakes?" I shuddered. "I'd scream if I saw one of those slithering around here!"

"Old house, so it happens," he reminded me.

I walked down the hallway, asking him, "Mind if I peek into the rooms?"

"That's fine," he said, "but they're not all finished."

"That's how my condo is," I smiled back at him. "But it's easier to do one room at a time, than to decorate a bunch at once."

"True," he replied, as evidenced by three of the bedrooms I peeked into, that were unfinished.

"Ah, here's a room that's done, nice!" I exclaimed as I peeked into the fourth room, which was set up as a simple home office.

"Half of the time, I work from home, so this is my home office. Not too exciting, but that's actually the original yellow-gold paint color," he said.

"Nice paint color, and your office furniture looks good in the room. Not too out of place," I said, closing the door.

I opened the next door, and gasped, "Nice bathroom!"

"Thanks," he said, "I just finished it two weeks ago, and it was such a pain, with all the tile, and getting the tub in there."

I glanced around, taking in the white tile on the lower part of the walls, with a bit of a sheen to it, the clawfoot tub, the pedestal sink, and other details that made the bathroom seem like a destination, not an afterthought.

"Really nice! I was thinking of redoing my bathrooms, since they're 1970s decor, really awful," I lamented, "and maybe getting something like a clawfoot tub. Am I copying you, if I ask where you got it from?"

"Not at all," Dan said, lounging in the doorway with his arms crossed, "it's actually flattering. I got it from a supplier, and I can give you the info whenever you need it. It's no problem."

"Thanks," I replied, just looking around and feeling very relaxed.

Suddenly, we heard distant obnoxious knocking and simultaneous doorbell.

Dan wrinkled his face in annoyance as he said, "That's probably my two best friends, Yuri and Matt. Guess we'd better go downstairs and let them in, otherwise I'll never hear the end of it."

"You mean you can't ignore them because you're giving me the tour, and expect to live through their comments?" I asked him, smiling.

"Exactly," he confirmed. "My friends are brutal with picking on me. But, I suspect your friends would be, too. Am I right?"

"No, we're delicate ladies," I said, trying not to laugh at my own words. "We wouldn't say anything improper, of course! It would be just like our lunches with the gang!"

We turned and walked downstairs, both chuckling over my last comment, especially because Dan and I knew how crazy our lunches out had been, with gossip shared and lots of wacky conversations about our lives and life in general. Dan had been the only guy in our lunch group, and been subject to our girltalk more than once; there were times we had returned to work and he seemed scarred by all the girltalk! But I never had the guts to tell him that sometimes, Hillary, Kim, and I would girltalk at those lunches to excess, simply because we knew it tormented Dan!

I smiled, thinking of that, as he opened the door to his friends, who greeted me with raucous hellos, then bounded off to the kitchen to stash their beer and other beverages they were carrying. After that, others started to arrive, and I wandered around and talked to others, introducing myself to whoever I didn't know. Hillary and Kim finally arrived, and of course asked me as many questions as they could about me getting there early, without being overheard by anyone else.

It was definitely a good party—Dan had good food: a make-your-own-taco station, and other Mexican foods, and some desserts, including my mini-cheesecakes, which always disappeared quickly.

And, everyone was charged up about the possibility of an impending blizzard, so there was lots of talk about who was prepared, and whether it would be a bad storm. So, everyone seemed to be happy to be out and social, before being trapped inside by a bad storm.

"Having fun?" Kim asked, as she sat down next to me in a corner of the living room.

"Definitely," I replied, glancing across the room to where Dan stood, talking to a few of his coworkers from his current job; they had introduced themselves to me earlier.

"You cutting out soon, or staying till the fun end?" she asked, not trying to be nosy but it was obvious.

"Part of me is dead-tired, but I get the feeling that he really wants me to stay," I replied in a low voice, elbowing Kim for being nosy.

"And then what happens?" she smiled at me.

"I don't know, Ms. Set Up!" I replied. "I don't have everything all figured out."

"Well, if you stay," Hillary said to us, leaning down, "you are sending him a message that you're interested. Cilla, are you?"

I looked from Hillary to Kim and shrugged my shoulders, then sighed. "I don't know if I am or not. Dan's great, but I just don't know, and I just don't know why, either."

Kim spoke up, "You kind of made the decision when you arrived early, though. Random people don't do that, unless they're weirdos, but girlfriends do."

"Um, great," I managed, feeling like something was closing in on me, and I was helpless to stop it. "Everything's figured out for me. I don't need to think at all. We'll live happily ever after."

Both of them looked at me oddly, and Hillary spoke up.

"Girl, get a grip here. Just hang out with him after everyone's left, because he's going to want you to stay and chat about the party and whatnot. Anything else is on you. Maybe you don't sleep with him tonight, though, since you're being all neurotic, ok?"

I took a deep breath, and replied in a calmer voice, "Ok, that makes sense. Not sure where that mini-freakout came from, but I can be normal and just relax. It's just Dan, right? He's cool."

"Of course he is," Kim chipped in. "He wouldn't do anything weird to you, unless you asked him!"

The three of us laughed at that, and changed topics to work gossip. A few hours later, most of the partygoers had left, and those of us who were left lounged on the sofas in Dan's living room. I think I dozed off around the point where Dan got up to start a fire in the fireplace, but I woke up when his friends Matt and Yuri were leaving, because Matt yelled, "Bye Cilla!" and then slammed the front door.

I yawned and sat forward.

"Did everyone else leave?" I asked Dan. "How long did I sleep?"

"Yes, they've all left," he replied, with a bemused look on his face. "You've only been out cold about twenty minutes, since 1:30 a.m. So I've decided to not take your actions as a reflection on the status of my shindig!"

"Oh come on, tonight was fun!" I confirmed as I threw a small pillow at him.

"Careful," he said, catching the pillow in mid-air. "Not near the fireplace."

"Oops, sorry!" I blushed. "Wasn't trying to mess up the fire."

"That's ok," he said, walking over to sit down next to me on the sofa.

"So, do you want to watch something?" Dan asked, picking up the TV remote and turning towards me.

"Sure, that sounds good?" I replied, waking up from my mini-nap, "Unless you'd rather kick me out so you can get your beauty sleep?"

"Nah, we can hang out, then I can make you help me clean up!" he grinned at me, then turned on the TV and settled on some random sitcom. "This party was your idea, remember? So, clearly you owe me!"

"Oh, that's not cool. I did you a service by suggesting you socialize again. It doesn't mean I'm your party cleaning bitch!" I protested, laughing.

"Yes, it does!"

"No, it doesn't!"

"Yes!"

"No!"

"Yeah!"

"No," I kept laughing at this point, "I'm too tired to clean, anyway!"

"Aww, poor thing," Dan said, picking up my hand and holding it.

I smiled at him and stopped laughing.

"See?" I acknowledged him holding my hand. "My hands are too delicate to do cleaning."

"No, they're all calloused and bumpy, good for cleaning up my kitchen," Dan teased me, holding my hand tighter.

"You're an ass," I told him. "I'm not cleaning! Not tonight, anyway. I'm too tired."

"Ok, well we can go to sleep and clean in the morning," he said, smiling.

"Honestly, that sounds good, because I'm too tired to drive." I said, surprising myself. "Is that ok? I'll sleep on your sofa."

"No, you can have my bed and I'll sleep here," he said, before I could react. "Don't argue, ok?"

He pulled my arm gently, so I stood up.

"I definitely am tired, so this is good, thanks for letting me crash here," I yawned.

"No problem," he said as I went up the stairs in front of him. "I'll accommodate a sleepy woman if it means I still get my party cleaner to help in the morning!"

"You do have nice dreams," I teased him. "And, yes, I'll help some in the morning. Only after coffee, though!"

"Good deal," he said. "I remember what you were like at work before you'd drink coffee. It was like working with a zombie."

"Yeah, you can't forget that. Everyone at work knows I'm not a morning person, except for my nice, yet slutty boss," I said, smiling, as we reached the doorway of Dan's bedroom.

"Slutty boss?" Dan asked, raising an eyebrow at me.

"He knows he is, and Kim refers to him as that," I explained as I leaned against the wall. "He's with different women all the time, and comes in and sometimes tells Kim and me about it. We're a bit horrified for our sisters in this state, for being duped by him!"

"He didn't dupe you, did he?" he asked, slowly.

"Oh god, no!" I exclaimed. "I'd never even date a boss, let alone sleep with one. Kevin's nice, but thankfully not my type even if he was single and someone I saw as available. Besides, I value my source of income too much to ever mess up my job."

"Yeah, I don't blame you for seeing him as off-limits." Dan said, leaning against his bedroom doorframe. "Speaking of work people, there's someone at my job that a few of my coworkers had wanted to set me up with, but I kind of refused."

"Really?" I asked in surprise. "Was she here tonight?"

"No, she wasn't, because she was out of town," he said. "I'm kind of glad about that, because I didn't want to encourage her."

"Or did you not want her to meet me?" I inquired, teasing him.

"Uh," Dan stammered, "something like that."

"Ah," I replied, then decided to be blunt. "So, what do you think your coworkers and friends will tell you on Monday about me, when you ask them what they thought about me?"

"I . . ." he started, then paused in surprise. "I guess they'll say that you're really nice and they see what I like about you."

"I have no idea what my coworkers will say about you," I murmured as he reached out and pulled me close to him. "Probably that they know you're nice but as much of a pain in the ass as you always have been."

"Cilla, they used to be my coworkers, so I hardly think you need to weigh in with them on the subject of me! Anyway, do you know that you talk too much sometimes?" he smiled down at me.

"Not true, but I'll quiet down, temporarily," I smiled at him, as he leaned down and kissed me.

We kissed for a while, nice, soft, sweet kisses. Until I gently pulled back.

"I'm getting a bit sleepy," I said, smiling some goofy cute smile at him.

"That's fine," Dan smiled back, patting my hair back. "I can leave a t-shirt on the bed for you to change into, if you want."

"Thanks, that sounds perfect," I replied. "I'll just duck into the bathroom for a minute."

After using the bathroom, I took out my contacts and put them into two small bathroom cups that I left on the back ledge, since I hadn't thought to bring my contact lens case. I went into the bedroom and closed the door, then found the t-shirt Dan had left for me, and changed into it. Left my clothes in a folded pile on the other side of his bed.

A minute later, there was a knock at the door.

"Tuck-in service?" Dan called.

"I guess so, come in," I called back, pulling the covers up as he came in.

Dan sat down on the bed next to me.

"You ok? Need more pillows or another blanket?" he asked.

"I'm good, thanks so much," I replied. "So, what does this tuck-in service involve?"

"Pillow-fluffing and kissing?" he suggested.

"Well, skip the fluffing, because I don't have time for that," I said as I reached out to grip his shoulder.

Dan leaned down and kissed me, and put his arms around me as I wound my arms around his neck. We kissed for a little while, and as the kisses became more deep and passionate, I broke it off.

"Dan, is it ok if we take things slow?" I asked, leaning back in his arms.

"Of course, that's totally fine," he said, pulling back and standing up. "Good night, Cilla. See you in the morning."

"Night, Dan," I replied, laying back down as he closed the door.

My brain started going into overdrive immediately, analyzing what had happened. Yes, I had enjoyed Dan's kisses, and yes, I wanted more. But did I really want Dan? That was the big question I felt too unsure about, as I dozed off to sleep.

Woke up to the sound of a very loud bird squawking outside of Dan's bedroom window.

"Shut up," I muttered to the bird more than once, in between flipping over and even trying to cover my head with a pillow, to make his noisy morning call go away. "If that's a mating call, I bet you're celibate."

I finally got up, put my clothes on, and shuffled into the empty bathroom to wake up and put my contacts in. Suddenly realized that the little bathroom cups I had put my contacts into were gone!

Looked around the bathroom, then went into the bedroom. No sign of the small plastic cups anywhere.

I squinted as I walked down the hall and went downstairs. Dan wasn't asleep on his sofa, but I heard signs of life in the kitchen, so I dropped my purse and shoes in the living room before going into the kitchen.

"Good morning," he greeted me as I sat at the table. I squinted and saw that he was getting coffee and bagels ready.

"Morning," I replied, because I didn't want to be all mean first thing. "I have a question: in the upstairs bathroom, what happened to those two little cups I had my contacts in?"

"Oh, shit, I'm sorry!" Dan said as he looked at me, guilt on his face. "I thought they were just filled with water, so I threw one down the drain. And, um, I used one before I even looked at it."

"You used one? So, you drank one of my contacts?" I asked him, then burst out laughing.

"Guess I did," he grinned. "I'm not going to die, am I? Can I just fart it out intact?"

I couldn't even speak, because I was laughing too hard!

"Need . . . coffee . . ." I finally sputtered out.

Dan was hysterical too, as he filled a coffee cup with coffee for me, and set it in front of me.

"Milk, please?" I was finally able to speak.

"Not saline?" he asked, sending us both back into laughter.

Dan brought over bagels, cream cheese, and two plates, then sat down.

"Thanks for breakfast," I smiled at him, as we both dug in. "If only it wasn't so blurry!"

"Shouldn't you learn to rely on your other senses right now?" he shot right back at me. "You can smell the coffee before it burns you, for example!"

I chewed some of my bagel and looked at him.

"Didn't you realize the water wasn't normal water when it tasted a bit salty?" I asked him. "And had my contact lens in it."

"Like you, I was sleepy last night. It just didn't register in my brain. I thought you were annoying to be wasting cups, and I didn't think when I drank the first one, because I had added a bit of tap water to it. I am sorry," Dan explained. "You're not going to let this go, are you?"

"Not by a long shot!" I confirmed.

"You're going to tell everyone, aren't you?"

"The only reason people don't know is because I haven't gone on Facebook yet," I told him, smiling behind my raised coffee mug.

Dan sighed.

"I'll release you from any cleaning duties, you know. Since you can't see."

"I don't mind helping you," I smiled, taking pity on his sad face. "You do have to drive me home, so I can get new contacts in, then you can drive us right back here."

"You sure? I don't want to be on your bad side any more than I already am," he said, looking doubtful.

"Honestly, you're not on my bad side at all. I was due for new contacts in a week, so it's not a big deal," I clued him in on the truth, as the coffee worked its magic to wake me up. "I'll just tell everyone to be very careful to not leave little cups of liquids unattended around you."

"Great," he managed, eating his bagel and shaking his head at me. "This really isn't my day."

I felt bad for Dan. He seemed like he really regretted drinking my contact lens, even though I knew it was an honest, yet totally funny, mistake. I wanted to cheer him up, or at least make him feel a little better, because things between us seemed weird at the moment.

"Dan," I started, standing up and walking around the table to him, "Don't feel bad. I know it was an honest mistake, ok?"

"Ok, thanks, Cilla," he nodded his head.

I stood behind him, then hugged him from behind. Dan leaned into me and turned his head to look at me, and I smiled back at him.

"We should get going, if we're going to get your vision back, so we can clean," Dan said, sighing.

"What is it?" I wrinkled my forehead as I asked him.

"I was thinking I'd probably have to feed you lunch, too," he said, as if I was suddenly a burden to him. "Since you've been blind because of me, and . . ."

"And?"

"And I want a few more excuses to keep spending today with you," he said, getting right to the point. "I like you, Cilla. Not just as a friend. I am fine with your request from last night about going slow, though."

"I appreciate that, Dan. I like you, too," I replied slowly, nervously. "But I never saw you as someone single and available before, so it's taking some getting used to, ok?"

"Ok, that's cool," he confirmed, squeezing my hands briefly, then letting go of them.

I let go from hugging Dan, so he was able to stand up. We cleaned the table up from our breakfast, and got ready to go out to my condo.

The rest of the day passed by in a blur. At my place, I put in fresh contacts and took a quick shower, then changed clothes. The cleaning that Dan had hyped up only took us about one hour, and was mostly washing dishes and tidying up his living room. Lunch was burrito bowls that Dan made from some party leftovers. After that, we hung out on his sofa and watched TV. I went home around dinnertime, because I didn't want to be out on the roads late due to the predicted snowstorm that night.

Back at home, I did a few chores, then started to get things ready for work in the morning, even though there was a chance I might be working at home. Being snowed in was a definite possibility, but I hoped it wasn't, because I needed to talk to Hillary and Kim about Dan. Kept wondering whether I was really interested in him, or if I was just trying to force myself to date him as an alternative to going back into the dating website.

Soon, I was in bed and completely unable to sleep. Tossed and turned for a few hours, I guessed. Suddenly, my cellphone, on my nightstand, pinged and lit up. I leaned over to see if it was Todd . . .

Instead, I felt completely disappointed when I looked at the display and realized it was Dan. I didn't touch my phone; I got out of bed and put the window shades up, then reached onto my dresser for my glasses.

Puffy snowflakes swirled around outside, while my thoughts swirled around in my head. Fuck, I had wanted that text to be from Todd, not from Dan! Thought I had moved on from Todd.

And, now that I was awake, all I could think about was Todd, and wonder how awesome it would be if he was here with me, snuggled in bed together, riding out the snowstorm. Proof that I had lost my mind.

I started to consider texting Todd, just a random "How are ya?" But, would that be a desperate move on my part? What if he wasn't in New Jersey right now, traveling for his job? What if he didn't even remember me?

How awful was I, thinking of Todd, when I had been starting something with Dan over the past day or two? I felt lower by the minute, and my eyes teared up. Dan was so nice, and I didn't want to lose his friendship. I felt awful for having encouraged him when I felt like I shouldn't have given him hope of dating me.

The snow outside was looking more blizzard-ish by the minute, matching the chaos of my thoughts. I walked back to my bed and laid down, hoping for sleep to claim me soon.

My alarm woke me up at 6:30 a.m. the next morning, and I slowly got out of bed. Walked over to the window, and looked out at a few feet of snow that blanketed everything outside. Clearly, I wouldn't be going into the office today. I brought my laptop downstairs, and switched it on in the kitchen while I got coffee started. Also turned on the TV to see the weather forecast, and to watch people whine about the blizzard. As if they didn't have the same four days' notice of the storm as the rest of us had had.

I started reading work emails, and there were the usual Monday morning emails about pending work. One from the director, cancelling work for the day because of the storm and state of snow emergency. One from my boss, saying that if we were still unable to get into work tomorrow, he wanted to know who could work from home on Tuesday. A few from coworkers saying they could work on Tuesday from home. I decided to send a similar reply, too, since I didn't want to waste a vacation day because of the snow.

And because I wanted to keep busy. My brain still churned with my dilemma: Todd or Dan. Part of me realized the lunacy of this even being a dilemma, but I knew that my heart wasn't being rational.

After I had a cup of coffee, I realized that my cellphone was still upstairs on my bedroom nightstand, so I retrieved it and went back downstairs to the kitchen. I decided to heat up some waffles and bacon for breakfast, and started them while I tried to figure out what I was going to do today.

I was in the middle of eating my breakfast when my cellphone pinged, and it was a message from Dan.

"Morning Cilla, snowed in?" he texted.

Out of curiosity, I also ready his message from last night, the one that had triggered my insomnia, "You up? Yeah, me neither"

I replied, "hey, morning Dan. snowed in, eating b'fast"

he texted a few minutes later, "me too. anything good? I'm having toad and fruit"

I laughed, then replied, "toad sounds gross. waffles and bacon. then I'm probably just going to watch some TV and be lazy for a bit. u?"

About thirty minutes later, he replied, "oh shit, i meant to type TOAST, not toad! my breakfast was good, I swear!"

We texted on and off during the day, just light funny banter. But, it started to stress me out; I kept thinking that I was encouraging Dan with each text I sent to him. However, I figured that if I ignored his texts, he'd call me and see if I was ok, then keep me on the phone for a while.

I sat in the living room with the TV on, but I mostly watched the snow continue to fall outside all day. Felt conflicted while I sat on my sofa.

Later that night, Dan called me.

"Hey, it's Dan," he said after I clicked to answer on my cellphone.

"Hi, how's it going?" I asked.

"Good, though I'm tired of being snowed in already," he admitted. "It's your fault I got back into being social, so now it's bugging me to be home all alone."

I laughed, then said, "It's not my fault. That was all you. It's good that you recognize you needed to shake things up and be more social, though."

"I wish the roads were clear," he said in a wistful voice. "Then I could come over and hang out with you."

I teased him, "I don't know about that—I haven't invited you!"

"Oh, that's cold," he protested. "Even colder than outside! Why are you acting all cruel to me?"

"Sorry, Dan," I said, trying to think of something that wouldn't encourage him. "I'm probably more cranky than I realized, because I'll be working from home tomorrow. I don't want to, but I don't want to waste a vacation day because of the snow."

"Aww, poor thing," he sympathized. "I'm probably working at home tomorrow, too. We'll suffer together, right?"

"Yeah, I guess so. I think I'm going to go start dinner and do a few other things, so I'll talk to you later or tomorrow, ok?"

"Sounds good, bye Cilla," he replied.

"Bye, Dan," I said before hanging up.

That night, I went to bed early. Laid there, just listening to music, on a random shuffle. Twice, it played Foo Fighters songs, and twice, I seriously considered texting Todd, to say–

What would I even say to him, if I did text him? Just a breezy "hey"? Or "want to meet up when the snow's thawed"? The messages had all been from him, so I didn't know whether it was even a good idea for me to message him. Fell asleep while my brain was pondering the issue.

*　　*　　*

I worked the next day, and talked to Dan a little bit. When I wasn't working, I was shoveling out my front steps and my car in the driveway. By mid-Wednesday, I was able to make it into the office.

Dan texted me that afternoon, "You out? Want to get together for dinner?"

"Sure, 6 p.m. at the diner ok?" I texted back.

"Sounds good, see you then," he replied.

I was nervous the rest of the afternoon, but I knew I had to be honest with him.

When I got to the diner, after fighting through worse-than-usual rush-hour traffic, I saw his car in the parking lot. I went inside and saw him wave at me from a table along the side, so I went over to him. We hugged, and I sat down, then Dan handed me a menu. We ordered dinner, then I took a deep breath.

"Dan, I have to tell you something, and it might make me seem like an awful person, but I have to be honest with you," I started.

He looked at me. "Cilla, you can tell me anything. Even if it sucks, I'd prefer honesty, because lies would mean you don't respect me enough to tell me the truth. As long as I've known you, you always told me the truth, no matter how much we pissed each other off at work."

"I know," I replied, nodding. "Ok, I know I said I wanted to take things slow and see what happens between us. The thing is, I think I'm still hung up on the last guy I was with. Which isn't fair to you. I'm so sorry, Dan, because you're such an awesome guy and I don't want to lose you as a friend. But I don't think I should be with you as a girlfriend, because I don't think the chemistry is right between us."

He sat back, looking at me, absorbing what I said. Not making a move to say anything. Our burgers and fries were brought to our table then, and we started eating.

"You ok?" I asked.

"Guess so," he replied, looking down at his fries. Eating them one at a time. I just sat there, nibbling on a piece of my hamburger roll, waiting for him to say something.

Finally Dan spoke, "I get what you're saying, that there isn't enough of a spark between us. I do really like you, but I did think that there didn't seem to be enough feelings between us. Are you going to be happy, though? Didn't you just have a fling with this other guy?"

"Yeah, it was just a casual fling," I confirmed, knowing how much of an idiot I sounded like.

"Then how can you still be into this guy? It was a fling, so he's been flung, right? You don't just hook up with former flings. Even I know this. You fling them and move on," he said, looking right at me.

"You're right that he was a fling," I said, not fully understanding what I was saying, but the words 'felt' right. "But, I just don't think that he and I are done with each other. The chemistry with Todd was so intense, that I think we'll find our way back to each other.

"Look, I know it doesn't make sense, but this is how I feel. I don't want to lead you on. Or lose your friendship. But, I understand if the friendship is on your terms for a while, if I've messed you up or something, I'm so sorry."

"No, I want to stay friends," Dan said, looking into my eyes. "Losing you completely would suck."

I was actually surprised; I figured he would be annoyed that he was being rejected for my romantic pipe dream.

"Dan, are you sure? I don't want to give you false hope or anything," I replied in a shaky voice.

"Yes, Cilla, I'm really sure I still want to be friends with you. We've been friends for about seven years, and I don't want to throw that away. Besides . . ." his voice trailed off.

"What?" I demanded, sweetly.

"Hopefully I won't piss you off with my next comment," Dan said, then took a deep breath. "I think if things go south or you're still into this guy and nothing ever happens with him, you'll need the support of your friends, including me."

I sat there and looked at him, a bit stunned. Couldn't figure out whether to be pissed or realize that he might be the voice of reason. Unless Dan was saying that to put doubt in my mind, and steer me back into thinking of him as the romantic partner I should reconsider?

"Are you playing devil's advocate by saying that to me, or do you have motives?" I asked him plainly, in between sipping my soda.

"Only devil's advocate, I swear," he confirmed.

"In that case," I slowly replied, "guess I should thank you for giving me something to think about. I do admit that I'm not being even remotely rational. But, when we were together, it was just so different, in a good way. Not sure I even understand it."

"I'll be honest," Dan commented, leaning his head on his hands in front of me. "I don't get it, but I respect it. Is that ok?"

"Yeah, of course," I replied, glad he was being as honest as I was.

I was starting to feel better about telling Dan the truth, and it felt good. Like I had stood up for myself and done the right thing. Not being with a guy just because I was worried about being alone.

"So, we're still friends?" I ventured. "It won't be awkward between us now, will it? Because we can still hang out, unless you realize later on that you hate my guts and think I'm a teasing bitch or something like that?"

"I promise you, still friends," he replied, smiling at me, "Besides, I think you're more of a pain in the ass than anything else!"

"That's good, because if you ever came back to work at the company, now it won't be awkward," I teased him.

Dan winced. "I'm not sure they could afford me now. Unless they're hiring and I can negotiate to work at home some of the time?"

"Honestly, I don't know if they are or not," I mused. "Of course, if you came back, none of us would get anything done and my boss would probably be jealous of you. He thinks he's the best-looking single guy there, and you might steal his thunder!"

Dan choked on his soda.

"Ok, you're not allowed to say things like that to me at the moment, ok?" he said, turning red. "Otherwise this nice, respectable decision is getting thrown out the window, and we start an affair, because that comment could easily mess with my head."

"Oh crap, you're right, I'm sorry," I stammered out, feeling like a jerk for saying something inappropriate. "Should I go? I'm an idiot, I wasn't trying to mess you up or anything."

"Yeah, go," he said, smiling sadly at me, and I stood up. "Don't worry, we're still cool. I'll email you soon, I promise."

"Ok, bye," I waved at him as I walked out of the diner, strangely feeling a bit of confidence in myself that I hadn't felt in quite a while. It felt refreshing and odd; it wasn't that I was happy to let Dan go, but that I felt it was clearer that my heart was heading towards Todd.

*　　*　　*

A few days later, it was Valentine's Day. I was in Washington, D.C. to run a training, but ended up stuck in my hotel because the city was a sheet of ice. After a morning of panicked work calls and emails, I went downstairs to the hotel restaurant for lunch, and left my almost-depleted cellphone in my room to recharge.

When I was finished with my leisurely lunch, I ended up finding a quiet nook off the lobby, and alternated between reading the paper and staring outside at the snow/sleet mix, which was a hazardous mess. Got tired of that after an hour, and decided to go back up to my room. Heard my cellphone ringing as I opened the door.

I just missed the call, and checked my phone: I had three missed calls, two from Dan and one from Kim. Apparently Dan had wished me a happy holiday, but got worried when I hadn't returned his text or call. And, texts from my family, also wishing me Happy Valentine's Day.

I called Kim back, but only got her voicemail, so I explained, "So, I guess Dan called you about where I am. I just came back from lunch here in the hotel. I didn't have my phone with me, so that's why I didn't answer messages or calls. I'll call Dan now. Talk to you later, and happy heart day!"

Next, I called Dan.

"Hey it's me," I said as soon as he picked up.

"What happened? I couldn't reach you, and heard D.C. was hit with an ice storm. Are you ok?" he blurted out quickly.

"Yeah, I'm fine," I reassured him. "I'm at the hotel, and can't get out to do the training. I went downstairs for lunch, and didn't have my phone with me. It was in my room, charging."

"Oh, that makes sense," he said, sounding relieved. "I'm glad you're ok.'

"Yeah, except I'm cooped up in a hotel, on Valentine's Day. It's me, other business travelers, and some couples. A little awkward to be alone and out today."

"Yeah, I get that. Well, spend some time relaxing in your room. Do room service and movies," he suggested. "Or, talk to me."

"Yeah, I'm definitely doing room service later. And movies or something. It depends what I'm in the mood for later," I said in a slightly shaky voice.

"Makes sense. Listen, I'm going to go, since I have work to do. But, happy platonic valentine's day, ok? And, it's up to you if you want to call me later," he replied.

"Ok, Dan, happy heart day, bye!" I said.

"Bye, Cilla," he replied, then we hung up.

I felt weird about his phone calls. It was nice of him to check whether I was ok, but it seemed obvious that he still wanted me. I sighed and fell onto the very fluffy bed, then gasped out loud. Todd's bed had been just as fluffy. I started thinking about him, then drifted off to sleep.

My cellphone rang, and I sat up immediately, waking up. It was a phone call from today's client, returning my call about the training we would need to reschedule. I went over to the desk and quickly switched on my computer to access my calendar, and within a few minutes we had it figured out. I hung up the phone, then emailed my boss with an update on the rescheduled training, and that I hoped to be able to come back in a day or two. It depended on the trains, but I'd be working in the hotel room until I could go home.

After I sent the email, I decided to order room service. While I was figuring it out, I got a call on the hotel's phone, "Hello, Ms. Langford, I'm the hotel concierge. I'm calling to tell you that Kevin Bauer called me, and you should place your room service dinner order with me instead of calling the room service button."

"Why is that?" I asked, confused.

The concierge explained, "Kevin gave me his credit card information, so he will be paying for your dinner this evening. He wanted to do something nice for you, since you're snowed in on a work trip on a holiday!

"Oh, thanks for letting me know! Could you please call me back in two minutes, and I'll have my order ready?" I asked the concierge if he could.

"Sure, I'll call back in two minutes," he replied then we hung up.

I went through the menu, and figured it out. Two minutes later, he called back and I ordered a citrus starter salad, seared scallops with vanilla sauce, a glass of white wine for dinner, and a small bottle of champagne and a red velvet cupcake for dessert.

After my dinner was delivered, I took a photo of it with my cellphone and texted Kevin the picture, along with a "thanks Kevinboss!" message. I watched the news while I ate my salad and entrée, and put the champagne and the cupcake into the fridge for a little while.

My mind started to wander to thoughts of Todd again, and I tried to think rationally. I did think I needed to *not* romanticize my fling with Todd. He was 27, for christ's sake. We had decided against a relationship. He was great, honest and very nice. He had *cared* whether I enjoyed myself.

I missed Todd. That was the unexpected, and very surprising, truth. I still didn't understand how, or why, but I did. Maybe he became a habit, or we became too close too fast. I wondered if he missed me, too, and struggled with that.

Or whether he had figured "out of sight, out of mind," where I was concerned. He didn't miss me. Maybe he had found another woman to fill his calendar, and his really comfortable bed. Would that bother me? I didn't know; I wasn't able to stake any claim on him. Did I wish I had? I didn't know, maybe I wish I had known to say something.

I needed to stop thinking; occupy my brain with something, anything, to push Todd out of my brain, as he had pushed me out of his life. I decided to watch some movies, and have my dessert. I didn't want to call Dan; it would be leading him on, and feel like we were enacting some *When Harry Met Sally* scene or something. It was better to lose myself in a random movie, so I did.

As the evening dragged, my heart felt like a jumbled mess. Swirled around like the sleet still pounding outside, till I didn't know what was going on, but the result was only one thing: that I missed him.

Over the next month, those thoughts endured in my head as I went through my life. Every few days, I considered texting Todd, but I talked myself out of it, every time. Or, I distracted myself from the texting. I felt frozen; I had no idea what to type to him, anyway.

Absence was messing with my heart, because I did miss Todd. The distance showed me that I definitely cared about him, and it was increasingly tormenting to know that he was so close, at the other end of the town from me. Also thought about just showing up at his apartment, but if he was entertaining another woman, I knew I would be humiliated.

As the days passed, I started feeling lower and lower. March didn't arrive like a lion, but like the worst bout of PMS I had ever experienced. This month, my body hated me even more than usual. Sucked.

A few days before St. Patrick's Day, Kim and I went out for lunch at a local Irish pub, and she knew I was in a bit of a funk over Todd.

"What's the problem with Todd?" she started in.

"The problem is that I miss him," I sighed heavily. "I want to see him. Not just for sex. I want to date him, but he clearly isn't into me that way."

"Maybe the problem is that you sold yourself short by sleeping with him, and now he doesn't know how to transition to dating you?" she theorized.

"No, I think it's that he was more interested in my vagina than my brain," I replied, resting my chin on my hands, picking at my fish and chips.

"Yeah, wrong anatomy for him to focus on. That's a tough one," she said, in between drinking her green beer.

"I don't know what to do. I think about him constantly. I like him so much. I want to text him; every day I open up his texts and read them. Or stare at his pictures. It's crazy. But, I think I screwed up by falling for him; this wasn't supposed to happen. We agreed to keep it casual and not attempt a relationship, and he might even be mad that my feelings changed. Plus, we haven't even texted each other since the day after the holiday party. Clearly, it's over."

"Are you truly positive that he's *not* into you?" she asked, very seriously.

"No," I had to admit to Kim, feeling more lame by the minute. "The thing is, this wasn't like a regular fling at all. We talked; we connected. He wanted to know all about me, and I got to know him quite well, too. So if it *really* was just a fling, he was sending me mixed signals."

"Then how do you know? Or are you assuming it because you put out some magical 'come-hither' look that he didn't respond to?" Kim asked, challenging me, in a nice tone.

"Something like that," I mumbled.

"Cilla, this is a reality check for you: you're an adult," she chided. "If you like him, contact him and tell him. You have a fifty percent chance that he has the same feelings."

"And a fifty percent chance that he doesn't, and I'll look like a desperate 40-year-old," I sighed.

"No, you're not desperate at all, you just fell for him," she said gently. "That's ok, it happens. You said that you think he's a great guy, so maybe it was going to happen anyway. But, you are still selling yourself short. You're worthy of so much more than a simple hookup or booty call situation. You *deserve* to be happy, and if Todd might be the one to make you happy, you should tell him. Don't have regrets, Cilla. Regrets will eat away at you, especially if you are continuing to see Todd, and still not tell him how you feel about him."

To my surprise, I started crying a little, and Kim hugged me. After a few minutes, I took a deep breath and calmed down.

"I know you're right. I am worthy of more. So is Todd. I do see us being together as a real couple. It's still crazy, because of the age difference," I managed.

"So what?" she countered. "Guys marry younger women, and now it's more acceptable with older women and younger men. Forget about a number. Contact him! You have his phone number, call him and ask to see him. Then, in person, ask him if he's interested in *dating* you, and seeing what happens."

"What if we're in two different life spots, and want different things?" I asked.

"That might happen. Or it might not happen. Take a chance, and see if he's the one. If he isn't, you don't have to see him ever again, because then he's clearly not for you," she concluded.

8

Is Shopping Organic Really Worth It?

I was shopping at the local organic market, exhausted from a long morning of a web training, then a meeting with Kevin about a bad review from a client. One hour of defending myself had left me in a lousy mood. Between the morning and the prospect of a slow work week, my last-minute request to take off from work for a few days was thankfully approved. So, I had a few days available to work out my aggression on some condo projects, and recover from the morning.

My mind was barely on my shopping list, which I had forgotten back on my desk. Rather than go back to the scene of the morning's crime, I was trying to reconstruct it in my head and failing miserably as I carried a hand basket around the market. Wasn't even paying attention to where I was going, and banged the basket into someone's cart in organic veggies.

"Sorry," I said automatically, figuring it was easier than a car accident, given my lousy mood.

"It's ok, Cilla," someone said, and I looked up sharply. Todd! I bumped into Todd's cart!

"Ohmygod, hey!" I exclaimed, setting my small basket on the floor, and then he leaned forward to hug me.

Please, I thought, don't let the hug end. If he only knew that I had been thinking about him, and that last week Kim and I had discussed me contacting him.

He pulled back from the hug, and I let go of him. Silence hung between us, a bit awkwardly. I couldn't think of what to say, but smiled at him, some dopey cute smile.

"So, what brings you here today? Aren't you usually working on weekdays?" Todd asked me.

"Yes, I usually am," I explained. "I had such a shitty morning at work today, so I decided to take the next few days off to work on some projects around my condo, and get my aggression out. I have those two really ugly 1970s-style bathrooms that I want to finally start to redo."

"That stinks about your morning. And I'm impressed that you know how to do this renovation kind of stuff," he said, looking impressed.

"Well, I don't have thousands of dollars for a master plumber, and they're both really ugly, so I figured out how to do stuff myself, for much cheaper," I explained. "So, how are you doing? Keeping busy with work?"

"I'm doing fine," Todd replied, leaning against his cart in a casual pose, "business is good and I've been figuring out some more cool work trips—might do a photo shoot in Vancouver, and I have jobs lined up in Miami and Florence, Italy."

"Wow," I said, smiling at him, "that sounds awesome! As long as I haven't completely screwed up at work, I might get to go to Philly and Baltimore next week to do trainings. How jealous are you of my travel?"

We both laughed, then just looked at each other. Wanted each other; I could see it in his suddenly passionate expression, and I was sure he could read it in my expression, too. It was as if we had flipped a switch and brought the chemistry back, right in front of us.

"Excuse me, you guys are blocking the broccoli," a guy said to us, clearly annoyed.

Todd and I both muttered, "Sorry," and I moved my basket while Todd moved his cart out of the way. We started laughing again, because we both knew the moment was clearly broken.

I decided to take chance, and asked him, "Do you want to get together sometime?"

"Ah, so you miss my body," he grinned at me.

I felt stung, but continued, "Actually, I miss *you*. I was thinking more like a date, so we could catch up. We really hit it off with some great conversations, too. So, it might be nice to do dinner."

"Well, I'm not sure about my schedule this week," he started, "but I could text you and let you know. Besides, we're catching up right now."

"Yeah," I replied, "but it's not the same, in the middle of the market. Come on, how about it? You know it would be fun!"

"I don't know, I'm not usually one for doing dinner," he hedged, tilting his head and looking around. "Besides, I usually don't have much money left over lately, since I just had to pay health insurance, car insurance, and upgrade some of my computer programs."

"Well, we could always do dinner over my place or yours," I suggested helpfully, feeling unsure about his responses. Was he trying to get out of seeing me? Or was he involved with someone else and just didn't want to tell me?

"Are you involved with someone else?" I asked. "If you are, you can say so."

"No, I'm not," Todd replied, with an unsure tone. "I'm not sure about my schedule, though."

"Well, what are you doing now? We could always do a late lunch together and catch up, as soon as we're both done shopping," I suggested, hopeful that he'd be interested in it.

He looked at me, with a blank look, while I waited expectantly, tension building in my neck. Then, he ran his fingers through his hair and winced.

"Cilla, I'm sorry but I thought you were still on the same page as me that we weren't in this for a relationship. We were just going to have some fun, and I really enjoyed myself with you. Did something change for you? Because I'm still not sure a relationship is a good idea for us to pursue," he said.

It was my turn to give him a blank look, because I just felt stunned. Couldn't speak. He had verbally kicked me in the throat with his rejection. I wasn't sure how he could stand there and say that it meant nothing, when his actions the last night we were together were so contrary to casual. And after what he said to me that last night we were together, how could he reject me like this? In the middle of the organic market.

He stared at me sadly. My brain and self-respect returned, and I turned around and walked calmly towards the register, lugging the loaded basket of groceries.

"Cilla, wait," he called behind me. I was in line at the register, behind two other people. He stood next to me. I glared at him, but said nothing to him. Out of the corner of my eye, he kept staring at me.

After some very awkward moments, it was my turn to check out. Todd put his basket of groceries up on the counter with mine, and the clerk asked, "Are you together?"

I wanted to scream, but Todd interrupted, "Yes, we are."

I felt frozen again, and just stood there watching our groceries get bagged up together, and watching as Todd paid for everything, and watching as he put everything into his cart. I walked out of the grocery store slowly, not having a clue what Todd was pulling now. I was considering pelting him with my organic apples, right in the crotch. At least he paid for them, so I wouldn't feel bad about wrecking the apples.

"Cilla, can we go to your place and sort this out?" he asked, holding the bags of our groceries, combined because he had lied in the store about us being together.

I was still stunned—why did he pull that stunt in the store? Was he prolonging our goodbye so he could try to keep me on the back burner as a lover who could give him an ego boost? Or did he feel guilt or pity for me? I felt exhausted and sad. Had no idea how to wrap my brain around this when my heart was feeling shredded like the organic brisket in my groceries.

"Fine," I said, beaten down mentally. "Follow me."

He took the grocery bags and trotted to his car, then loaded the bas into it, and started the car. I pulled out of my spot and waited. His car soon pulled up behind mine, and we began the caravan to my condo, a few miles away.

I pulled into the driveway, and he pulled in behind me, blocking me in. I got out of my car and opened my front door, leaving Todd to deal with the groceries yet again. Especially since it was his genius idea to combine our purchases. I did hold the door open for him; I was nice that way.

"Wow, your condo is nice," he said, looking around as he set the grocery bags on the kitchen counter. I started rummaging through them, pulling out my groceries, then putting mine away.

"Thanks," I said quietly. "I love living here. It's a lot of space and very peaceful. I'm still working on fixing it up—I'm kind of into French country, with some bohemian/eclectic thrown in. I guess as long as the décor doesn't run to French whorehouse style, it's successful."

Todd chuckled as he watched me from the doorway between the kitchen and the living room. I kept busy with the groceries, to distract myself from the reality that he was actually, finally, here in my home. How many times had I imagined him here, in my kitchen, having dinner and fun conversation with me? On my sofa, cuddled up and sharing a movie? In my bed, holding each other and talking about random things from our day, or just talking about us? More times than I wanted to admit.

Now he was here, he'd wrecked my feelings, and part of me just wanted him to get the fuck out, so I could have my cry without witnesses.

I finished with my groceries, and Todd's eyes met mine. He asked, "Could you please stash my stuff in your fridge? Just until I leave? We do need to talk, and I'd like the tour of your home."

I put his bags into the fridge, then walked towards him. He smiled at me, but the smile slowly faded from his face as he really took in my stony expression. Todd backed into the living room so that I could enter the room.

"This is my living room. It's where the entertaining happens," I said, without emotions. "Dining room is back through the kitchen. Half bath is right over here—it works but it's scary 1970s ugly orange, so beware. Up ahead on the right is the laundry room, which is free but not open to the public."

"Nice," he approved.

"At the end here, on the left, is the grand staircase. We ascend it to reach the master bedroom, guest bedroom, office/salon, and master bath. FYI, the master bath is also scary 1970s, but pea soup green," I continued as I went upstairs, Todd right behind me.

I could feel him staring at me, checking me out. And wondering if I still wanted him as much as he wanted me. Deep down, I hoped he thought he was going to have sex with me today, so that I could turn him down, and then he'd miss me and fall for me. I had no idea what else to say or do at this point, to make him see *me*. Me the potential girlfriend, not me the hookup partner.

If he had an epiphany, maybe it would be worthwhile. I didn't like the idea of being manipulative, but I was still pissed over his blunt rejection and then the bagging stunt in the organic grocery store, which was definitely manipulative.

I was completely confused by his actions. Why would he want to talk to *me*, when he said he didn't want more than our casual situation? Did he remember what he said that night, over two months ago, about wanting "me, only me"? Or did he just want to apologize for it?

I still remembered his anger over my condom-counting. He had been enraged by the thought of me being with any other partners—was it jealousy? Or had he simply been territorial, and expected exclusivity even though it had *never* been agreed-upon? Was I supposed to have been faithful to just him, implicitly, and was that why he had stopped text-summoning me?

At the top of the steps, we turned left and entered the first door, to my bedroom.

"Here's the master bedroom" I said, gesturing around. "Note the custom curtains, acquired from the Marquis of Ikeadom, and the rare machine-carved wood bed frame, bought online."

"Very nice, this room is huge," he said, looking around and admiring my décor. I was glad that the room was neat and clean, no dirty laundry laying around.

"This is really nice—aqua and navy look good together. I never would have put those two colors together, but they look perfect in your room," he complimented me.

"Thanks, only an artist type would notice that. It was difficult trying to figure out how to make the colors work, since I didn't want any crappy lame flower or country-style patterns to take over," I replied, glad to have something impersonal to talk about, to keep the conversation from turning awkward.

He continued, wandering around the room, "Your bedroom really reflects you, and it's really nice. Maybe I need to shoot this room. Or at least spend more time in it."

"We'll see," I replied, my throat tightening up. I couldn't handle the idea of him working in my bedroom, if he wasn't mine. Especially with his last jerky comment about spending more time here. How dare he confuse me like this? It was cruel of him. Speaking of wanting to be in my bedroom, yet he rejected me and was still just stringing me along.

"Nice mattress," he said then, sitting on the bed near the footboard. "Come over here and enjoy your mattress, Cilla!"

I turned from looking at my perfume bottles on my dresser. He sat there, smile on his face, and patted the mattress next to him.

"I know what my mattress feels like, Todd. I sleep on it every night," I snapped, knowing that if I did as he asked, we wouldn't talk; we'd have sex instead. I felt a pull to him on the bed, and sat down on the floor in front of my dresser instead.

"Oh, so, I guess things are different now?" Todd asked, the smile now long gone.

"Todd, I guess so—I told you that I have feelings for you now, and you said that you don't. You rejected me in the middle of the store. I don't know what or even if we have anything to salvage, so I'm at a loss for what to do now. You wanted to come over so we could talk. So, what should we talk about?" I laid out the facts, feeling so much turmoil inside that I wanted to scream and cry. Somehow, I was still holding it together, but not for much longer, I feared.

"Cilla, I'm sorry I can't be who you want me to be," he finally managed, his voice sounding stiff, not like his own. "I wish I wanted the same things you did, or that you really were in the same place that I am. I do wish we could continue on as we have been. I'll miss you, I really will."

Tears slowly started escaping, and sliding down my face.

"How could you?" I asked softly. "How could you sit there and say you don't feel the same way, when you've acted like you wanted more from me? We had sex, but it was *never* like any hookup I've ever had. It was too personal, too intimate. It was emotional. You know that, you have to admit it—"

"—That's just my style," he interrupted. "I told you I was different."

"How about when you flipped out over my condom-counting joke? You were really angry, Todd, why?" I asked, then waited expectantly for his answer.

"You were nosy and you know it," he said, getting irritated and defensive. "What gave you the right to question me?"

"I call bullshit. You were jealous and possessive over the idea of me being with other men," I replied, looking into his eyes, directly confronting him because I knew I had to be honest, even if saying the truth meant I'd lose him. My hands started to shake a little, because I was very afraid that I was going to lose him, today.

He stood up then, stretched, and I watched his movements. I figured he was ready to leave, but then he kicked off his sneakers and laid down on my bed, reclining on the pillows.

"Thought I was going to leave, did ya?" he asked with a sly smile. He seemed so sure of himself, that I guessed it was his only move to try to regain the upper hand. It was such an asshole move, though. Cruel of him, but I felt too mentally exhausted to call him out on that, when there were enough issues already in play to figure out. I could tell that he was definitely trying to regain control of what we had, or what was disappearing between us. Were we breaking up? How could we, when it had only been sex and a pseudo-friendship, and actions that had implied feelings and romance? And the chemistry between us that was so amazing, the chemistry that seemed to be the only tenuous element keeping us together and speaking.

I knew then that I had to ask him about his alcohol-infused confession to me. I took a deep breath.

"Todd, do you remember our last evening together?" I asked, looking at him through my occasional drippy tears.

"Yes, I think I remember it all, even though we both drank too much whiskey," he replied calmly.

"Very true," I agreed. "Do you remember what you said to me, after our last time together, before you fell asleep?"

I looked at him, but he was looking at a point on the wall above my position still on the floor. At that moment, I knew he *did* remember, but he wouldn't admit it out loud to me. Because that would be admitting his vulnerability, and that no matter what he might or might not feel for me, he had *no* intention of acting on it. And I knew, I knew that I had lost Todd. I wanted to launch myself up from the floor and slap him across the face, and scream at him for being a coward. I wanted to shake him by the shoulders and beg him to tell me the truth. But I couldn't, because I couldn't make him be something that he wasn't willing to be: a partner in a relationship with me.

He finally spoke. "Hmm, I'm not sure what you're talking about. Could you please refresh my memory?"

Damn, he was a cruel jackass, to manipulate me into saying what he knew he had said that night.

"You said that you wanted to have babies with me, and to be married to me, forever. Any of that ring a bell?" I asked him, standing up slowly, clutching the top edge of my dresser.

"Huh," he mused, still avoiding eye contact with me, "sorry, but I don't remember. Cilla, I'm so sorry I led you on . . ."

His voice faded out as he finally locked eyes with me. He looked sad, backed into a corner by my inquisition. And I felt despair. And so devastated.

I took a few steps forward, and walked past the bed. Couldn't look at Todd, still reclining on my bed, and I walked towards the stairs. Heard him mutter, "Damn, this sucks, really sucks."

I walked out of the room, and at the top of the stairs, I held the railing firmly to steady myself, and made it downstairs safely. Sat on the sofa, and leaned back. I felt numb, couldn't even tell if I was crying. Had no idea how long I sat there. Eventually, Todd came down the stairs and stood in the corner of the room, leaning against the doorjamb. He stared at me, and I stared back, feeling defiantly numb.

"Cilla, I wish . . . I'm sorry, so fucking sorry that this isn't working out," he managed, sounding agonized.

"Don't forget your groceries," I said, in an eerily calm voice that astonished even me. What the hell did I care if he took his groceries? His gaze changed, and he nodded. Walked across the living room to the kitchen, opened the fridge, and took out his bags. Then, he walked back into the living room and looked at me.

I took a final chance.

"I know you remember what you said that night. I wish you would be honest and admit it. Bye, Todd," I said, in a flat tone that was foreign to me.

"Bye, Cilla, I wish we were ok, but I'm sorry we want different things," he finished calmly, then left.

Heard his car start, and back down my driveway and out of my life. Let out a breath, then the tears started to flow, and didn't stop. Cried because he had blatantly lied to me. Cried because my heart was broken. Cried because I was pretty sure I'd never see him again. Cried because I thought we'd be so good as a couple. Cried because I couldn't believe he could reject me, when we both knew the attraction and chemistry were so intense. And, cried because I ended up losing a contact lens somewhere in my living room. Lost forever. Like Todd. Cried some more.

Fell asleep on my sofa that night. The next morning, my cellphone alarm woke me up. Went upstairs and looked in the mirror, and looked like sheer hell: one contact lens still in and stuck to my eye, puffy damp hair, and swollen face from so much crying.

Instead of working on my bathroom renovations, I moped around the house. Cried, ate too much ice cream, and watched a lot of shitty daytime TV, wearing the same clothes for a few days.

Thursday, I pulled myself together and went into work, but left there around lunchtime to go home sick. Told my boss that my allergies were making me miserable, even with medication, so he was cool about it and ordered me to go home and rest up.

I didn't even chat with my girlfriends that day; isolation was my mode of dealing with life at that moment, because I was constantly on the verge of crying. Instead of going home and climbing into bed, I drove over to the park and wandered around the muddy, early spring-thawed landscape. The woods were pretty, with a few trees budding up, and a few early spring wildflowers visible on the ground, that I was careful to walk around. The park was coming back to life from the bleakness of winter, slowly but surely.

Just thought about my situation—I admitted to myself, for the first time, that I was definitely in love with Todd, and it was not a beautiful fairy-tale love. It was passionate and all-consuming, bleak and vulnerable, and I knew deep down that I was scared by my feelings. It was so incredibly stupid—falling for him was never supposed to happen. Like Todd, I was supposed to be detached from my feelings and keep our meetings casual and fun, no strings attached. I had known that, and agreed to that. I had nobody to blame for my idiocy but myself.

Sat down on a bench near the shore of the lake, and just thought about what to do. If there was anything to do. Fall out of love with him? Or tell him how deep my feelings ran for him? Was very afraid of his reaction. Would that change anything? He had already cruelly rejected me for telling him I liked him, but if I threw love into the mix, I didn't know if he'd care. After wandering around and sitting at the park for the entire afternoon, felt too mentally drained to cry, even though my eyes felt as if they had been ready to spill threatening tears all day. The spring air felt too chilled, but I didn't care. I was still trying to figure out what had happened, and what to do.

Pondered my heartbreak, which felt surprisingly different than any other breakup in my life. Still felt raw and empty, and more alone than I had ever felt in my life. I was actually physically exhausted from all the crying; my head had been pounding from headaches and my sinuses were also swollen and raw. My very existence felt like an agony unlike anything I had ever experienced.

I was sure of one thing, though–I was glad I had called Todd out that day on whether he had remembered his comments. He had lied to me, for whatever reason. And, because he had lied about something so vital to our possible shared life goals, how could I trust him, or hope to build any relationship with him because of the lie? It scared me—did I fall for someone who just didn't want or know how to be in a relationship? Was he completely wrong for me? Was I wrong for him?

*   *   *

That day at the end of March, when Todd had seen Cilla again, he drove home from her condo with his groceries. Couldn't believe what had happened between them; he had honestly thought they could have renewed their casual, no-stress relationship. Had no clue that she was going to freak out and accuse him of misreading signals.

Well, yeah, he had said some stupid shit when he had been drunk that night, but who usually remembers the stupid things? The women you didn't want to, that's who. Of course. So, yeah, he was pissed and defensive when she accused him, and threw the stupid comments back at him. Especially pissed because she and he had had a great connection—he would have texted her for some more fun, if she had been cool with it.

Since Cilla, he hadn't sought out any other women; he hadn't been that interested in them. Women had pursued him, especially when he had been on that work and leisure trip to the Mexican resort. Random women would talk to him, and he was nice, but not as friendly as he might have been. Maybe he was even more choosy than he had been, but the strange part, even to him, was that he was fine with waiting.

Waiting? What was he waiting for? Even that thought had him stumped. Waiting for Cilla to come to her senses and apologize to him? Did he even want to see her again? Not sure, but he was very surprised to see her at the park later that week, just wandering around aimlessly.

It was a mild day, with temperatures in the 50s, and Todd saw her from his vantage point on a hill behind the rangers' office. He was there to take a few photos of the park for an art gallery show he might be entering later that spring. Hopefully she couldn't see him. He doubted she would recognize him, since his hair was covered by a black hat, and he had on a leather jacket that she had never seen before. He had his camera, and looked at Cilla through the lens.

Pressed the shutter to take a few pictures, then changed lenses, and started taking some more of her. Something in her expression made him feel sad, but he couldn't look away. Couldn't stop taking photos, and feeling guilty that he might be the reason her eyes looked so sad and bloodshot.

*   *   *

9

Pondering the Crime Scene (i.e., My Dating/Relationship Past)

After that day at the park, I knew I was feeling awful. I tried hard to hide it, but wasn't sure if my family and friends were really fooled. I seemed to be quite motivated at work, which I threw myself into as a distraction from my pain.

Didn't want to date at all, though. Didn't even visit the dating website. I had no desire to move on to someone else, when I was still carrying a torch for Todd, even if it was futile. Felt like I was slowly sinking into despair, though, no matter how hard I tried to keep my own demons away.

I sat down in front of the TV on a Saturday morning in mid-April, to watch a random movie. It was about two weeks after I had seen Todd and had my heart broken. I tried to watch the movie, but I just stared through the screen, not at all captivated by the movie. After ten minutes, I switched off the TV and tossed the remote onto the coffee table. It was 11 a.m. and I had no idea what to do. Felt restless and lost. Stood up and wandered through my home, going from room to room.

Paused in the doorway of my downstairs bathroom, and realized that maybe I should channel my frustration and heartbreak into the bathroom renovations I had planned to start two weeks ago.

Ten minutes later, I had music blasting, and I was chipping away at ugly burnt orange tiles, evicting the ugly tiles from my walls forever. My heart didn't feel any better, but I was relieved to be distracted with a purpose. And, I was using my rage and elbow grease for a good purpose, since it actually didn't seem to be too difficult to remove the tiles. While I removed tiles, I thought about my dating past . . .

Unfortunately, I had been rejected because of my reactions to some dates' strange behaviors. Rejected by one guy over my reaction to being licked as a "sexy" kissing move; the guy actually licked me with his tongue, from chin to nose (and yes, his tongue went inside my nostril as it went up my nose), and I could tell that he considered it a choice move in his seduction repertoire. No dog had ever licked me in this manner, so why was a human doing this? I kept wondering.

I didn't know how this guy came up with his move. When it had happened, I tried to play it off and be nonchalant, since I didn't know if he was going to turn into a creepy guy that I'd have to fight off. However, I must have had some subconscious facial expression or body language that he noticed, because he didn't text or contact me after that.

That was probably a blessing in disguise, because I didn't think I could handle the licking long-term. If that was a wedding kiss, my dress would have been slobbered on, and I didn't want to feel like I was in a Tom and Jerry cartoon while in a lacy dress.

Sucked. Another guy I had met on the dating website was an emotional con artist type. He flirted with me in messages, and seemed very interested in me and my life. Sounded great, right, as if it could go somewhere? We made plans to meet up, and the day of, suddenly something went wrong or there was a credible emergency. He said he would contact me as soon as he could, but never did. Coward.

A variation of the previous guy just messaged and messaged, until they were as intimate to my everyday life as my best friend was. It was a pseudo-relationship in the making, but the real problem was that they never made plans to meet me, and I couldn't push them because they were so busy at work and they were trying to pull away and couldn't wait to meet me. Virtual pals. Now, I knew to assume that they were just keeping me in rotation, and I wouldn't ever meet them, unless my number came up to win the "meet-an-unreliable-player" lottery.

There were other guys who I didn't really get off the ground with: one guy had dated me briefly, then invited me over his house so he could make me dinner, and he was proud that he was incorporating ingredients from his veggie garden into the dinner. That was definitely a cool thing, and he was a good cook. He made veggie kabobs and some barbeque ribs for dinner. After dinner, he took me out to his yard to show off his garden and his chickens.

I looked at the coop, swarming with about fifteen different chickens, and teased, "Wow, that's a lot of nuggets!"

He stopped and looked at me seriously, and said, "That's real nice. They're my pets."

And proceeded to tell me all their names. It was a very awkward moment, and I was speechless for a bit over my faux pas. The evening got better, but I still felt like a dope over my comment. We tried to get together after that, but schedules didn't really mesh. I wasn't too broken up about that, since I didn't feel that we were very compatible.

I stood up in the bathroom and looked around—there was no longer tile on the walls or on the ground. The bathroom was a mess.

"Do I continue with this room? Or should I go upstairs and remove that tile, now?" I asked myself, aloud. "I still have a lot of frustration I can take out on the tile. But, do I want two messy bathrooms at the same time?"

I decided to take a quick break for lunch, and checked my cellphone after putting some leftover pizza in the oven. A missed call and voicemail from Dan.

Hmm, he was my renovation expert. I checked his voicemail and it was a basic "Hi, just seeing what you're doing this weekend" message, so I pressed the redial button.

"Hello?" Dan answered.

"Hi, it's Cilla, returning your call," I replied. "Guess what I started?"

"Oh, the bathroom renovations? That's great, how's it going?" he asked, enthusiastic for me.

"It's going decently," I replied. "I got all of the tiles removed from the downstairs one. I'm debating whether I should remove them from the upstairs one today, too. What do you think?"

"Well," he hesitated, "you'll be living in a mess until it's all done. It'll be dusty and piss you off, especially since both bathrooms will be out of commission until they're finished. You understand that, right?"

"Yeah, that's why I'm conflicted," I told him. "On the other hand, I have a *lot* of energy to burn off, to keep going with removing the tile, while I'm motivated."

"Energy to burn off, huh?" Dan asked, sounding curious. "Where did you get excess energy from, too much caffeine and vitamins?"

I was conflicted. Should I tell Dan the truth or not? Would it hurt him, or would he be my friend and understand? Or would he go the "I told you so" route?

"You still there?" he asked.

"Yeah, sorry," I said, trying to find the words. "I have a lot of excess energy because I actually saw that guy and we had a dramatic run-in–"

"–No way!" Dan interrupted. "What happened?"

"We fought and he rejected me," I said in a shaky voice. "Hence, my energy spike, that I'm trying to use to advantage on the ugly bathrooms."

"Jesus, I'm so sorry. He's an ass to reject you," he said, sincerely. "Is there anything I can do? Do you want me to come over? I can help you with the renovations, you know."

"If you want to come over and help, that would be great, actually," I said gratefully. "It would definitely help if you helped to make all the bad tiles go away, because it looks like *The Money Pit* around here. I have tile piles and grout piles. And, I'm a bit unclear on the whole 'how do I know if my subfloor is level and ready for the new tiles, or if it needs fixing' issue."

"Ok, let me get a few things together, and I'll be over in one hour, if that's fine?" he checked with me.

"Dan, that's awesome of you," I replied. "I really appreciate this!"

"It's fine," he assured me, "I prefer this call to the 'oh shit, I messed up the floor and what do I do now' call!"

I started laughing, and he said, "See ya soon!" and hung up.

I got my pizza out of the oven, and started eating it at my kitchen table, while my thoughts strayed back to my past . . .

I thought about the relationship I had been in with Jeremy when I was younger. It had been love, but it had taken me so long to realize that he was emotionally controlling. I could see clearly that he wasn't the guy for me, especially when I had felt very "the world is my oyster" after I had ended things with him.

About two years ago, I had dated, or tried to date Dylan, but he was always too busy for me. That was definitely lame— what was the point of dating if he wasn't going to make a bit of time for us to actually get together? How can you really get to know someone, to enjoy being with him, when he doesn't make the effort to spend time with me? That felt like a rejection. It was lame, especially when I had always believed that people made time for what they wanted to in life.

Another guy I had dated for a while last year was nice, but also very busy, so I was often left buying our movie tickets or booking a hotel room for us. It translated into me spending too much of my own money. In general, I didn't mind paying my own way sometimes, since I wasn't out to use a guy for his money. Being equal would have been fine with me.

However, it would have been nicer if we had split costs, or alternated paying for stuff. I couldn't figure out if he was clueless or just cheap, but I was turned off when it became obvious that he expected me to keep paying for stuff. It wasn't as if I made more money than him—I knew what he made at his job, and he knew my salary too. Lame, when it felt like he was cheap and using me.

I cleaned up my lunch dishes while I remained lost in my thoughts. At one of my public trainings last year, I had met a very good-looking executive, Parker. He had come up to me near the end of the lunch break (I had gotten back from lunch early, and was perusing my notes for the afternoon part of my training), and asked me a question about the material. I answered it, and was impressed by him.

At the end of the training day, he came up to me and asked me another question, which led to us talking. Which led to him asking me out for a drink that evening. Which led to us dating for a few months, until he randomly started calling me and wanting me to dirty-talk to him. At times like an evening at home, that was fine. But during my morning break from a training, not so fine. He got pissy when I refused, and ended it with me. Clearly we weren't that compatible, either.

I heard a knock at the front door, and went to answer it.

"Hi," Dan said as I opened it, then leaned down to hug me. I hugged him back, then pulled back.

"Thanks for coming," I smiled wanly. "You're the best!"

He looked at me very seriously, and was about to say something, but I stepped back and waved him in instead.

"I don't want to go into details, ok? Just don't ask," I told him. "Otherwise I'm using that tile-chipping tool on you!"

"Ok, ok," he said, still giving me that serious look. "But if you do, I'm here for you."

I nodded.

"Oh, shifting gears—Matt and Yuri wanted to see me, but I told them I was coming over here. So, they might want to bring dinner over and hang later," he informed me.

"That's great, as long as nobody has to pee," I smiled at him in relief.

"Good point—maybe we'll have to go out to a pizza place instead?"

"That's fine," I replied. "I don't care what I look like this weekend. So, do you want to start in this bathroom, and I'll work on the tile upstairs?"

"Yeah, that sounds fine. You know, I should call the guys over earlier—I can rope them into helping, and we'll pay for dinner," Dan finished as he started walking towards the downstairs bathroom.

"Oh, that would be awesome, especially because of the upstairs bathroom!" I exclaimed as I started up the stairs, to wreak havoc on the puke-green tiles in the full bathroom. Went into the bathroom and started chipping away at a corner tile on the wall, and chipping away at my past yet again . . .

Maybe I was just a magnet for freaks and guys who didn't want to commit. Maybe I was a practice girlfriend, who guys dated, then ditched for the next woman, who they then committed to.

I started to wonder about my demon: being alone, no, that was wrong. I was afraid of being lonely. Was that my destiny in this convoluted life of mine? I hoped not; I never saw myself growing old alone. Always pictured some good-looking man growing grayer, sitting across from me at our dinner table, decades into the future. And kids, grown up, with kids of their own, causing lots of chaos at a family dinner together, maybe at the holidays.

If I wanted that scenario, I had to wonder, was I doing anything to sabotage it from every being a possible destiny? Part of me was terrified that I might be subconsciously doing something in present relationships/dates to mess up the possibility of being serious with any guy.

Maybe I wasn't always assertive because I didn't want to lose the guy. Didn't want to be alone. Compromised myself, so I wouldn't end up alone and lonely.

I heard the three guys chatting downstairs in low voices, though I wasn't sure what they were saying. Until I moved so I was mostly outside of the door, chipping away at some of the tiles in the doorway.

"So you're helping her, and not getting any? And we're helping, and that still won't get you any? Man, that's kinda fucked up," Matt said.

Dan hissed, "Shut up, what if she hears you?"

Yuri added, "My question is, are you over her and really ok with just being friends? Because stuff like this can just keep you thinking you still have a chance with Cilla, especially when she's made her feelings clear . . ."

That was all I heard, since their voices faded to a whisper after that. I knew I'd have to pretend that I didn't hear anything, and act like everything was just fine when I went back downstairs. I went back to my thoughts . . .

I did feel a bit proud of myself for asserting myself to Todd when he had denied remembering his comments. I had insisted that he speak up about what he had said. My own heart and needs had been at stake that day in March, as had been his. It was a huge step for me, a woman who was never good at rocking the boat or being dramatic. Even though it had gone to crap, I didn't have any regrets. I had taken a chance with my heart.

I was interrupted by Yuri, who poked his head into the bathroom and asked, "Want to go out for pizza now? We were thinking we'd come back tomorrow and finish getting rid of your tiles up here, and you could start tiling the downstairs bathroom tomorrow."

I smiled at him and replied, "Definitely, I'm starving! Give me a few minutes and I'll be ready to go, ok?"

We went out for pizza and had a lot of fun. I tried to pay, because I was very grateful to the three guys for their help. However, Dan was sneaky and insisted on paying.

After they dropped me back off at home, I decided to watch a bit of TV, but my mind wasn't on it . . .

I didn't want to feel any more pain; I wanted to feel happiness, and enjoy sharing something special with a significant man. Wanted the happily-ever-after as a realistic destiny. I hoped it was possible, because I didn't want to envision decades of being lonelier and slowly decaying like an abandoned house, until there was nobody left to give me the time of day.

Didn't sleep well—most nights I was still wide awake at 2 a.m., alone with my thoughts. It was the hour that I replayed every moment I had ever spent with Todd in my mind, and tortured myself with the memory of his rejection. Like replaying the same DVD every night to a toddler, for comfort.

In these moments, it actually felt familiar to me, the same emotion: heartbreak. Bizarre but comforting. As long as that DVD replayed in my mind, I would keep my heart and psyche stagnant, in perpetual pain.

After two-and-a-half weeks of this routine, I looked awful. Dark circles under my eyes remained, no matter how much concealer I spackled on them. And, I applied it as though I was Van Gogh, a few inches thick and swirled around my eyes. I was starting to get two tension lines or wrinkles on the center of my forehead. Was I actually starting to look like a 40-year-old? Damn, life was being extra-cruel to me, if that was the case.

*   *   *

I worked on finishing up the two bathrooms over the next few weekends, with a bit more help from Dan. By mid-May, I had a downstairs powder room that was pale green and very modern in design. And an upstairs full bath that was light blue, with a more antique French look to it, including an oversize clawfoot tub. My condo was definitely improved, and I spent a lot more time in it than usual.

I invited Mel over for coffee, to show off my renovated bathrooms, and we marveled over the major improvements together. We sat at the kitchen table, drinking our coffee, with some gourmet biscotti I had purchased on one of my training trips.

Mel went through my cellphone, which was sitting on the kitchen table. Hers was out of power, and she needed to call her oldest kid to find out what time to pick him up from music lessons. She casually scrolled through my contacts, and I thought nothing of it.

She came upon Dan's entry in the address book and had to ask, "So, what's the deal with him?"

"That's Dan, I've told you about him. We're just friends," I replied.

"Oh, yeah. You sure you just want to stay platonic with him? He's cute!" she persisted, while still going through my phone.

"I'm sure that we're just friends. I can't make myself be with someone I don't have chemistry with. It just wouldn't be fair to Dan. We do still hang out here and there, though," I finished on the subject of Dan.

Suddenly she gasped.

"Hey, I know him!" she exclaimed.

"Who?" I asked absentmindedly glancing over, then realizing she was looking at Todd's contact info.

"Todd Albrecht! He's the cute yearbook consultant I've mentioned to you before," Mel explained.

"Oh my god, he's mentioned doing the yearbook to me. I don't know why I never put it together with your description of him! I'm an idiot, because that's *the Todd*!" I started laughing in surprise.

"Yeah, you are," Mel laughed back. "I also don't know why you never showed me the picture of the guy who's made your heart so crazy this year."

"Me either," I replied, shrugging my shoulders. "I don't think you ever asked me, and I didn't think to show it to you when I first saw him."

"Ok," she confirmed, "we're both idiots! Well, now you know why I like yearbook so much! If I was single, I'd be all over him."

"Enough, please," I said, getting irritated. "No need to rub in that, no matter what, I don't have a chance with Todd."

"Cilla, it's not like that," Mel protested. "I'm not trying to hypothetically steal him away from you."

"I know that. I just realized that you get to see him. And I don't."

10

Going Out . . . and Getting Kicked in the Heart

Went to Mel's barbecue, on the Saturday of Memorial Day weekend. I hadn't been in the mood to go, but her kids missed me, so I had to cave in and see them. Hopefully, their kid-happiness would rub off onto me and make me feel a little bit better, or at least better than the anti-depressants my doctor was on the verge of prescribing to me.

I parked my car next to the driveway at Mel's house, got out, and gathered up the food items I had made: a huge bowl of pasta salad and two peanut butter icebox pies. Called out "knock, knock" through the screen door, since I didn't have hands available to knock or even open the door. One of Mel's teacher friends let me in, and Mel and I started chatting in the kitchen as I helped set out food.

"Cute dress," I complimented her on her diagonal-striped sundress.

"Ditto," she replied, eyeing up my polka-dot sundress. "We'll have to borrow each other's dresses sometime."

"So, everyone's outside?" I asked, not sure what to say.

"Well, you know who I invited, right?" Mel started right off the bat.

"No, who?" I blanked out. "Wait, oh shit, oops, Todd?"

"Yeah, and as far as I know, he's coming," she said.

"You kidding?" I gasped, having totally forgotten that Mel worked with him on her high school's yearbook. "I don't want to see him again. Ever. He's such a bastard."

I just looked at her, annoyed that she had invited him.

"I had to invite him—I always invite the entire yearbook staff, you know that," she reminded me.

"Then how come I never saw him here before? I would have remembered at least meeting him in previous years."

"Last year he couldn't make it because he was out on an assignment. The year before that, he came. You were away then, remember? At your college friend's wedding in Aruba, I think," she recalled.

"Oh, that's right, wedding and vacation trip," I said. Both of us got lost in our thoughts for a few minutes.

"Cilla, I can see you guys together. Todd's a decent guy. He doesn't know we're friends, does he?" she asked.

"I never told him. When we hung out, we were usually talking about other subjects, or not at all," I replied, annoyed I was thinking about him too much again.

"Ah, so is he good in bed?" she asked me, whispering so her kids didn't happen to overhear our conversation.

"Mel, come on. I don't want to think about that right now. He stomped on my heart, remember? He's the reason I'm miserable."

"Don't avoid the subject—you brought it up! Back to the sex, is he good?" she persisted.

"Yeah, very good size, fantastic skills, and I miss him and his skills. Happy?" I finally managed, to shut her up.

I stalked out of the kitchen towards her backyard, still angry with her, and got involved in hugging her kids. Then I started to chat with her husband, until their youngest child, the five-year-old girl, pulled me away. We sat at one of the picnic tables and drew pictures of birds and butterflies together, while I felt as though the butterflies were flying around inside me.

*   *   *

Todd pulled up in front of Mel's house. She was the coordinator of the high school yearbook that he consulted on. He worked with a great group of people, but he had no desire to go inside and party with them. He had attended Mel's parties in previous years, and enjoyed himself.

This time, he just wanted to go home and do his own thing. Mel had said that she'd invite a single friend or two for him, but even that didn't interest him. He tried to keep busy with work these days, especially with an upcoming gallery show that he would be participating in, and trying to forget her. Cilla. And failing, miserably.

Took a deep breath, and got out of the car. Then went into his backseat and brought out the two stacked trays of barbecued ribs. One of the other teachers let him in the front door, yelling, "Mel, guess who's here? Todd, with real food that smells amazing!"

"Thanks, Kay, let me get past you so I can put these in the kitchen," he smiled at her.

Got into the kitchen, and Mel quickly made space for the trays of ribs.

"Wow, these smell yummy," she said as she peeked under a corner of the foil.

"Thanks, it's one of the few things I can cook for more than one person," Todd grinned at her. She was always nice to him, and they hugged hello.

"Come on, I'll take you outside, where all the drinks and the other yearbook people are," she said, linking arms with him.

"Ok, sounds good. Where are your kids?" he asked her.

Before she could answer, her two boys, ages nine and eleven, came up to them, arguing fiercely. Mel took one look at them and barked, "In the house, now," then said to him, "Go have fun, I have to put these two into their cages, then I'll be back out. Go enjoy yourself, Todd!"

He walked over to her husband, who was manning the grill, and greeted him with, "Beer is in the tub there, drink now!"

He was nice, and they chatted about random subjects for a little bit. Then, their youngest child, a girl, came over, saying, "Daddy, look at my butterflies! Cilla helped, aren't they pretty? They're way better than Mommy's butterflies!"

Cilla? Todd felt instant shock at the sound of her name. It had to be a coincidence; this was a friend of the little girl's, not his Cilla. Turned towards the little girl and saw his Cilla, and choked on his beer in mid-gulp.

*   *   *

Saw him in person, standing by the grill, for the first time in two months, and I just wanted to cry. He looked so hot, in a plain black t-shirt and jeans, and once he stopped choking on his beer his expression turned to anger. We just looked at each other, saying nothing. Mel's husband paused from admiring his daughter's pictures to look at me curiously, but said nothing to either of us.

Finally, I decided to speak up.

"Sorry we're seeing each other here. I only found out today that you were invited and attending," I said, and stood up and walked over to him.

"How do you know Mel?" he asked in shock.

"We've been best friends since we were about ten years old," I answered.

"Oh, wish I'd known that," he said tightly. "Now this feels like I'm being manipulated, thanks."

"Hey," I said grabbing his arm and pulling him to the back of the yard for privacy, "don't get angry with me. Take it out on Mel, I know I plan to."

"Oh, I will," he said.

"Besides, if you must know, Mel didn't even know that she knew you until two weeks ago, when she was going through my phone and saw your picture in my contacts," I confessed.

"Oh, okay," he said, calming down a little. "How are you doing these days?"

"Miserable a lot of the time, though I do try to stay a bit positive. It's not easy, though," I said in a small voice. "How about you?"

"I'm doing alright. I've tried to keep busy with some assignments, but I'm in between some of them. So it's a bit frustrating to be planning, but not doing as much now as I want to. June should be a big month for me, though."

"That sounds good," I said, as casually as I could. Figured it was a little easier if I spoke to him as though he was some random acquaintance I saw on the street, promised to do coffee with soon, but that future get-together never materialized. Hopefully I was fooling myself into feeling more sane, at least.

After that, a friend of Mel's interrupted us to say hi to me, and as she and I got deeper in conversation, Todd drifted away to talk to some of the yearbook guys by the beer. We spent most of the rest of the barbecue avoiding each other, but were both aware of each other's location at any given second. I had no idea how many times we locked gazes, I just knew that seeing him was sheer torture.

I didn't care what we were eating, or what funny conversations I was part of. I couldn't wait for the day to be over, so I could stop feeling anguished by Todd's presence near me; it was so painful, even after two months without contact. Just agonizing.

I wasn't able to get Mel alone until the tail end of her cutting up cakes and desserts. It was clear that she was avoiding me and Todd, because she was never one to be far from the life of the party and all the action. I went into the kitchen and confronted her.

"Todd told me he didn't even know that we were friends, and he had no idea I would be here. I only found out when I showed up. What's the deal, Mel? You can't just do this to people, you can't just throw us together and expect us to end up together. This is my life—" I rambled, until she interrupted me.

"—Yeah, it's your life, and you've been miserable in your life because you want the one thing you were too afraid to go for. That's all I've heard for the past few months, Todd this and Todd that."

"That's not it at all! Haven't you listened to me? I *told* Todd how I felt, and he rejected me. There's nothing between us; he made sure of that. So there's nothing that can really be salvaged because you think throwing us both together today is a good idea," I told her, getting more frustrated.

"You don't see what I see—the way you both looked at each other today. It's love, and I don't know why you're fighting it. Just talk to each other, and work it out like adults," she said to me, and to Todd, who had walked into the kitchen while Mel was speaking. I glanced at him and could tell that he was as angry as I was, but if you didn't know him, he appeared calm and slightly serious. I turned back to Mel.

"What kind of a friend does this? You have *no* right to meddle in our lives like this! I'm too pissed off, can't think straight!" I yelled at her, my voice becoming more shrill with every word. I grabbed my purse from the counter next to me, and stomped off, determined to leave as soon as I could.

"Cilla, wait!" Mel called after me, but Todd said something to her in a low voice that I couldn't hear as I opened her front door, then slammed it behind me. Stomped down the driveway to my car, then got inside it and burst into tears. I couldn't even handle driving yet, between the tears and the trembling.

After a few minutes of crying, I heard tapping on my window. I rolled it down, and Todd was there.

"You ok?" he asked, looking seriously concerned.

I shook my head no, because my throat was still too tight to speak.

"Do you want to get the hell out of here?"

I shook my head yes.

"Will it bother you if we leave together, maybe we can go to my place?

I shook my head yes once, then no once. I was definitely undecided on whether his suggestion was wise.

"At least you're honest," he smiled slightly. "How about if you get into the passenger seat, and I'll drive your car?"

He opened my driver's side car door and I got out, still sniffling, and walked around my car to the passenger side. Got into the passenger seat while he got into the driver's seat. Heard him muttering obscenities while he adjusted the seat, which was set for my 5'4" height, so that he wouldn't be in pain, being 6'.

The drive from Mel's house to Todd's apartment was mostly quiet, punctuated by my dwindling sobs and sniffles. I looked out the window at the setting sun and the random Saturday evening traffic. At one point, he was driving and held my hand, and it felt so nice. I couldn't tell if he was doing it to be a friend or because he felt guilty he didn't want me, but I was too mentally exhausted to object to him comforting me.

We arrived at Todd's apartment complex, and got out of my car. He put his hand on my back and we walked slowly to his apartment. I was still sobbing a little bit, like an intermittently dripping faucet. Just enough that it was still embarrassing, of course.

Got inside his apartment, and kicked off my shoes, then sat on his sofa. Felt myself just sink into the cushions. Was drained, so damn drained.

He called from the kitchen, "You want a drink, Cilla?"

"Just water or soda, please," I replied.

"You sure? I'm not trying to drug you or anything, but the whiskey might calm you down a bit."

"Ok, sounds fine. Thanks," I replied.

He brought the drinks over and handed mine to me, then sat, sipping his.

"Do you want me to put on some music?" Todd asked.

"Sure, otherwise we could talk," I said quietly, not sure if I was being sarcastic or funny.

He grabbed his phone from the coffee table so quickly that I could tell the notion of talking was horrific to him, and put music on, an early Foo Fighters album.

"So . . ." he started.

"So, how are you?" I asked him, then sipped my drink.

"I've been ok," he replied. "Busy with some different photos."

"What type of photos? Can I see them?" I asked, trying to distract myself.

"Oh, it's all corporate stuff, nothing that you'd really like," he said very quickly, seeming a bit nervous.

It was really awkward. I sipped my whiskey, because I had no idea what to say.

"So–" we both said at the same time, then awkwardly laughed.

"You go–" I said, while Todd said, "After you–"

I started, "Sorry about wrecking the party for you. I almost didn't go. Maybe I shouldn't have. I swear that Mel only knew that you and I knew each other two weeks ago, when she was going through my phone for something."

"That explains it," he said, more to himself. "Mel acted really weird to me the week before the party, when we were chatting about it.

"So, how's work?" he asked then, turning to me and sipping his drink.

"Work is mediocre. I just phone it in these days," I said, honestly. I stood up and slowly wandered around his living room, looking at some of the photos on his wall. I felt his eyes on me, as I walked from photo to photo, just looking at them.

"What's on your mind?" Todd suddenly ventured.

I glanced over at him, and he was still lounging on the sofa, looking straight at me.

"On my mind?" my voice said, hollowly, as I set my drink down on the nightstand, then turned to face him.

"You, Todd. You're on my damned mind these days. I've missed you."

My words hung in the air, and I felt so vulnerable as I stared right into his eyes. He stared back at me from across the room, and I couldn't read his expression at all. Finally he spoke.

"I missed you, too."

Todd stood up, walked over slowly, and stood in front of me. His expression was turning passionate, but with something darker behind it.

Clearly, talking about us wasn't going to happen. Neither was an apology from him. I wasn't sure if I cared about an apology at that moment. And I started to feel a bit frightened, not of Todd, but of my own state of mind. Was I losing it? Was I depressed? Was I letting him use me? The questions swirled around in my head, and I knew I wouldn't have any answers for them tonight.

I wanted Todd, and was sure that desire was evident in my expression, too. I reached out and put my hands on his chest and grasped his t-shirt, pulling him closer to me.

His lips seemed to fall right on mine, and the first kiss was deep, like coming home. We hadn't kissed since mid-January, and it felt as if we had spent months trying to find each other since then, and the kiss was a perfect end to that search. The kissing quickly became deep and frenzied, and it felt like I couldn't kiss him enough.

After a while, he stopped kissing me, and whispered, "Turn around."

I did, and he started to lightly kiss my neck, while taking my dress and underwear off. He started to caress my body, then pulled me tight against him and caressed my breasts, a bit rougher than he had previously, but it still felt good. I moaned quietly at his passionate touch.

Todd walked us over to the bed, and lightly pushed on my shoulders, so I sat on the bed. I watched as he took his shirt off, and helped him with his jeans and underwear. I started to caress his body with my hands, and he started to do the same to me.

After a bit, he stopped my hands with his, and pushed me gently to lie down, then he put on a condom and we started to have sex. As the passion started to build, Todd stopped.

I looked at him in surprise, and he suggested, "New position?"

I nodded, and he requested, "Turn over, I promise you'll enjoy it."

He moved back, and I turned over, face-down on the bed, and he entered me again. Then he put an arm around my waist, pulling me back up so we were kneeling on the bed together. I turned my head back to look at Todd, and he looked back at me with a seductive expression that probably mirrored mine.

"Having fun?" he whispered.

"I think so," I smiled at him, as his hands moved up to knead my breasts. After that, I was lost in the pleasure, and my fingers reached behind me to grip his thighs and pull him ever closer, until we were both in a frenzy from our shared delight. Suddenly, we both pressed our bodies even closer, as I cried out and Todd's breath hissed through his clenched teeth.

Eventually, we let go of each other, and he gave me a quick hug, then went to get rid of the condom.

After a few minutes, I went into the bathroom, which Todd had just vacated, with my purse, got out my contact lens case, and took out each of my contacts, quickly putting them in the case. I closed it up, and went back to the bed, tossing my purse on the dining room table on the way.

I fell onto the bed, inching up until my head was on the pillow, turned towards "my" nightstand. I felt him get back into bed, and I glanced at him. Todd was wearing boxers with a pattern of guitars all over them.

"Cute boxers," I said, smiling at him tremulously.

"Thanks, pretty girl," he replied, turning off the light. "Night."

"Night," I whisper-parroted to Todd, as he snuggled up behind me. I was too drained to think, and sleep claimed us both, very swiftly.

Slowly, very slowly, I woke up. Felt slightly trapped, but then I opened my eyes and realized Todd lay against my back, holding me in his arms. I gently unclasped his arms from around my stomach, and slid out of the bed to stand on the cold wood floor. He didn't stir, and I tiptoed to his bathroom, to see if I looked as awful as I felt.

I looked in the mirror. The face that stared back at me was tired and sad, with pillow marks on my right cheek, bloodshot eyes, and eyeliner and mascara smudges around my eyes. Scary face was framed by wavy hair that looked pretty good—Cosmo could have done a photo shoot on this morning's hair. As I stood there, though, my eyes started to water, just thinking about how last evening had ended. The sex had felt so impersonal and lonely near the end. Even though I had enjoyed a great orgasm, emotionally I felt even less connected to Todd than I had before we had actually slept together last night.

I wasn't sure if he had even looked at my face when we went to sleep, and that bothered me. I remembered him going to the bathroom, and then coming back to bed, embracing me from behind, and saying good night. Not a kiss or anything personal or romantic that showed me he was happy to be with me. I could have just been a teddy bear he hugged during the night.

Clearly I was fooling myself, to think that I meant more to him than a random fling. Kept feeling lower and lower, the more I thought about it. A few tears escaped my eyes and started to slowly drip down my face. I reached for my contact lens case, and put the contacts in my eyes pretty easily, but of course my eyes started to burn from the tears after my contacts were in. I took a few deep breaths to attempt to calm down, since my eyes were stinging and tearing up. I was trying my hardest to hold it together emotionally.

I quietly crept out of the bathroom, wiping the tears away. Found my clothes and started putting them on as quietly as possible, because I didn't want to talk to him—I was close to sobbing out loud. Put my empty whiskey glass in his sink. Finally got my purse, shoes, and hoodie together.

While I slowly pulled my hoodie on, I chastised myself for thinking that Todd would be interested in me as a person, as a girlfriend. Unfortunately, he just didn't see me that way, and he probably never would. Realized that I was just holding onto my feelings for him, and it just kept getting me hurt, every time I saw him and expected more from him than he clearly wanted from me. It sucked, it really sucked to think about it.

I kept grasping for some reason. Maybe he just didn't want me, because he was holding out for someone younger and prettier. Was I just holding onto hope that he could be my happily-ever-after, just because he had wanted me, months ago? So he was just over me? Maybe. I didn't think that was it, though. He wouldn't have left the party with me last night, I was sure of it. Todd wouldn't have walked headfirst into our dramatic evening just for sex.

No. Maybe it was the major one staring me in the face: our age difference. Maybe if we were each five years in age closer to each other, he'd be more into me. Which meant that the reality was clearly futile, hopeless.

We hadn't ever discussed the future, other than Todd's drunk declarations to me, which he had later denied. We hadn't even discussed the possibility of being an exclusive, monogamous couple.

I didn't feel secure that Todd would ever be on the same timeline for settling down as I was. I wanted to settle down, get married, have a family. Todd seemed like he was fine with his slightly messy apartment and his slightly chaotic freelance work that took him away from New Brunswick at unpredictable moments. Maybe Todd was at a different point in his life than I was. I wasn't sure that he was thinking of reality beyond his photography assignments and making sure he paid his bills. And found a lady to keep him company when he felt like it. Maybe that was the reality that I was afraid to see, that I was his plat du jour, and I was replaceable.

As my thoughts kept building, I slowly looked around his apartment, at all the clutter that he knew he could clean up, but that he left out just to be a bit lazy, at his sleeping cats, barely visible under the sofa, and finally at him. Just at him.

The chemistry between us was so strong, I felt the pull to climb back into bed so much that it scared me. I touched the doorframe behind me with one hand, as if to anchor me so that I wouldn't move one step towards the bed. Promised myself that I wouldn't move unless there was some sign that he really wanted me the way I wanted him. I knew I wanted to date him, not just have a hookup/casual encounter with him anymore. I wanted to walk into a restaurant with him holding my hand. Wanted to snuggle with him in a darkened movie theater, and share a soda and popcorn. Wanted to do stupid ordinary things with him, such as laundry, which meant we were together in domestic bliss. I thought all these thoughts, and still no sign delayed me from exiting his apartment.

Carefully, I turned and unlocked his door. Opened it slowly, then looked back at Todd asleep on the bed. He hadn't moved since I left the bed. I re-locked the door and quietly pulled it shut behind me as I left. Put my shoes on in the hallway, then went outside the main door and down the steps. Walked down the path to the parking lot, and got into my car. Spent about ten minutes fixing the seat settings back from Todd's adjustments to the driver's seat last night. After starting the car, I started sobbing and sniffling, yet again. And that's how I spent the car ride back to my apartment.

*   *   *

Woke up and realized two things: he was never drinking that much whiskey again, and Cilla wasn't in the bed.

"Cilla? Where are ya?" Todd called, in case she was in the bathroom. No answer. He got up to check and the bathroom door was open, and her contact lens case was gone from the back ledge of the sink. Walked slowly back, and as he looked around he realized that there was no sign of her—no purse, clothes, or even the glass she had used last night.

He wandered into the kitchen for some water. No, wait, the glass she had used last night was in the sink. Wow, that was odd. If her glass was in the sink, Todd wondered, it meant she had left on purpose; wished he knew when she had left.

He walked around the bed and sat on the side Cilla had slept on, that he had started to think of as "her side." Wondered why she had left. He knew she didn't have any plans, because she had said to someone at the party that her Sunday was going to be "blissfully boring."

Todd realized that he would have to text Mel. His car was still over her house, so he'd need her to come get him.

He grabbed his phone from the nightstand and texted her, "Mel, can u pls come pick me up sometime today, so I can get my car?"

She texted back, "Sure, no problem—is it ok if i come get you in 2 hrs?"

"yes, thx so much," he replied.

Wasn't looking forward to her interrogation about him leaving the party with Cilla yesterday, but at least he could rip Mel a new one over her interference and deception.

Todd decided to ponder the issue of Cilla's sneaky exit later, since his pounding head clearly needed a bit more sleep. He set the alarm on his cellphone, then lowered his head to the pillow—her pillow—and it smelled like her, citrus-sweetness.

Sleep didn't claim him, though, as he kept thinking of Cilla and how good it had felt to hold her in his arms. Fuck, he wasn't sure if he wanted more from her, but it also scared him to admit that he was glad she had been with him last night. When he said that he had missed her, though, he was honest.

Todd did miss Cilla, and he was afraid to say it. So he was glad she had said it to him first.

But, did that change anything between them? She was gone, and he hadn't said some things that he should have.

Stared at the nightstand, with the dwindling supply of condoms on it. The condoms that she had counted, in jest, which had angered him that night, months ago.

And kept staring at it. No matter how awful he felt, sleep wouldn't claim him. Because he was the biggest jackass ever. It was the photos, which she didn't even know about. He had thought a lot about showing her the photos, and asking her for her permission, but he didn't.

For most of the month, Todd had been on the verge of texting her a few times each day. His finger would hover over the "send" button after each time he typed a message, but he never pressed the button. He knew he was worried about her reaction: Cilla might refuse to let him use the photos, or she could start yelling at him, or cry. He had no idea what his reaction would be, in any scenario.

Last night was a wasted opportunity. He should have shown her the photos, and secured her written permission for the use of them. Every day, he tortured himself over those photos, which drew him closer to her, yet also kept him from seeking her out. Todd knew he was a coward over the photos and where Cilla was concerned.

*   *   *

11

Climbing Out of the Black Hole;
Just Need a Ladder!

It was a week after seeing Todd. I sat at work in the morning, just zoning out mentally. Couldn't concentrate on anything. I drank my coffee, trying to figure out what I was going to do that day. Finally turned on the computer, and started to go through emails.

Later that morning, I was still parked in front of my computer, finally deep in thought over an issue I was trying to troubleshoot. Barely heard the knock at my door.

"Come in," I called, absent-minded.

The door opened and Kevin sauntered in and sat down.

"Langford, we need to talk," he started.

"Give me two minutes?" I requested. "I'm just going to get to a stopping point with this troubleshoot."

"Sounds good, I'll nap," he replied, slouching in the chair and closing his eyes.

I made a few notes on my yellow pad about the graphics issue, and saved and closed my file.

"Kevin, thanks for waiting. What's up?" I asked him.

"I need to ask *you* what's up, actually," he countered. "Something's going on with you. You're not yourself; you seem like a ghost around here, lately. Your job performance is fine, by the way. But, I'm only bringing this up as someone concerned for your well-being."

I sighed heavily. "No, I'm not myself these days. I don't even know where to begin, to tell you."

"Then summarize it. Whatever you're comfortable with telling me. I don't want to push you, but if there's anything I can do to help you out, I will."

"Remember the photographer that I was seeing back in January?" I asked Kevin, who nodded.

"We've seen each other since then, and it's been up and down. And, he ended up stomping on my heart," I summarized.

"I had no idea, I'm so sorry," Kevin exclaimed. "If there's anything I can do, just let me know."

"I think I'm alright. Just working on getting over him and moving on, at this point," I said, hoping it might start to become that easy for me.

"Ok, I understand," he said. "By the way, what happened last week, when you left Caty's baby shower abruptly? You snuck out, but I noticed."

"You notice everything," I said wryly. "It was the song that was playing, a Foo Fighters song. That's Todd's and my favorite band—it's a weird thing, I guess, side effect of the rejection."

"Ah, I see," he remarked, and it was just awkward then.

"Is it ok if I get back to this, since I've reached my limit on talking about me?" I asked, feeling a little shaky.

"Yeah, of course," Kevin replied, standing up. "Cilla, I'm serious—if there's anything you need, just let me know, ok?"

He walked to the door, and I called, "Thanks, Kevin, bye!"

He waved in response, and I went back to burying myself in work.

*   *   *

Life had definitely lost its flavor for me. My social life was sad these days—I rarely went on the dating site. Didn't want to see any guys. Didn't want to see my friends, even, but I forced myself to go to happy hour or go to the movies with them. I did it mostly because I knew they'd yell at me for being antisocial, and I didn't want a lecture about how I wasn't moving on from Todd. I knew I really should have been, since he wasn't such a good guy after all.

I was still sad over having my heart broken, and I wasn't sure how to recover from it yet. It felt unlike any rejection from any other guy in my entire life. In my heart, I knew he was different from anyone I had ever met, and that we could have had something special together.

Each night, I felt the heartbreak as though it had just occurred, to be as fresh in my mind as if it was that day's news. And, every night, the pain resurfaced, like clockwork, as if I had scheduled it on my cellphone's calendar.

*   *   *

I had dodged seeing Mel since her cookout, but she was sneaky. She ended up contacting Hillary by email, and the two told me that I'd be meeting them for happy hour. Not asked, told. I figured I'd go along with it to get them off my back, but I felt as enthused for tonight's happy hour as I did during my yearly mammogram.

I saw Mel's car in the parking lot, when I arrived at Typesetters' parking lot, and I parked near her car. I sat in the car, touching up my makeup. Then I just sat there, taking a few slow, deep breaths. I really didn't want to leave the car cocoon, but after a few minutes I forced myself to gather up my purse and exit the car.

Went into the restaurant and saw Mel sitting at a table near the bar, so I went over to her.

"I'm here," I announced to her, with my arms outstretched.

"Hey, Cilla, I've missed you!" she exclaimed as she hugged me. "I'm really glad you're here!"

"Surprisingly, me too," I admitted reluctantly, starting to feel glad that I had pushed myself to get out of the car.

She asked me, "How are you doing? I've been thinking about you, sweetie."

"I'm surviving, but that's about it," I admitted. "I'm still a mess because of Todd."

"I know, I feel lousy for throwing you guys together at the party," she said, looking guilty.

"Thanks, Mel, I needed to hear that," I replied, squeezing her hand across the table, while I looked at the wine list. "If you didn't address the issue, I was considering throwing a drink on you and stomping out !"

"I'm glad I'm not drenched in alcohol yet," she smiled.

The waiter came over and I ordered some red wine, and some appetizers for us. After a few minutes, I had my wine, and we toasted.

"To not killing each other, once again," I said as our wine glasses clicked, then we laughed.

"So, am I allowed to ask where you stand with Todd, what the latest is?" she asked hesitantly.

"Sure, you can ask," I offered, as I sipped my wine. "Ok, we went over to Todd's apartment the night of the cookout, we had really hot but emotionally distant sex, and slept together. I woke up early the next morning, and just wanted to cry. So, I left before he woke up."

"Did you guys talk it out?" Mel said, after absorbing my sad tale.

"No, we specifically didn't talk, except for saying that we missed each other," I offered. "It was clear that Todd didn't want to open up, and I had no idea what to say to start any type of conversation."

"Maybe you just have to corner him somewhere and jump him, so he's forced to confront your love?" she suggested. "Tie him up and convince him, any way possible!"

"I wish it was that simple, Mel, I really do. But I feel like it's insurmountable, like he's just immune to who I really am," I replied, in despair. "You know him, how's he doing? Is he upset over me? Or is he going on and acting like everything is just fine?"

"He's doing his job for the yearbook when he's with me. But he does seem more quiet and serious than usual, and it's noticeable. The kids always laugh and joke with him, but this season, he's more 'all business', especially around me," she said, reluctantly.

"Does he ask about me? No, wait, I don't want to know. Yes I do!" I felt conflicted.

What would her answer solve? It would only torture me.

"He hasn't asked about you, but it seems like he doesn't know what to say to me anyway. It's been awkward ever since the day after the party," Mel said.

"The day after? What happened then?" I asked, confused.

"He texted me to come get him, so we could reunite him with his car. You know, since he drove your car that night when you guys left my house," she cleared up.

"Oh, that's right. I hadn't even realized that when I left his apartment that day," I mused. "Guess I didn't even consider that I could have given him a ride."

"He texted me, and I showed up around lunchtime," Mel started. "He got into my car, and started right in on me."

"How pissed was he?" I asked, curious. I didn't know how mad Todd could get, and I didn't envy Mel one bit.

"Livid. He was mad that I hadn't told him that we were such great friends, and that he'd be seeing you at the party. And then he was angry that I meddled," Mel recalled.

"Well, you did meddle," I agreed. "Anything else?"

"He was angry with himself. Muttered that he wished he had discussed some photo issue with you, and regretted that he hadn't said anything. Then told me not to mention it to you."

"Good job on that," I said, laughing. "What photos was he talking about?"

"I have no idea. So you guys really haven't spoken since then? What are you waiting for? You should call him," Mel urged me.

"No, it's over," I said, feeling sadder for having said it out loud. "Todd's had too many chances to tell me how he feels. He has my phone number and his fingers have the ability to dial the number or text me. He just isn't going to say the words to bring us together."

"Then, the hell with him," Hillary said, finally showing up and sitting down at the table.

"Seriously? Have you seen them together, like I have? Cilla and Todd are into each other. They should be together. They deserve to be happy together," Mel said confidently, as if she knew we'd become a couple because she had prophesized it.

"Except that he's broken our girl's heart more than once," Hillary countered. "She's given him so much time and ample opportunities for him to step up and declare his interest, and he hasn't. I think she needs to work on healing her heart and moving on to someone who *will* tell her how he feels about her. Someone who will love her!"

"What do *you* think?" Mel said, as they both turned to me.

I had been sitting there, just sipping my wine and absorbing their advice.

"Ladies, I'm torn," I started slowly. "I wish that Todd was into me. The fact is, last time we were together, I feel as though he used me. And, I feel like total crap that I let him—I wanted more from him that night, but he disappointed me.

"So, I don't know that my heart matters much at the moment. Bottom-line is that he doesn't want me. I need to move on," I finished, then downed the rest of my glass of wine in a very long gulp. Really ladylike, especially with my raised pinky finger.

Both of my friends sat there, munching on mozzarella sticks and looking at me sadly.

"Well, I guess that's that, Cilla," Mel finally said. "When do you want us to start setting you up with some new guys on blind dates?"

"Oh, damn, how about in a few months?" I said, laughing hollowly. "I don't know that I'm ready for dating yet."

"Well, when you do date again, don't settle for some anonymous hookup or encounter that leaves you feeling empty. Let the guy know you want to date him, not just be with him in bed. Don't let him talk you into sex—make him see your brain first, not your lingerie," Mel told me emphatically.

"No, I disagree, how about some sex? Like a hookup?" Hillary asked, giggling a bit. "Sorry, I couldn't resist!"

"Funny, that's what got me into this mess in the first place!" I said wryly, smiling at them.

"Just go on the dating website and find a hot young guy to do a one-time recovery-bang with. It'll help you," Hillary urged me. Mel sat there silently, looking wistfully across the room.

"I'll consider it, Hilli. You ok, Mel?" I asked her, noticing her zoning out.

"Yeah, I'm just thinking about Hillary's 'recovery-bang' comment. I could use that, to recover from this school year!" she laughed. "As long as they're legal, and the husband approves!"

"Well, if I end up with an overabundance of young, virile hotties, I'll send some your way," I promise-teased Mel, then we all started laughing.

The next day, I felt slightly boosted by that conversation and my girlfriends' support. But, as the days progressed, I started to sink lower and lower again. Getting out of bed each morning was still a herculean struggle, as was being outgoing, pleasant, and professional at work. Every night, I went home and had a routine: get clothes, coffee, and food prepared for the next day, then collapse into bed and toss and turn for hours.

Days passed, in much the same way: sadness, survival, repeat. I felt like I was building towards something, but I had no idea what, or even why I had that feeling. Maybe it was just wishful thinking.

*   *   *

A week later, Hillary called me at work, "Guess what? I got the tickets to that art gallery show! Come with us!"

"Wait, what?" I asked, wondering where the beginning of the conversation had been.

I frequently felt lost at work lately, even with trying my best to pay attention. And, it was rare that she called me; she hated talking on the phone, so we usually had all of our conversations in person.

"It's this Friday night. I got the work tickets that were advertised in email the other day. Come with me and Doug, please?" she explained.

"Um . . ." I managed, feeling overwhelmed by a simple invite from my close friend.

"Cilla, please, you're floundering here. Let's have a fun evening out. We'll dress up, drink some wine. It's supposed to be a great gallery show. Please?" she asked. "Don't say you have nothing to wear—the dress you wore to the Christmas party is perfect!"

I closed my eyes and took a deep breath.

"I'll go, since it sounds like you'll counter any excuse I can think of," I replied softly. Hillary squealed, right through the phone into my left ear.

"It's going to be a lot of fun. I'm so glad you'll go! We'll pick you up, ok?" she said, and I barely heard her past the ringing in my left ear.

"Ok, sounds good," I replied. "This does sound like a fun event, thanks so much for asking me, Hillary!"

"You're welcome!" she said. "It'll be good for us to go out and do something much different than our usual happy hour, just to shake it up."

Two days later, I left work early, and went to my salon. I was in desperate need of a haircut, so I finally got that, while catching up with my stylist about my dating ordeals. After that, I got a pedicure and a manicure, since my nails were a neglected mess.

I arrived back home after my afternoon of pampering, and pulled the dress out of my closet. I sat on my bed, just looking at the dress as though we both had loaded guns pointed at each other. A Wild West standoff was the last thing I needed.

I groaned out loud and stood up, then picked up my phone and went into my bathroom. Sat on the edge of my nice, new clawfoot tub and looked into the mirror. Looked down at my cellphone, and set it to record a video, then stood the phone on my sink counter, facing me.

I started speaking, for reasons I couldn't explain, "I'm going out tonight, for the first time in a while. It makes me feel nervous, especially because I'll be wearing that dress.

"I need something more, something better, from my life. I need to stop pining after Todd," I continued as my eyes teared up, "and move on, so that my heart can heal.

"I need to be happy again, for me. And I need to work on making my life a happy thing, because I'll be living it for a long time."

I paused, to take a deep breath. Reached for the phone to shut it off, but then sat back and continued talking.

"Oh, and maybe I need to not throw my 'cat' at the next guy, unless I really want to," I laughed, the sound echoing through the bathroom louder than I had thought it would be, and it seemed more alive to me.

"I need to make sure the next guy really appreciates me, before tossing my heart into the ring. Ok, enough of my self-help-life-talk-crap for one day!" I stood up and switched the video off, then went into the bedroom and stood in front of the dresser mirror. Felt better already, so I started applying makeup, then switched my music on—went to Foo Fighters, and started playing "These Days."

I sang along to it and felt the smile on my face as I put jewelry on, then the dress and finally shoes. Then I looked over at my everyday purse, and realized I had to switch to my navy silk clutch. After finding it in the back of my closet, I transferred purse contents into it, then I grabbed my lavender pashmina, just in case I got chilly later, and went downstairs.

Hillary and Doug, her husband, picked me up to go to the art gallery opening, and I teased her for being on time, for once.

"Sometimes I can get it together and be ready, you know me!" she laughed as she turned around in her seat to chat with me, in the back seat.

"Yeah, you like to make an entrance; then the party's started!" I chimed in.

Doug interrupted, "I told her the time about fifty times, that's how I broke her cycle of tardiness tonight!"

Hillary glared at him, then at me for giggling. I changed the subject.

"The weather's perfect tonight. I think the last time I wore this dress, it was freezing!" I said, and then realized the last time I wore the dress. At the work holiday party. And then I went over to Todd's, which had been an almost-perfect night with him.

"What is it? Thinking about him again?" she asked, knowing the answer.

My eyes started to tear up a bit as I replied, "Yeah, just thinking about that night of the party, when I ended up at Todd's after. I'm still sad, and just wish the hurt would go away."

"I wish I had an answer for you," she said, "We all want you to feel better, you know. How about if we work on making tonight a fun, special night, ok? Maybe we'll find you someone here tonight to make you smile?"

"That sounds good," I agreed, and flashed her a cheesy smile. We giggled as her husband pulled their car into the parking lot. Traffic inched along to get to empty parking spaces; it looked like the event was going to be packed.

"Wow, this is really fancy," I mused as men in suits and women in sequined cocktail dresses walked past the car.

"Yeah, I heard from a few people at work that it was *the* event of the year around here, so I'm glad we were able to snag the tickets from work," she said enthusiastically. "Not having to pay $150 a ticket is pretty awesome, right?"

"Very true, since I need my money to put towards a vacation," I said as her husband pulled into a parking spot, far away from the gallery.

We got out of the car and followed the crowd. I noticed that even the path along the edge of the parking lot was decorated for the event, paper lanterns lining the walkway, and lanterns glowing in the trees nearby. It looked magical, and I could feel my mood lifting, for the first time in a few months.

Finally made it to the entrance of the art gallery, and we could see through the windows that the opening was packed inside. And, heard the strains of music from the entrance, as we had our tickets checked.

"There are six different exhibit rooms, so make sure you go through all of them. Some of the artists exhibiting are local residents, who are here tonight. So you could meet the artists, isn't that exciting?" the greeter's enthusiastic rhetoric went on, and then we excused ourselves as she started on the group behind us.

The gallery exhibit party was very elegant—it felt almost like a wedding reception, except there was a purpose, to enjoy the art. Paintings, sculptures, photos, and other works of art dotted the rooms. Some were modern-bizarre, others interpreted or were inspired by classical works, and some of the works were unique and I couldn't place what might have inspired them. It was eclectic and definitely surprising to have something so worldly in our suburb, so I could see why Hillary called it "the event." Waiters brought trays of hors d'oeuvres and champagne around, and the crowd was so dense that we had to squeeze our way in to see some of the works of art.

By the fifth gallery room, my feet might have been in pain from my high-heeled sandals, but I had imbibed a lot of champagne. I didn't really feel my feet, so I was standing and walking fine. Couldn't help it, I was parched and waiters brought them around, so of course I was going to drink it as if it was an energy drink, being on an art marathon. Wondered why they didn't do this in the Metropolitan Museum of Art or the Louvre? My ass would be in the museums every weekend!

The fifth room seemed less crowded than the previous rooms; maybe some of the people hadn't paid attention to the greeter's spiel, or maybe they were too lazy to fight through the crowd. Each room had also had its own music, whether it was a DJ, band, or others. Here, it was a guitarist, strumming in the corner, accompanied by someone singing some Spanish ballads. Hillary and I wandered around the room slowly, while Doug stood in the corner, and looked exhausted.

"Do you mind if I go back to Doug, since he's looking like a zombie?" she asked.

I waved her away gently, "Not a problem, go keep him awake!"

I slowly wandered around the room, then turned a corner, and suddenly I saw it—three different photos of me. *Me.* Me, on large black-and-white photos. In one of them, I was standing on a hill, looking at something with a sad expression on my face, a lake in the background, and my hair was blown around by the wind. In the second one, I was standing against the edge of some newly-budded springtime woods, head down and very forlorn posture.

My thoughts raced—where and when was I in these photos? Finally, my brain settled on the day—I remembered the day the photos were taken. It was a bleak chilly spring day in early April. I had felt so low that day, since it had been a few days after Todd had rejected me so cruelly. The day I had left work early, and just wandered around the empty park.

Now, I realized that he had not only seen me, but watched me. Waited for the perfect moments to take each shot. Taken these photos of me and avoided me. On purpose, months ago.

I could feel that I was on the verge of either sitting or fainting at that moment, because my legs were started to feel a bit shaky.

I glanced around the gallery sharply, to see if Todd was around, but I didn't see him. People milled around the gallery here and there, but this room felt so quiet to me. Breathing seemed so loud to me, as I took a deep breath and turned back to the photos.

Finally decided to look at the third photo, which was a direct shot of my face, with tears in my eyes and agony etched on my face, and the lake's shore in the background.

"What the . . . ?" was all I could manage. I stood there in front of the photos, just amazed at how they captured *me*, and all the pain I had gone through. And my eyes teared up as I stared at the photos some more. I tried to stop the sobs escaping, but couldn't help it.

"Miss, are you ok?" a gallery worker asked. She seemed like a snooty, self-absorbed type.

"Oh, my goodness, it's you! From the photos! We all cried over these photos too. Aren't they spectacular? Such emotion, such life is captured in them. Your essence and beauty. It's wonderful that you're here to see them—all of these photos were sold, within the hour, I believe, and I'm still getting requests for them! I keep directing them to Todd's website, but I think they'd bid on these photos if they could!"

I couldn't even follow her, but nodded and managed, "Thanks, I had no idea the photos would look like this."

"Oh, well clearly Todd Albrecht is talented," she continued. "These works are a triumph for him. I told him earlier that we will expect great things from him in future shows!"

"Is he here?" I asked, still feeling shaky.

"He's definitely around here somewhere," she said. "We do request that the artists stay within a room of their gallery exhibit, since many patrons like to find out about the artists' upcoming shows, what inspires them, and if they do any exclusive commissions. You know, typical artist business."

"Of course," I said, still staring at the photographs, amazed. Wondering if Todd was nearby, and even now watching me? I couldn't turn away from the photos to even think of checking. Hillary came up to me then.

"Oh my god, I can't believe it, Todd did these photos of you? Did you pose for these?" she gasped, as stunned as I was.

"I did, but not with my knowledge," I muttered. She hugged me.

"Should we find and kill him?"

"No, but he's actually around here somewhere," I said, raising an eyebrow wryly.

"You're going to confront him, aren't you?" she asked. I suspected that Hillary was ready to be my second, if there was to be a duel with Todd to the death, or at least to the pain. I decided to let her know that I wasn't going to be making a huge dramatic scene.

"I'll say something, but I don't feel like screaming at him. It's not worth it, because I can't change his mind on anything."

"Ok, well, Doug and I will be in the corner in case you need us," she said, hugging me again.

"Thanks, you're the best," I flashed her a shaky smile, trying to draw a bit of strength from her ironclad support.

She walked away, and I looked around, and saw him suddenly, at the gallery doorway. He was talking to two people, and I watched him blatantly, mesmerized by how different he looked in a suit. Todd was just ridiculously hot, and his hair looked neater and also a bit blonder.

He started to turn towards me, and I panicked and pivoted back to immerse myself back into the photos. My eyes still dripped a bit, so I delicately dabbed at them with a tissue, to try not to mess up my makeup.

I suddenly, slowly glanced all around, and as I looked in his direction, our eyes met. Shock on his face met with shock on mine, at him acknowledging me. We just looked at each other, and any external music, chatter, or other ambient noise seemed to fade away. It was only us in that moment of frozen recognition.

He glanced back at the people he was talking to, then walked towards me, taking two glasses of champagne off a passing tray on his way over to me.

"Cilla, you look so beautiful," he said, holding one of the glasses out to me. He didn't smile; he looked shocked to the core.

"Thanks," I replied, taking the glass, then holding it up. "To your artistic achievement."

We drank our champagne, then he took my glass and handed both empty glasses to a passing waiter.

Todd hesitated, because I could sense that he wasn't sure if I was sincere or if I was plotting some type of revenge or embarrassing psychotic scene calling him out, but then clinked his glass with mine. Maybe it was a bit mean of me, but I relished that he hesitated to trust me, and that he was concerned about my reaction to seeing him and the photos. I felt more power than I had in months; it was a rush to not feel as if I was floundering around in a fog.

"I had no idea you would be here–" he started, but I interrupted him.

"–Neither did I, but I am glad I'm here. Your photos are just amazing, unlike anything I've ever seen of yours."

"Cilla, I have to tell you something," he leaned down and whispered in my ear, quite serious. "I fucked up in a major way. I was supposed to get your permission before showing these photos, since you're the subject. I'm *so* sorry I didn't; I've been a bastard and a coward for months, but I can disclose that to the gallery owners and withdraw from the show now."

"So, what happens if you do disclose it?" I whispered back angrily.

"I'd be asked to leave the show, and it would be a serious blow to my career. It would ruin my credibility," he answered, still whispering in my ear. "But I'd do it. I'd do anything to win you back."

"Todd, I was never really yours," I was blunt as I whispered. "You made sure of that. And FYI, it hurts that you didn't tell me about the photos, when you've had months to do it. *Why?*"

He reached for me, but I took a step back and glared at him. He couldn't just hope to solve our issues with some affection.

He asked, "Can we go outside and talk?"

I hesitated, then replied angrily, "No, let's stay here and discuss this."

"Ok," Todd explained quietly. "I panicked, because I realized how much you meant to me. It took me forever to realize that the more I thought about you, the more you were firmly cemented in my heart. I was fighting a battle against my heart, which refused to let anything come between us.

"I was afraid to show you the photos, because I didn't want to make you angry at me again. And, the last night that we spent together, I wanted to be close to you, but I know I guided us into having sex when we should have been talking. I know it was cowardly, and I'm so sorry. I don't blame you for walking out on me after it.

"That day in April, at the park, I wanted to approach you; I was dying to hold and comfort you. I saw the sorrow in your eyes, on your face, even in your body language. At the same time, I was conflicted and afraid to cause you more pain by continuing our contact. So that's why I kept my distance."

I nodded and he continued in a low voice, "Every day since I took them, I've looked at those photos and tortured myself over how much agony I put you through, after the way you fell for me. I've hated myself so much for being too chickenshit to go the next step with you."

"The next step?" I asked him, feeling my anger dissipate like a storm cloud being blown away by his words. Was he actually talking about what I hoped: us being a couple?

"This is why I wanted to go talk somewhere else, away from the gallery," he muttered uncomfortably, running his hands through his hair as he stared at the floor.

"Oh, have I said how incredibly handsome you look tonight, all dressed up?" I said, to distract Todd.

"No, you haven't, but you can now," he grinned at me, clearly glad I distracted him with our flirty and friendly banter that had been part of our communication since our first night together.

"Ok, here goes: you look incredibly handsome tonight. Who knew that you even knew what a suit was?" I grinned back at him. "Now, your turn."

"You're not wearing a suit," he said, "so I don't know what you want me to say!"

"Guess I can't help it if you really don't like seeing me in this dress again," I nudged him with my comment.

"Actually, I do have a thing for that very silky dress," he smiled slightly, looking at the floor. "And a big thing for you, Cilla."

I stepped closer to him, so that I intercepted his gaze to the floor. He looked right at me then, and I saw slight tears in his eyes. And the one thing I had been waiting months for: his soft expression of love directed at me.

Finally.

My heart started to beat faster. My eyes teared up too, and I reached for his hands. He ignored my hands and instead pulled me close to him, so his arms went around my waist. My hands went around his neck, and we kissed, the best kisses of my life.

Until Todd pulled back and looked down at me, with the sweetest smile I had ever seen on his face. I felt my face breaking out into a goofy smile.

"I love you," he whispered, then let out a nervous breath.

"Love you, too," I replied, smiling more, if that was even possible.

Todd pulled me in for another magical kiss, and I felt my heart beating against his. After a few minutes, we both pulled back and looked at each other. I motioned for him to lean in, and I whispered in his ear.

"Just so you know, I'm not completely angry with you anymore," I told him. "I'm also officially giving you permission to show those photos."

"Are you absolutely sure?" he asked, looking surprised.

"Yes, I'm sure," I consented. "I heard that they all already sold, so I guess congratulations are in order!"

"Thanks, I really appreciate that. I'll split the money with you," he said.

I smiled very sweetly at him, saying, "Actually, you could give it all to me. I'll find something suitable to do with it."

He looked a little surprised, but then replied, "Anything for you, my sweetie."

I turned then, looking at the photos, while he kept one arm around my waist. My cellphone suddenly pinged with a text message, and I reached into my fancy clutch for it.

I looked at my phone, and then started laughing and turning pink in my face.

Todd leaned down to look at it: a picture of us kissing, with the message, "WAY TO GO!!!"

I turned towards Hillary and Doug, who were still in the corner, both smiling at us.

"Come on, you can meet my girlfriend and her husband," I said, as we started walking towards them.

I introduced them to Todd, and we exchanged pleasantries.

"So," Todd said to Hillary and Doug, "I know you guys brought Cilla, but do you mind if I take her home? I'm thinking that I should take her out somewhere for a very late dinner. And, I owe her more apologies and explanations."

"That works for me," I said, smiling up at him.

Hillary looked at Todd pointedly until he started fidgeting, then she looked at me.

She leaned over and whispered in my ear, "Are you sure this is what you want? You're making a conscious decision to be with him tonight. What if he breaks your heart again? He could be—"

"—Hillary, he's completely different tonight. He apologized and almost cried over it. I do believe him, and we're going to talk," I whispered back.

"Really?" she whispered in surprise. "That *is* a good sign. Just remind him about something—you were honest about how you felt, and he really made you feel bad about it."

"I agree," I nodded at her. "I'll be fine tonight, thanks so much!"

"Ok, then I think we're going to go," she said as Doug fought back a yawn.

We said our goodbyes and they left, leaving Todd and me in the gallery room.

"Do you want to sit on this bench, while I deal with any of the patrons?" he asked me. "The show's on for one more hour, so I don't know if your feet are hurting."

"No, I had some champagne, so I don't know if my feet hurt," I admitted, laughing. "I'm fine hanging out with you. Besides, if anyone asks about your photo model, I can tell them firsthand about the circumstances behind the photos and how I was all upset because of you."

"No, don't tell them that, you brat!" he hissed quietly.

I smiled at Todd to soothe him, since I knew that I wouldn't do anything to make him look bad. For the rest of the hour, he made small talk with anyone who came into the gallery room, and introduced them to me. It was so nice just to stand next to each other, and finally feel like a couple.

After the show ended, Todd found out he had a few things to tie up. He gave me his car keys to go sit in his car and wait for him, so I walked to his car slowly. Found his car, and got into the front passenger seat.

I relocked the doors and just sat there, thinking about what had happened. I felt so happy and content, but I also wanted to shake Todd by the shoulders for having driven me so crazy with heartbreak over the past few months. I did agree with Hillary that I needed to discuss with Todd how much he had hurt me; saying "I love you" couldn't just erase the pain I had gone through. I did feel hopeful that he finally understood we needed to have that serious conversation; otherwise I would have left with Hillary and Doug earlier.

I must have dozed off with those thoughts, because suddenly there was loud knocking. I bolted awake and realized it was Todd. I unlocked the car door, and he got into the driver's seat.

"I'm sorry it took so long," he explained, "but the people who bought my photos were arranging for their photos to be sent to them. I couldn't leave until that was all figured out."

"That's fine," I replied sleepily, "I dozed off. Now we can hang out."

"Yes, we can, Ms. Cilla," he said, smiling broadly at me. "How about if we go to a diner? We can eat and talk, and see what we're in the mood for after that."

"Good plan," I smiled back.

We got a corner booth in the diner, and ordered breakfast. I drank coffee and he had an orange juice. We stared at each other in the too-bright diner, suddenly not sure where to start.

"This is definitely new territory," he said nervously.

"It is," I giggled, "it's weird that we're both tense. We've done much crazier things than we currently are, so we shouldn't be tense."

"Actually, yes we should be tense," he corrected me. "It's always been easier to lose myself in being physical with a woman than it is now to open my heart up to you. I'm not used to this at all. But, Cilla, being with you is the most important part of my life experience."

"That's good, I've felt for some time that you're the only one I want to be with," I told him.

"I know," he said as he squeezed my hand across the table. It was the only contact we had since entering the diner, and it felt like magic.

"In the beginning, the age difference really did bother me," he said, after a pause. "But I think I also used it as an excuse to try to keep you away, so I didn't have to attempt to change from being 'me' to becoming 'we.' I spent seven years trying to forget the pain of losing a baby and someone I loved, and losing the potential family. And, in you, I found love again, and you helped me re-ignite my dream of a family. One that I could put ahead of my existing not-so-great family. I'd be happy to come home to our family every day, and feel content with it. All those thoughts scared the shit out of me. I was worried I could lose it again; I guess I just freaked out over everything changing, and I took out my issues on you."

I closed my eyes for a minute, letting his words sink in, trying to figure out what to say next, to help us build what we both wanted.

Our food showed up then, and as we slowly ate our breakfast-at-night, we kept the conversation flowing.

"The age difference did bother me in the beginning, but then I saw who *you* really were, and I stopped caring about two different numbers," I told him. "I didn't realize that I fell for you until after you stopped texting me. I just knew that you were unique, mature, and I found you fascinating. Not just your body, but also your mind. And it didn't help that you were interested in talking and getting to know me. Don't you see that your actions sent mixed signals? Be honest: have you ever had a hookup before us, where you talked so much and wanted to know all about your partner?"

He nodded, chewing his pancakes, and answered after thinking about it, "You're right, actually. I'm sorry, so sorry. I never picked up on it, I just thought you were the most beautiful woman who I could actually talk to. You were interesting, and it was refreshing that we really seemed to be so comfortable around each other. When we were together, I never wanted you to leave."

I continued, "You do need to understand that trust is a huge component of us being in a relationship, and you already broke my trust."

Todd looked sad, and asked, "Over the photos? I'm sorry, you have to believe that!"

I waved him away with my fork full of a waffle piece, telling him, "No, it was when we were in the market and I told you how I felt about you. I opened up to you, and your rejection confused me, because you were sending me mixed signals by trying to keep the conversation going. It was as if you were trying to convince me to not care for you. Then, when you blatantly lied to me about not remembering your drunken confession, that broke my trust even further."

Todd sighed, put down his fork, and drank from his orange juice.

"Yeah, I know I was the worst jackass that day. I have no explanation other than I *was* trying to maintain our casual status quo, and you were pulling the rug out from under me. I felt like you were rejecting me because you rejected our original agreement," he said, looking straight into my eyes.

"And yes, I did remember what I said, after all the whiskey and all the sex that night. I know I sound like a jerk, and I was one. I'm so sorry. I'll keep apologizing to you as many times as I can, and I still fear it won't be enough," he said, in raw honesty. "Again, I'm sorry for what I put you through, and I would spend every day trying to make it up to you."

"Apology accepted, of course," I said, choking back tears. "When there's love, there's forgiveness."

Todd leaned forward and kissed me softly, another perfect kiss.

We got our check, and he paid it before I could react. He stood up and helped me up, then led me out of the diner to his car. Once we got into Todd's car, he turned to me.

"Cilla, your place is closer than mine. You have a nice big bed I haven't spent enough time in. Can I invite myself over?"

"It's highly possible, since you're on my good side now," I replied, smiling. "Enjoying getting your way?"

"I am, but it's also you getting your way, too," he smiled back, as he drove to my condo, then parked behind my car in the driveway. We exited the car and I led the way to the front door, fishing my keys out of my small purse. I unlocked the front door and we went inside.

"Do you want any water or something else?" I asked, going to the kitchen to get myself some water.

"No thanks, I'm fine," he called from the living room, taking off his suit jacket and laying it over the back of a chair, before sitting down. "Mind if we relax? I'm full from the diner."

"That sounds good to me," I replied, returning to the living room with my water. "I didn't realize it was 1:30! It's been a very eventful evening."

"It has been," he said, flipping around the TV channels with the remote.

I sat on the sofa and took off my high-heeled sandals, then pushed them under the coffee table so they were out of the way. Leaned back, to cuddle with Todd.

"I love you," he said, randomly, then squeezed me.

"I love you too," I replied, smiling. "This feels so nice."

Silence fell for a while after that, and we watched a comedy movie for a little while.

Todd looked at me, and simply said, "I want you. Is that still ok?"

"Of course it's ok!" I replied slowly. "We started out as lovers, and tried to become emotionally closer right from the beginning. We can work on our relationship any way that makes us happy. That way, we both get to feel close to each other, right?"

"Definitely," he said, then kissed me. "I think we should go upstairs now and work on our relationship!"

I smile and stood up, pulling him up. We went upstairs to my bedroom, and had one of those perfect evenings together, working on our relationship . . .

The next morning, we woke up slowly in bed, still cuddling each other from last night.

I said quietly, "Morning. I know what to do with your money."

"You mean from the photos?" he asked, drowsy.

"Yes, it can be for moving in," I offered, hoping it was what he wanted, too.

"I don't need it for that—Matt has a truck. And my friends are my moving crew, so I don't need money for it," he said, sounding more awake. "Try again."

"How about we save it for the future? Our future together?" I replied.

Todd looked down at me, and nodded, "That sounds great. You fine with that?"

"Yeah, I am," I smiled up at him, then we kissed, both ready to start the day together.

Epilogue

Are They Still Happy?

Lately, I could only subsist on cappuccino and cookies for breakfast, pizza for dinner, and a little bit of gelato at other times during the day. I figured that our baby, currently cooking, was already smart because the baby clearly had my favorites down. Todd and I were in Rome—he was doing a fashion shoot, and I was the smart wife to help turn his work trip into our honeymoon, too!

Yes, wife and mom-to-be! We had gotten married only a few days ago in a very small wedding that we had planned quickly, or thrown together, almost as soon as I had found out that I was pregnant. Our family and friends found out on our wedding day that we were expecting, so there was a lot of excitement and celebrating that day. And, also important, a lot of cake.

I sat at a cafe near the Piazza de Spagna, the Spanish Steps, sipping a cappuccino and people-watching on Memorial Day weekend. Thinking of how different my life had been last year—I had been in despair, at rock-bottom. Currently, I was floating on a gelato-soft cloud of happiness. It seemed a bit unbelievable at times, but I figured that helped me to remember to not take it for granted.

"Guess who?" Todd covered my eyes from behind me.

"Not sure—is it the father of my baby? Or my husband?" I teased him. He dropped into the chair next to me and sighed.

"How are you feeling, funny girl? Hopefully better than I am," he said wearily, motioning for the waiter to bring the check.

"Feeling like the baby wants to shop a little," I smiled at him.

He frowned, then said, "That can't be right. Baby doesn't like to shop."

"You're wrong, the baby wants to shop. I'm just not sure which designer is the baby's favorite yet, so we'll have to explore them all on this street," I grinned.

"Oh god, I got here just in time–" he looked scared.

"–To carry my bags. You do love me!" I confirmed.

"Of course I love you! I'd rather show you, back in our hotel room, instead of shopping right now. What have you been doing for the past few hours? You could have shopped then."

I wrinkled my nose, and admitted, "More nausea, unfortunately. I did plan to shop earlier, but it just didn't happen."

"Ok, then we shop now," Todd replied as he left money on the bill, then stood up. "Sorry, I didn't know how bad the nausea was for you today."

"How about two stores, then we go back to the hotel? You are supposed to show me how much you love me, right?" I suggested, standing up too.

"Sounds perfect, my love," he said, as we started down the street together, smiling at each other and linking arms.

About the Author

Jenny is a native of Central NJ, and currently lives and works there. She has a BA in English with a minor in Print Journalism. Jenny has always enjoyed creative writing fiction, romance, and poetry) and received writing awards in high school and college. She wrote a good portion of this novel as part of Camp NaNoWriMo, in April and July 2013. She also enjoys bike riding, kayaking, and traveling. Jenny is single, but a hopeful romantic for the next guy that might sweep her off her feet!

If you liked this book, or have any feedback, please feel free to contact me at my website, http://www.jennybaskwell.com, or through my Facebook author page, http://www.facebook.com/jennybaskwellauthor. Happy reading!

Acknowledgments

This book would not have been possible without the support of some great people in my life:

My parents, Helena and Jack: The tuition was finally worth it, right? Thanks for letting me freeload sometimes while I was writing—it's nice to not be a totally starving writer!

Ryan and Angela: Thanks for letting me put you both to work, Rye for web and PR help, and Ang for reading sections of the final draft.

Harrison: My cutest nephew ever, who I'll give a copy of this book to, once you're old enough to date!

Jill: You gave me a nugget of an idea after being entertained by a dating story, at one of those VIP meetings months ago!

Waleska: Thanks for always giving me great advice, and for all the crazy-fun happy hours!

Jen, Natalie, and Casey: You ladies always help to keep me sane with our girls' outings!

Alex: Thanks for helping me think about a better title, and with all the money stuff!

PWG: Without the excellent resources I found about here, I would have never learned about or participated in Camp NaNoWriMo in April, and I highly doubt I would have found my motivation to complete the book. This is truly a fantastic writers group, and that is especially because of so many enthusiastic writers banding together for support and camaraderie. I especially want to thank Shen (the awesome leader), Scott (my self-publishing guru), Katie and Jenny (for setting up Monday nights!), Bill (the original "monkey in the box"), the "Monday collective", and the Thursday gang.

The Foo Fighters: Thanks for making such awesome music, which I often listened to when I was writing parts of this book. My extreme apologies for writing that the main character couldn't listen to your music at one point! Can't wait to see you guys in concert again!